Revised edition

1

For my mum, who always believed in me.

'Our posturings, our imagined self-importance, the delusion that we have some privileged position in the Universe, are challenged at this point of pale light. Our planet is a lonely speck in the great enveloping cosmic dark. In our obscurity, in all this vastness, there is no hint that help will come from elsewhere to save us from ourselves.'

Carl Sagan *Pale Blue Dot: A Vision of the Human Future in Space*

Chapter 1

When I was born, my arrival coincided with a momentous and terrible milestone. Our mark on the planet had become indelible, irreversible, signalling the beginning of the end of human history. Or at least, the moment when most of the governments of the world finally began to quietly admit it. And yet, you would have struggled to find it reported on the news if you didn't know what you were looking for. Only a handful of people spoke about it or openly lamented it. Because – what was the use? We had lived through the short window of time when something could have been done, and we had allowed the window to close. And that was that. What was the point in troubling ourselves with something that could no longer be changed? Besides, we had generations left to us. The changes were creeping, imperceptible; easy to ignore.

So it was that, by the time I turned ten years old, the Earth had already been stolen from us. By generations past, steadily chipping away almost without being noticed. Slowly at first, maybe unwittingly. But then consciously, fuelled by greed, a desire for progress, and the unfathomable need for power by which our species is characterised. But we, the ones born afterwards, didn't even know anything was wrong. How can you truly be aware of something when it's never been any different?

Until that summer, when everything suddenly changed forever, I was young and oblivious. A small-for-my-age, inwardly focussed child content with my lot. And 'my lot' was a comfortable home in a modern compound, living with my precocious little sister and adored mother. I am an ordinary, unremarkable person who has lived through extraordinary, remarkable times.

We were happy – at least, I can certainly say my childhood began very happily. The cynicism that began to grow in me then would have me believe I was just naïve, and of course I was, up to a point. It was easy to be when you were protected from reality. And I am the first to admit that my early childhood was very sheltered. That shelter was my mother; it was all very deliberate. She told us what was what, and taught us right from wrong – even when the lines between the two were blurred – but we were protected from most of the bad stuff. The hardships of life and… yes, the truth. I don't wish to suggest she misled us – she certainly never lied to us. You'll come to know that about my mother. We knew about the power blackouts and the floods, the wildlife that no longer existed outside zoos and the endless streams of displaced, involuntarily nomadic people. Those were the facts facing us every day. But she didn't discuss the hopelessness of it all with us. The fact that it shouldn't have been that way, or that it was simply too late to put the brakes on now. If I had asked she would have told me everything, but it took something pretty huge to prompt me to do that. I was sheltered in the literal sense, too. We lived, like most of the fortunate ones, in our small, gated community. Protected from the evils and uncertainties of the outside world.

I have to keep reminding myself that that wide-eyed girl didn't exist all that long ago, even though it feels like another lifetime. But she wasn't clueless, that child, and certainly not ignorant. How could she have been, when she spent so much of her time listening in?

My mother was a big deal. At home, of course, to us, she was the whole universe. But I mean in her work, too. Since the latest pandemic she had worked more and more in her home office, and in turn our schooling became split between online learning at home and lessons in school. So although I was meant to be doing my home school work on the days when it wasn't my shift to be in the classroom, I found it far more interesting to listen in on her business meetings. I was always sure I was pretty stealthy when I did this, but once she turned around unexpectedly and, on seeing me sitting there in the doorway, she didn't even look surprised, let alone angry. So anyway – that was how I knew she was so important. She spent so long in those meetings, thrashing out problems I barely understood, but my inkling told me her views mattered, that important changes hinged on her responses. She was a senior consultant negotiator in world affairs. I loved to say this to myself under my breath, sometimes when I became bored (she would sometimes speak languages I didn't understand, or the conversation would be out of my brain's reach), and resorted to playing with the dolls I was far too old for just to please Shelley, my five-year-old sister. I would often take on the role of senior consultant negotiator, and Shelley would put up with this just for the joy of having me deign to play with her when I was so far beyond such things.

So despite being ignorant of perhaps the only truth that really mattered, I had a grasp of some world affairs that was beyond my years. But also perhaps a little beyond reality, if I'm telling the truth, because when I didn't completely understand what was being said in these meetings my imagination would fill in the gaps. And all that time, I had no idea that something would happen that would be beyond even anything I could dream up. Because all this time, we were *all* oblivious, going about our days and living our routines with our eyes closed.

I said Mum didn't mind me listening in while she worked, but that's not completely true. Not long after she caught me that day, she came to chat to me in my room.

"You know," she began, "that I will always be truthful with you." As I have hinted, this was her 'mission' (I should say, one of her missions. She had quite a few, mainly to do with how she wanted to raise us), shared with us often on the understanding it would be a mutual agreement: complete honesty at all times, however awkward or difficult the situation.

"...So." She continued. "I'm not going to tell you not to listen in while I'm working. I'm actually pleased you find it interesting. But you must promise never to discuss anything you hear outside this family. Can you do that? Lots of it is rather sensitive, and top secret, so I could get into quite a bit of trouble if you did. Does that make sense to you?"

And of course I agreed. I've already said Mum was the centre of our universe, and I suppose that sounds a little over the top. Every child's parent or caregiver is, up to a point, I'm sure. But for us it was more than that. It was only the three of us for most of the time, and that was exactly how we liked it.

Perhaps surprisingly, given my interest in the world, I didn't pay much attention to the news. But then, my interest was not so much in the machinations and events of my mother's job, more in my mother herself. So when things began to change and events were repeated in the headlines around the world, I didn't even notice. It was actually Shelley who picked it up first (as I said, she was precocious).

The three of us were sitting at the breakfast bar one morning. Mum always insisted that we share meals together when we were all home, no matter how busy we were. She had only broken her own rule a handful of times, if there was a crisis at work or she'd had to be called away unexpectedly. She didn't always work at home, she sometimes had to travel around the country or overseas, although this was less frequent now. Actually, on this particular day when we were all sitting there enjoying our breakfast I would have struggled to remember the last time Mum had been called away on business. We didn't mind too much when she was because Frankie, our neighbour and Mum's best friend, came to stay and look after us and she was nice, but it was always better when Mum was there, however preoccupied she might be.

And she was, on this day. She looked like she was reading the back of the cereal packet even though it just had some cartoon characters on it and a simple word search, and she kept tucking the same bit of hair behind her ear.

"Mummy, what's a nextra terror strall?" Shelley was a clever kid, but she often got words a bit wrong. I remember she had me confused once telling people her friend lived in a 'colder sack'. But it was another mission of Mum's to always answer our questions, no matter how frivolous or complex or uncomfortable. This one, once she had grasped Shelley's meaning, wasn't really any of those things. In fact, I answered it instead through a mouthful of cornflakes.

"It's a creature from outer space."

"I wanted Mummy to answer!"

Mum smiled indulgently, as she often did with Shelley and 'her ways'.

"She's right though, darling. Extra-terrestrials are beings that don't live on our planet. Have you been hearing about them lately?"

"Yes, lots on the TV and Newsquest."

Newsquest was a news app for kids that I was meant to use for school, only Shelley seemed more familiar with it than I was, even though her schoolwork only seemed to consist of phonics and painting projects.

"Hang on… why would extra-terrestrials be in the news?"

Mum and Shelley both looked at me in that way they each had; slight concern on one face and sheer disbelief on the other. It was amazing how small my tiny little sister, half my age, could make me feel sometimes.

"Darling, you must have heard a little bit about it?"

"Heard what? There's not some kind of alien invasion is there?"

It was a joke. A pretty stupid one, admittedly, but Mum's face sort of changed. She didn't look cross – it took a lot to make her cross – but she looked determined.

"No. Absolutely not." It was the seriousness of her response that somehow made me feel less than reassured. I'd been expecting her to laugh or something, and a little tingle went up my spine. Perhaps it was a sense that something was about to change.

"There are some scientists in China who have picked up some electromagnetic signals that they don't recognise, and they can't quite determine the source. So of course there's lots of speculation about where they're coming from, from the wild to the rather ridiculous."

"Ridiculous like… they might be aliens?"

"No, darling. That's actually not ridiculous at all. There's every chance it's intelligent life from elsewhere in the universe.

12

The chances of ours being the only inhabited planet is, frankly, rather egocentric of us. But then," she scraped her chair back and gathered up the breakfast bowls, "that's the human race for you!"

But as I put the milk and cereal boxes away, I couldn't help feeling strangely uneasy. My imagination started to run wild with all those books and TV programs I'd seen about hostile aliens waging war, wondering if it could actually be a possibility. But it was more than that. My mum sounded like her usual bright and breezy self, the calm, sensible person I could always cling to whenever I felt afraid. But she was concerned, I could tell. That was why she'd seemed distracted. The thing that I got wrong at the time was what exactly had been worrying her.

Chapter 2

I didn't spend too much time thinking about it then. In fact, it more or less went out of my mind as schoolwork and other things took over. There was a lot of background talk about some project. Comet, it was being called. I had no idea then what it stood for; certainly not how significant it would become. So I didn't even think about or hear the strange signals mentioned again for a couple of weeks. And by then, it was all everyone was talking about.

Mum came into my room one morning to fling open my curtains and proclaim it morning, as she was fond of doing. I was a premature teenager in that I liked to lie in for as long as possible in the mornings, dozing or reading or simply staring at the ceiling and allowing my mind to go blank. But Mum was a morning person and didn't think lying in bed all morning was a healthy pursuit. This morning was worse than usual, because she didn't have her usual loud sing-song voice. Even though I hated being woken up like that, it was preferable to the stern voice and grim look greeting me that day. Mum rarely got angry with us, in fact she never really did, so when she was unhappy about something we had done there was no mistaking it. I think her displeasure with us was actually made worse by its rarity.

"I've just checked the EdApp, young lady."

Another thing – she never let us stew for long, always telling us exactly what it was we had done wrong. And this time it was to do with my school work.

"Oh."

"You haven't done any of the stuff set this week? Really?"

"I have done some!"

"Ten minutes of maths does not count. I trust you to get on with it and take responsibility for your own learning. We've talked about how important this is, Faye. Am I going to have to watch over you? Or get Frankie to come over and sit with you?"

"No, Mum."

Frankie lived next door and was on her own, so was allowed to come over and help with childcare. But she was also Mum's closest friend, and she would often appear at the door and end up staying for dinner, and she and Mum would sit up late into the night drinking wine and talking and laughing. Shelley and I liked her – she was like an older version of Mum, although I don't think she could have been that far into her fifties. She was tall and beautiful with the deepest, brownest eyes I had ever seen, and always had a slight air of glamour about her, even when she was dressed casually. I think it was the way she carried herself: like someone proud of her height, proud of the person she was. I used to watch her with some fascination, wondering if that sort of confidence just came naturally as you grew older. I didn't think it did. I wondered what she would say to me now – probably nothing, but she would look at me in that probing way she had that always made me want to confess all my worst deeds (which really weren't that terrible. Slacking off with my schoolwork was probably as bad as it got).

Mum sighed and sat down on my bed. "So, what's the solution? You spend two days a week at school, that's not

15

enough learning time. That's why the teachers set you the online stuff. You need to work harder, Faye."

"I know. I'm sorry."

"What are you going to do?"

"Work harder. Spend more time on it. Make sure I get it all done."

"Right," she flipped the duvet back. "Starting now."

I sighed. It was Saturday and I'd planned to catch up with my friends, but I knew there was no point in arguing. And so it was that I had to spend the next couple of weeks proving to my mother that I could be trusted to complete my school assignments. It wasn't that I found the work too difficult, or even that I was disinterested. I just found it hard to focus when I was given such a free reign and trusted to get on alone. And I preferred reading alone, or, as I've said, listening in on my mum at work, fascinated by how much respect and admiration she seemed to command from anyone she spoke to on the screen, whoever they were and wherever they were from. It filled me with pride, but it wasn't just that. It was good to see that others saw her as I did. She was the one with all the answers, all the knowledge in the world to make everything okay.

I mentioned my friends, and I should probably say more about them. I only had two friends, or two that I would call proper friends: Daisy and Aaron. I talked to other kids at school but didn't hang out with anyone else, and that was fine by me. I didn't see the point of having more friends than that. Apart from that, I only mixed with ten other kids at school, and only two days a week, because of the staggered school shifts preventing too many of us from mixing at one time. This was the way it had always been so I had never thought it was strange, but Mum had told us it hadn't been like that when she was growing up. Thirty or more kids would mix in classes, and people would even crowd together to celebrate or party or watch events. When she and my dad first met there were still places where people would squash together to dance in a hot, sweaty room. That was normal then. Now everyone has just got used to living life at arm's length, so that those days my mother describes just sound strange, and rather unappealing.

Anyway, Daisy and Aaron were twins so we were allowed, according to the complicated ever-changing rules, to meet outside of school as they lived in the same house. We saw each other most weekends, but now I had to message them to say I couldn't.

So that was life as I knew it at ten years old, before the events. There was my dad too, I really should have mentioned him properly, although I couldn't remember when we'd seen him last in real life. It must have been sometime when Shelley was still a baby because I barely remembered him being around. He lived in New Zealand and sent us emails and presents in the post, and we spoke on the holowall, or 'wall', which was the video link program Mum used for work, but that was about it. He was doing some important conservation work over there which was very cool and exciting, but I felt as detached from it as I did when I watched wildlife documentaries, because he was almost as much a stranger to me as the presenters of those. I realise I should have been more aware of what was happening with the world simply because of the nature of his job, but it really wasn't something I thought about much, then. Sometimes I forgot he even was my dad, which sounds strange and probably quite callous. But I don't think he'd have minded; I think there were times when he forgot too.

Chapter 3

Everyone remembers where they were when the announcement was made. It was one of those rare moments that are felt across the world, like the effects of the first big pandemic or the death of someone really huge and important. Things changed almost overnight, in our own lives but more noticeably in the outside world. On Newsquest it was all they ever talked about – it was all anyone talked about. Except for Mum, who spent more and more time in her office, often with the door shut, much to my indignation and concern.

Shelley was the one who alerted me to it, as usual. I was in my room daydreaming (as usual) with my homework spread out in front of me, and she barged in, making me jump.

"I think you should come and listen to the TV, Mum says something important is going to happen. About the extra... the extra... trestralls."

"Really? All that stuff about the weird signals was ages ago."

"It wasn't, it was just now. Come and see!"

I rolled my eyes, but followed her into the living room, where Mum was stretched out on the giant sofa staring at the big screen on the wall.

"Shelley says..." Mum held up her hand and waved it at the sofa: be quiet and sit down.

There was an important-looking woman on the screen wearing a suit, and the text underneath said she was indeed someone important, the Outer Space Consultant for the UN

(Shelley and I were fascinated that there could be someone with such a job title). The reporter in the newsroom was interviewing her.

"So how much can you actually tell us at this moment about Comet?"

"Well, the signals are still being carefully analysed at NASA and here at the UN, and we're working together to decode them, and work out exactly where they're coming from."

"But is it true that this morning the messages changed?"

"That's right, where up until now they've just been signals sent via electromagnetic waves, no actual messages but just a signal originating outside the Earth's stratosphere, today they appear to have been sent in several different languages."

"You mean... our languages? So, you can understand what they're saying?"

"That's right. So far we've detected English, French, Spanish and Chinese."

"And they're still originating from the same source?"

"Yes."

"So... what are they saying?"

"That information is classified at this moment, while we look at the best ways to transmit a signal in response, if in fact that is the course of action world leaders decide upon."

"Thank you, Miss Khan." The woman disappeared from the screen and the reporter turned to the camera. "In a moment we'll be hearing from the Prime Minister, but later today there is to be an emergency video conference involving leaders from every country in the world, an unprecedented event. This meeting is expected to last several hours while it is decided what the best course of action will be, as we heard just then from Aisha Khan from the United Nations. But one message has been relayed to us from the government, a very clear message that is: do not panic. There is no indication at this time that these are even extra-terrestrial beings trying to make contact, much less that any such contact is deemed as hostile. Later on, top astrophysicist Eduardo Mendez will be joining us to…"

"Mum, what's for tea?" Shelley broke in. Mum looked away from the screen for the first time since I had walked into the room.

"Faye, can you just order a pizza?"

"Yay!" called Shelley, running out of the room to look up the menu. "Pizza, pizza!"

"Mum…?"

"Darling, I really need to watch this. Go and help your sister pick the toppings."

I wandered out into the kitchen, which was actually not really a different room as all our living areas were open plan. But it was far enough from the lounge to let Mum take in the news in peace.

"Were you even watching that?" I asked my sister, who was jumping around singing some inane made up song to herself.

"Yep, they're talking to someone in space."

"And you don't think it's something we should be a little bit worried about?"

She stopped and looked at me, and I felt guilty for putting the idea into her head. She thought for a moment.

"Nope. They can be our friends. Maybe they'll save the world."

I grabbed the tablet off her. "Save it from what?"

"I don't know. Baddy aliens?"

It was a school day the next day, and before we'd even got on the bus the other kids were going on about it. We had to wait at different sections and get different buses, but the bus stops were close enough together that we could overhear. And red section were going on about UFOs.

"My dad says we won't know anything about it. One day we'll be here and the next, ZAP!"

"We've got to keep looking out for them. Hey, what's that? That weird dot in the sky?"

"A cloud, stupid."

"And that thing moving up there and leaving a trail behind it is a plane, before you ask!" One kid punched the other on the arm.

"Actually, technically 'UFO' stands for 'unidentified flying object', so if you don't know what it is it's a UFO. Doesn't mean it's a spacecraft." That kid got a slap round the head.

Daisy and Aaron were none the wiser when they arrived at the bus stop. Apparently the Prime Minister had said the same about not panicking, and had said the public would be kept informed as soon as all the important leaders had finished their meeting. But that already wasn't true, because the woman from the UN had said they weren't telling us what was in the messages.

The bus pulled up and we all filed on.

"Why do you think they're keeping that secret?" I asked Daisy. "Surely if they're being friendly they could just have said so?"

"I don't know. Maybe they just want to check all the messages are the same. You know, in all the languages."

"How did they know how to speak our languages if they've come from outer space?" Aaron said ominously, "That's what I want to know."

"Hey, look!" Daisy called, and everyone leaned to peer out of the front of the bus. There was a crowd of about twenty or thirty people gathered, most holding placards and looking grim faced. I wasn't sure if I was more surprised that there were so many people gathered together – I hadn't seen such a crowd in ages – or by what was written on the boards they held up.

'THE END IS NIGH'; 'SAVE OUR SOUL'S', and even 'DEATH TO ET's'

"Look at that!" said Aaron. We stared as the bus swooped past them, their voices muffled by the windows but their expressions and signs leaving no doubt as to their message.

"I know, right? There's no need for random apostrophes!" We stared at Daisy and then, the tension released, we began to giggle.

After that I veered between the slight hysteria we had all felt at seeing the protesters, to outright panic. Mum was no help – usually she was my beacon whenever I felt worried or sad, but right now, when I'd begun to have nightmares about strange beings watching me while I slept and kidnapping people for experiments, she was nowhere to be seen. Well, I knew exactly where she was, but it felt like a silent understanding that we didn't disturb her when her office door was closed. It didn't help much that Shelley was so calm. I'm not sure quite what I expected from a five-year-old, and I knew it was better for her to be slightly oblivious, but it just made me feel like more of a big baby because I was so much more worried about the situation than she was.

It was mostly the unknown I was fearful of. I had gone from watching barely any news at all to obsessively scouring Newsquest for information, but it all seemed so vague. The more they told us not to panic the less calm I felt. My imagination was my worst enemy, not just my subconscious at night time attacking my dreams, but during the day too, when in normal circumstances the nightmare monsters subsided and seemed like nothing. I found myself scouring the skies like that kid at the bus stop, catching my breath every time it looked like something unfamiliar, ominous, and blinking to see it was just a bird.

When, finally, there was more news (it can only have been a couple of days later, but in my semi-petrified state it had felt much longer), it did little to calm my insides.

"I wish to confirm this afternoon, that contact has indeed been made by extra-terrestrial beings." I stared at the face of the Prime Minister, larger than life on the screen in the lounge. It was difficult to read his expression; it was like a mask that revealed nothing, looking both stern and sincere. "Before anything else, I must reassure the British public that there is no cause for alarm. In fact, Comet scientists have been able to send a return signal and have in effect been conversing, and all indications at this time are that their intentions are nothing but peaceful. Further information will be available as soon as we know it."

As soon as he stopped speaking there was a flurry of questions from the small group of reporters that had been selected to ask them.

"Mr Prime Minister, do we yet know where the visitors are from?"

"How many of them are there up there?"

"How long have they been observing our planet?"

"You say their intentions are peaceful, what actually are their intentions?"

"Have we got any missiles in place to defend ourselves?"

He held up a hand, "I must ask for calm. I will answer two questions now, but I'm afraid most will have to wait until we know more ourselves. The scientists are trying to communicate constantly and are keeping world leaders updated as to any developments. All I can say for sure is: there is no cause for panic or alarm, no reason why we can't all carry on our daily lives as before."

He was about to address the questions when Mum's smartwatch buzzed. As she answered I tried to hear the PM's responses.

"...at this time, as communications are still somewhat primitive between us. We hope to ask these questions of them in due course."

"Right, I see." My focus shifted to Mum. She was looking shocked, but I couldn't work out if it was bad news she was hearing.

"Mum?" she held up a hand but smiled to reassure me.

"Yes of course," she was saying. "I'll get on to it right away. Send me the details and I'll start a report. I'm available straight away as all my other projects have been put on hold. Certainly. Thank you."

She tapped her watch to end the call, and stared ahead.

"Mum? What is it?"

She looked at me with a slight smile.

"That was work. ComET have requested me to be the chief liaison and communications leader."

My mind was blank. "What… for who?"

She gestured at the screen,

"For them. The visitors! You know, Project ComET: Communications with Extra Terrestrials."

I couldn't do anything but stare at her.

"How? I mean… You've said yes?"

"Of course I've said yes, it's an amazing opportunity. They're going to encode my messages and transmit them for me, but they want me to be able to keep the peace, as it were, and find out as much as I can about them whilst keeping them happy and calm, with no sense of threat on either side."

"And you're okay with that?"

"Darling, it's what I do!" She laughed. I groaned and rolled my eyes at her cheesiness, but couldn't quite join in the frivolity. "Also, it's a huge honour. Right, if you'll excuse me I need to get prepared."

Chapter 4

The news continued to buzz and I wasn't allowed to tell anyone that my mother was going to be talking to whoever it was that was sending the messages. The 'don't panic' slogan had started popping up everywhere, on billboards, bus stops, even posters at school. We had a special assembly where the head teacher spoke to us all, at home or at school, via the wall. I was in school that day, and watched from my classroom as she told us how exciting it all was, how it gave the human race the potential opportunity to find out more about outer space and our universe than we had ever known. This echoed some expert or world leader (I was losing track of them all) who had spoken on the news the previous day, telling us we were at the cusp of realising things we hadn't discovered in years and years of research. What Mrs Daniels, our headteacher, didn't add was that we, the human race and our representatives and experts, were proceeding with caution. And next to the 'don't panics' were increasing amounts of other slogans and messages, graffitied or written in shop windows and houses. They shouted out, silent and hysterical. 'There's nowhere to hide!' 'Let's fight back – join the resistance' 'Are you prepared to fight for your planet?' And as I read them I carried my secret around: my own mother was going to be communicating with these beings: messages of welcome and peace.

But no one had actually seen the visitors yet, or found any trace of them. That was soon to change, of course, but for several days as tensions and anxiety bubbled, NASA was using its powerful telescopes to detect Near Earth Objects which looked unusual or could resemble a spacecraft, with no significant results. Astronauts aboard the many space stations out there were on high alert, although we were told anything seen from the thermosphere, where they were orbiting Earth, would probably be spotted from Earth first. Mum was spending more and more time in her office, but this time she was sometimes leaving the door open, so one day I sneaked into my old spot by the threshold to listen for any information that wasn't already being churned out on repeat in the living room. We had the twenty-four hour news channel on every day and its presence was unnerving – the dramatic music playing out over the headlines and the serious voices of the reporters – but none of us had brought ourselves to switch it off in case we missed something.

"I realise we have to be careful," Mum was saying. "But this is the approach we need to take. It is vital that we do not refer to any sort of potential hostilities when nothing like that has been hinted at in these transmissions."

"I get what you're saying Helen, but I really feel we need to set the boundaries now, and make it clear we mean business if any sort of threat is detected." This was from one of the people on the screen, a dark haired woman with a nasal voice.

"No. Absolutely not. That is no way to begin delicate proceedings such as these. I'm sorry, but you want me on board and this is the way I operate."

"I agree with Helen," an older man spoke up. "We've worked together several times, admittedly never on anything quite like this, but her approach works. It really does."

"Right, well if we're all in agreement, we'll transmit Helen's communication today," said another guy on the screen with a strong accent I couldn't quite identify. "If at any time a threat

27

is perceived then we can go with a more... direct approach. Everyone happy? Kate? Rishi? I know you weren't too sure about this."

Everyone nodded and after a few more exchanges the conference ended. Mum sighed and went to drink her tea, which must have been stone cold. I had a sudden urge to hide or make myself scarce, but at that moment she turned around.

"Ah, hello my little eavesdropper! School work all done I suppose?"

I made a gesture with my hand out flat that was meant to say 'sort of but not really...' accompanied by a sheepish look.

"Well. I need a break and hot cup of tea. Keep me company in the kitchen?"

I followed her into the kitchen, which was bright white already but almost dazzling with the warm sun streaming through the windows and bouncing off the surfaces.

"You really should be outside in the garden on a day like this, if you're up to date with your home learning. I'm sure Shelley would love to join you out there."

"She'll just try and get me to play dolls with her." The truth was, I rarely ventured outside unless I really had to. It was too much effort to put on the sunblock and make sure I had the right clothing to avoid sunburn. Especially as the hot days of spring were approaching. We had the air conditioning set up so that the humidity and oxygen were at healthy levels, so I told myself it was just like being outside anyway.

I watched Mum fill the kettle. "Mum, can I ask you something?"

"Always."

"Are you sure you want to be the one who talks to the aliens?"

"I prefer to think of them as visitors." She looked at me, "welcome visitors. Imagine all the information they must possess! Talking to them will be fascinating. I feel hugely honoured to be one of the people chosen to do so."

"So you're not at all worried?"

"About what?"

"I don't know... about them being... hostile?"

"No. I think if they had any evil intentions we would know by now. Or we wouldn't, and our planet would have been blown up!"

I didn't see the funny side of her flippant comment.

"Mum! I'm serious!"

"I know you are darling." She tucked a strand of hair behind my ear. Flat, dull brown – although it was as unruly as my mother's, I hadn't inherited her deep auburn colouring with all the different highlights that showed up in the sun, like they were now. "I know," she replied. "I shouldn't have joked. But I really do think we're very lucky these people have found us. We may be able to learn a lot from them."

"People?"

"Yes. Why not? They may not be human people, but I feel like they are people. Until we know what they'd prefer us to call them, of course!"

"And what sort of things do you think we'd learn?"

"Well from a scientific perspective there's an awful lot of course. The technology they've used to find us and get close enough to transmit signals, and to learn our languages." An involuntary tingle sent prickles onto my skin. This was the first thing that had unnerved me about the whole situation, I realised, when Aaron had asked how long they had been watching us. Mum didn't seem to notice my unease. "But more than that, we as humans have so much to learn. About avoiding conflict and reversing the damage we've done to our planet. So much."

She gave me one of her sudden hugs; these were one of the best things about my mother. Her hugs were fierce and reassuring, leaving you feeling slightly breathless but intensely comforted all at once.

"Don't worry, darling. I know the unknown can be scary, and you must have seen and heard all those angry and frightened people declaring war before we've even had the chance to find out why they're here. Those are people that take the propaganda they read and the films they see far too literally, I think. And a lot of them are quick to believe the worst and spread conspiracies. But trust me when I say, handled in the right way, this will only be a good thing for our planet."

And I suppose she was right. Sort of. And most certainly not in the way she had meant at the time.

The next day, the visitors were spotted.

Chapter 5

It was NASA with those huge telescopes. A spokesperson admitted on the news that the craft had initially been missed because it was identified as a comet, but because it was unexpected and seemed to have come from nowhere, it was double checked. Sure enough, it was making directly for Earth, approaching our exosphere faster than any comet or asteroid spotted before. The spokesperson told us that NASA had a record of all the space objects that were on a possible collision course with Earth, and that this hadn't been one of them until a couple of days before. It was estimated that, should it continue at such a pace and trajectory, the comet/spacecraft would hit the Earth in less than a week.

Mass panic ensued. I had thought people were already panicking, with their protests and threats of violence against any invaders, but I realised that had been nothing. There were reports of riots, lootings, even shootings in some cities around the world. The suicide rate was alleged to have gone up, people were digging underground bunkers, and the shops had empty shelves. The food and water rations usually stopped people from taking more than their fair share, but somehow people were still stockpiling huge amounts of flour, rice, bread, tinned food, toilet paper. And it was happening around the world, footage was shown of people in America, Europe and Asia, crying in the streets, fighting to get into the shops. There were even people being mugged for their shopping; ordinary groceries turned into precious currency. The latest pandemic that had hit a year or so back had been forgotten, as people jostled and shoved each other in the streets, getting closer to each other than they had done in months. I watched it all with a sense of unreality, as though watching a film. It all just seemed too far removed from anything I knew.

The government emergency response tactics employed in previous crises meant that even stricter food rationing was quickly introduced in most towns and cities in the UK, with the army even stationed in the doorways of many supermarkets. The stocks slowly rose again. But it couldn't be said that calm was restored. In fact, I didn't quite realise it at the time but I'm sure I had an inkling in the pit of my stomach, where fear had made a permanent home, that things would never go back to how they had been. I tried to remember my mother's calming words, and she spoke many more reassurances to us both as the world lost its mind around us, but none of it quite got through. Shelley was her usual pragmatic self, asking rhetorical questions at every opportunity. "Do you think they look like us?" "I wonder if they go to toilet?" "What must they eat?" and so on, so that it was hard not to be affected by her infectious good humour. And I was grateful for it, because every time I saw the news it seemed that chaos reigned.

There wasn't even much respite at school. The kids at the bus stop and even those in my class talked of nothing else, which wasn't all that surprising I suppose, but I was surrounded by them doing daft impressions of alien beings speaking with strange robotic voices. "We come in peace"; "I will exterminate you."

"Give it up, Aaron, you look more like a zombie than an alien," Daisy sighed, without even looking up from her maths.

"How do you know?" Aaron replied, leaning into her with an inane look on his face, before the teacher called out to restore order.

And then, when I thought the world couldn't get any more strange or scary, news hit that momentarily stopped us all in our tracks, before sending out a yet more hysterical wave of fear in the already less than stable minds of many.

Several 'pods' had been spotted hovering in the outer reaches of the Earth's atmosphere. The comet-like object seen hurtling towards us just days before had now inexplicably and abruptly stopped, and was orbiting the Earth along with around twenty others. I imagined them, hovering there, waiting.

Mum sat us down one evening to tell us classified information that could have seen her disgraced, or far worse, but as I've said she was never one to hide information, especially not when it was causing such disruption and fear all around us. Sometimes the unknown is worse than the actual truth.

"I know this is a very strange time for you both, and probably a little scary too. But I want to reassure you that I'm not scared, and I don't feel we have anything to be afraid of."

"How can you know that though, Mum?"

"She's been talking to them, of course she knows!"

"That's right Shelley, I have. And I'm going to tell you what we've been saying. But you have to know that I really shouldn't be doing this, and I could get into lots of trouble if anyone found out. I hate to ask you, but can you promise me this will stay between the three of us?"
Shelley nodded solemnly.

"Of course, Mum," I answered. "I doubt anyone would believe us anyway."

"Thank you girls. The only reason I'm telling you is to reassure you."

She picked up her tablet.

"Okay. I'm going to read it out to you." She took a deep breath and a sip of her wine. "Initial communication, recorded in five languages, sent repeatedly within the three days it took us earthlings to decide how to respond.

"Hello. Are you receiving.

Hello. Do you receive us. Etcetera.

(Our reply)

Hello. Who are you.

(Theirs)

We approach your planet. To find out information.

(Us)

Where are you from?

(Them)

Our sun is (we couldn't decode their meaning here, but I guess they're telling us how far they've travelled. The problem is they would use different measurements for miles or light years and so on)...

(Us)

Why have you come here?

(Them)

To find information. We have found no other planets with complex life forms.

(Us)

We are happy to tell you about our planet. Can you tell us about yours?

(Them)

We are pleased to exchange information.

(Us)

How can you speak our languages?

(Them)

We have studied your signals sent out beyond the surface of your planet. (By this we think they mean satellite signals and communications with the space stations.) We have algorithm technology which decoded and translated your language.

(Us)

What is your planet like?

(Them)

It looks similar to yours, but is somewhat smaller. We request to enter your atmosphere to discover more about your world.

(Us)

We will need to confer on this. We will get back to you when we have made the decision.

(Them)

We will allow you some time to confer.

She looked up. "And that's it for now. We've barely touched upon any of the things we need to say. There are just so many questions…"

"Mum, what do they mean by 'we will *allow* you time…'"

"Just that they'll let us discuss it and then wait and see what they have to say, I suppose."

"And what if we don't answer them soon? Or they don't like the answer we give them?"

"I think a lot of what they say may come across as slightly cold and clinical, but we need to remember that they are beings from another planet. They've learnt our language through computer software and will have no idea of the subtleties of our speech or how tone of voice affects meaning. Translators have already seen some discrepancies between the different languages they're using to talk to us, what means one thing in Chinese can mean something different in French, for example. This is why we haven't released any of the transcripts to the public yet. It's just far too open to interpretation. But you can hear there's no obvious suggestion of threat of any hostility, can't you?"

I wasn't so sure if I could hear what my mother was clearly so eager to believe.

"And they want to come and see us!" Piped up my sister. "Please can we let them Mummy, please!"

"Well, it's not up to me, darling. I'm just there to make sure communications are clear and friendly from our side." She winked at Shelley, "But I can put a good word in if you like?"

"Yay, yay!" She jumped up and down and twirled around, "I'm going to meet a nextra trestrall!"

"You really need to learn how to pronounce it properly, then," I muttered. Mum caught my eye and gave me what was meant to be a reassuring wink.

Chapter 6

Mum was busy for the next day or so negotiating the best way to respond to the knowledge that there was more than one spacecraft orbiting Earth. It wasn't my shift at school so I was at home, and found it difficult to settle to anything. I half-heartedly got on with my school work, tried to read a bit, called Daisy and Aaron for a wall chat. But none of it helped – none of it got the image out of my mind of the flying saucers (as I saw them) suspended ominously just outside our atmosphere, waiting to descend. We had more of an idea now, from the constant chatter of the news channel, of the size of the crafts. Just a bit larger than a large family car, apparently. There were around twenty five of them, positioned all around the Earth, and it had been speculated that they could have come from a much larger craft, waiting further away, but the telescopes, intently poised and scouring the tiny area of space we thought we knew, had yet to pick anything up. And all the time the tensions in the world outside grew and grew.

Information was slowly released about the nature of the communications so far. Information we at home had, of course, already seen. Most of the world leaders, news reporters and scientists were still sure the visitors' intentions were peaceful, that there had been nothing sinister about the crafts appearing in our atmosphere without our knowledge. It was admitted that it had been rather alarming at first, but communications remained civil and no attempt was being made by the crafts to approach any closer. The situation was at a stalemate while world leaders had meeting after meeting to thrash out the pros and cons of allowing extra-terrestrials onto our soil for the first time in the history of the universe (at least, to our knowledge). Obstacles such as cross-contamination, logistics of landing the craft and military defence, should the need arise, were all mentioned, and still no decision could be reached. It was the leaders the decision rested with, but the people were making their voices heard too. There were the protests, some peaceful, some becoming angry riots, and some more paranoid branches of society around the world shouting that we should not co-operate. But there were also others – lesser politicians, religious leaders – who were voicing their concerns or words of support (the latter seemed quieter, to me). I saw footage of one man warning his congregation the 'aliens' were 'messengers from God, sinners should beware. He is cleansing our society like He did in the Great Flood…'. It all just added fuel to the panic and confusion.

In the midst of this, we were surprised by a call from Dad. We thought he was deep in a rainforest in Fiji, and hadn't heard from him for several weeks. He usually emailed, or sometimes phoned, but this time it was a wall chat. It was the first time I'd seen his face, apart from in the photos he sometimes sent, for longer than I could remember. Shelley, usually so chatty and animated, was strangely quiet.

"Hi girls, great to see your faces."

"Hi. Where are you?"

"Back home in Wellington, where my office is. Well, my room in my apartment with the computer, anyway."

He'd aged from the man I remembered – not surprising, I suppose. His hair had gone greyer and he had a bit of a beard. He also spoke with a strong accent I hadn't noticed before, as though he had lived in New Zealand all his life, not in Dorset until he was at least thirty-five.

"Is it nice there?" It sounded like the sort of question Shelley might ask, had she been acting like herself, so I was sort of asking on her behalf. I felt strangely shy myself, talking to this man who was a virtual stranger to us.

"Beautiful. Hey girls, I don't want you to be worried about all this stuff that's going on."

"Oh... it's okay, we're not really."

"Mum's handling it," blurted Shelley. I gave her a look and a sharp nudge. Of all the moments to pick to finally speak, she had really chosen it. I was worried Dad might pick up on it and ask what exactly she meant, but it seemed to go over his head – either that or the connection dipped out at the right moment.

"Great, great. But look, you're a bit in the thick of it there, close to the hub of things and all that. I just think you might feel safer elsewhere, you know?"

"What do you mean, the thick of things?"

"Well, you're not far from London, and I reckon if these aliens wanted to attack they'll go for the larger capital cities first."

"London is two hours away from here."

He gave a sort of scoffing laugh, "Love, these guys have travelled however many light years to get here. I doubt a couple of hours will make much difference to them!"

"Well, they're not going to attack..."

"No, Mum says so." Shelley again. I nudged her again.

"Well, I'm sure she doesn't want you to worry. But honestly, I think you'd both be better off down here. We're kind of forgotten about a lot of the time, which is fine by me. With any luck the aliens would forget about us too."

"Down there... in New Zealand? With you?"

"Well, yes. I'd have to talk to your mother about it of course, but I'm sure she'd agree that the most important thing is to keep you safe."

It was a few seconds before I could speak. Dad had never shown this much of an interest in us before and it was hard to understand why now should be any different. We had barely even thought about going over to visit – Mum had mentioned it a couple of times but it had never seemed like a realistic – or even that desirable – prospect. I wanted to see the place he talked about, experience those vast mountains and lakes for myself, but I knew Dad was busy and the reality would be that we'd spend more time on our own or in a hotel than with him.

"What about Mum?"

"Well – she could come too, of course."

"So you haven't mentioned it to her yet?"

"Not yet. Wanted to sound you girls out first. The schools are great out here, and the nurseries for the little one."

Shelley suddenly lost her inhibitions, "I'm *not* little, I'm at big school! And I don't want to leave Mum, or England, or my friends!"

Dad held his hands up as if in defence, even though he was nearly twelve thousand miles away.

"Okay kiddo, it's just a thought. I think when me and your mum have talked, though, it'll be decided it's in your best interests. It's really not that bad a place, you know. Some would even say it's the best place on the planet."

Mum must have known she was being discussed; she had given us some space to talk to Dad privately when the call came through, but now she peered around the door of my room.

"Everything okay here? Hi, Mark."

"Helen. You're looking good."

"Well – thank you."

It was strange – I hardly remembered hearing them speak to each other before. They were like acquaintances making painfully awkward small talk.

"I'd like to have a chat sometime if that's okay with you, Helen. I've just put an idea to the girls that I think they're pretty excited about." I was at a loss to know where he had gained that impression from. Shelley's mouth dropped open slightly, mirroring my own.

"Oh? That sounds interesting. Well, there's no reason why we can't all discuss it now then." Mum sat down on the edge of my bed.

"I think it's best left to the adults to discuss, if you get my meaning."

"You've already discussed it with Faye and Shelley, so I don't see the need to exclude them now."

"Right. Okay, well it's my thinking that they'd be better off here."

"There?"

"Yep."

"With you?"

"Yes."

Mum didn't give anything away about what she was thinking, or even appear that surprised.

"Why?"

"Helen, this is why I wanted to discuss this alone. You know the situation, things are getting pretty scary with aliens literally above us, ready to crash down and start a war, or just outright destroy us at any moment. The girls would be safer here."

"Okay. And that's because the aliens will leave New Zealand alone? When they destroy our planet?"

I found myself trying not to smile, and coughed behind my hand, not daring to catch Shelley's or Mum's eyes. I knew that this was a serious discussion, but I was also confident that Mum would not be talked around into agreeing to this bizarre suggestion. Having seen her at work, I knew she would never agree to anything she didn't truly believe in.

"I just think we're more... cut off here. You know?"

"No Mark, I don't. I know your heart is in the right place, but we are under no immediate threat. The girls will be just as safe here as they would there. Besides, aren't you pretty busy to be looking after two young girls?"

"Well, I was saying you could come over too. You know – if you wanted. Get an apartment nearby. Look, maybe we should talk about this another time."

"I don't think so. I'm sorry, but I can't just uproot our lives for no reason. Things work very well as they are, and I really don't think there's any danger here." She looked at us, "I'm sorry girls, I would never usually make a decision like this without you, but I just don't think it's necessary."

I turned to look at my dad on the screen.

"Sorry Dad, I think I want to stay here. I like it here, this is my home, and I think Mum is right that the visitors are going to be friendly. If they weren't then we'd probably know by now."

Dad looked at us for a moment. "Right, okay then." He seemed very accepting of my decision, but I suddenly felt pity for him. Perhaps he was genuinely worried for our safety? Or maybe he was lonely out there.

"Do you agree Shelley? Say if you don't."

"I want to stay here with you and Mummy."

"Thank you for the suggestion, Mark. When all this has calmed down I'll bring the girls out there for a visit. I know they're desperate to see the place. And you, of course."

"Yep… yes, you must do that. Pretty busy right now though, so I'll be in touch. Take care of yourselves, won't you."

After he had gone, Mum looked a bit sheepish.

"I'm sorry to have barged in like that. I meant it about going to New Zealand. We will go, as soon as this project is finished. I never want you to feel cut off from your father, or as though I'm keeping you from him."

"We know, Mum." Shelley nodded in agreement, and then gave her a sudden tight hug, as though she was anxious Dad was about to burst through the door and take her away.

The truth was, it had felt a bit surreal hearing Dad talk like that. But later, it wasn't the suggestion he made that stayed in my head, it was the language he used to describe the aliens. *Could* they destroy us all, just like that? I had heard Mum's assurances, and mostly believed them. But the truth was, no one actually knew.

Frankie came over that day, and later that night, unable to get to sleep, I listened around the corner as they sat talking in the kitchen. I hadn't meant to eavesdrop, I'd gone to get a drink of water, but they were so deep in discussion I hadn't wanted to interrupt.

"...I spend my life negotiating with terrorists and criminals and politicians – and more recently extra-terrestrials! – and not once have I felt that wound up!"

Frankie laughed, but didn't reply.

"I mean – he hardly even knows the girls! And he chose that life – it works. I felt like he was suggesting I don't know how to keep them safe. I've managed very well so far!"

"Yes, you have."

"I know he meant well, though. And now I'm wondering if the girls felt pressured into saying no because I was there."

"Of course they didn't, Helen. They know very well that they can tell you anything, and if they say they want to stay, then that's the truth."

"Thank God, Frankie. I mean – it would be impossible anyway."

"Absolutely. If you think I'm letting you move away then you're crazier than I thought."

It was strange, hearing my mother talk about feeling uncertain, doubting herself. I wasn't sure I liked it. I crept back to bed.

Chapter 7

There were debates upon debates taking place everywhere. Between world leaders behind closed doors, in the House of Commons, on Prime Minister's Question Time – even at school and in people's homes. The same arguments made and questions asked, over and over.

"Can the governments of the world ensure our safety?"

"What exactly do they want from us?"

"Are they being properly monitored by NASA telescopes?"

"Is mankind doomed?"

Among the many voices of dissent that had been so loud, though, were other voices, quiet at first but gaining in strength and number. Voices asking why we couldn't accept the visitors, allow them the insight into our world they were asking for, and in turn discover more about space than decades of scientific research had afforded us so far. And these voices, put next to the angry hysteria and, sometimes, violence of the dissenters, sounded reasonable; calm. It was acknowledged that caution was needed, but also argued that, with the right measures in place, why couldn't we co-operate? Some arguments were that we should do so because the consequences of trying to send them away could be far worse, but most people with this view felt that it was simply the right thing to do.

Sometimes these huge life-changing, global events bring people closer together. They unify us with a common cause, and a desire for things to change for the better. Often, though, fear of that very change is what divides us. And so the world's opinion was largely split into two camps: the 'Welcomers' and the 'Protectors', as they called themselves (although each group had different labels for the other. The Surrenderers and the Hostiles being the most polite). Even celebrities, big and small, were using their platforms to add their voices to the cacophony (a few of whom from the safety of palatial, purpose-built shelters). Opinions were fierce on both sides, accusations were thrown and the anger inevitably spilled out onto the streets.

But eventually the time came for the leaders of the world's nations to vote. All the debates still raged on among the ordinary people, but a final decision had to be reached, not least because to do nothing seemed in itself an act of hostility. And that decision lay with these two hundred or so powerful people, at the virtual UN conference that had been in progress now for several days.

I wondered what the extra-terrestrials were thinking, up there in their capsules, if indeed they did think in the way that humans did. How many were in each pod? Were they lonely there, wishing they had stayed at home instead of being light years away, suspended over this blue unwelcoming planet? Did they have a plan for what they would do if the answer was no, you are not welcome here? Would they simply drift off, continuing their search for life on other planets? How long had they been away from home? Did they have families, loved ones, waiting at home, or knowing that once they set off on their mission they would never see them again? I realised that I wanted to know. I was curious about these creatures, if that was the right term for them. The longer they stayed up there, waiting in a state of limbo, the less threatening they seemed, somehow.

It wasn't as though my fears had evaporated – they were still there, niggling me now and then, but I had a unique insight from everything Mum was telling us. And also, the sight of those angry people, destroying property and setting things alight in the name of their beliefs; so certain that these beings we had never seen were intent on world domination or destruction. But it was these humans who were the destroyers, that much was clear to me. And the calm voices of reason, although far quieter, had more impact on me.

The live streamed result was another moment in history that I knew we would never forget. There seemed to be so many lately. I knew I would remember insignificant details: how the glass of milk in my hand felt and tasted, the feel of the blanket over our legs, the bright glow of the TV screen in the darkened room – just as much as the fluttery feeling in my stomach, as we watched the result unfold. Mum had allowed us to stay up to watch, although it wasn't that late, probably about eight o'clock, but we knew there would be more information after the result of the vote itself. Whichever way it went, there would be questions to answer, details to iron out.

In the end it was a pretty clear cut decision. It had been decided beforehand that every nation would have an equal say, regardless of its size or power. Each country had its own way of reaching a decision depending on the state – or lack – of its democracy, but I knew that here the Prime Minister had made the decision following debates and votes among politicians from all parties. So even though a couple of the largest countries voted no, the overall decision was a yes. The extra-terrestrials would be landing here on Earth.

I wasn't sure exactly what I felt, but it wasn't dread. It was even perhaps some sort of relief, a sense that the right choice had been made. When it came to it, the human race had pulled together and taken the open minded route, the route that led to discovery and experiences beyond our imaginations. Shelley was clearer in her feelings.

"Mummy! Does that mean they're coming down to see us? Yes yes yay!"

While she was dancing around with her teddy bear I glanced at Mum, and we shared a smile that told me she felt the same way.

Chapter 8

I suppose it had been inevitable, but the hysteria of the 'Protectors' intensified almost immediately. The next day on the way to school, Red Zone's minibus was just ahead of ours and had stopped in the road. Craning our necks to look out of the windows we could see why – a large group of protesters, probably over a hundred people this time, was marching along the road, ignoring the angry blaring horns of the traffic. But the placards that I could see were calling out similar messages to the ones before: 'WE WILL NOT SURRENDER!', 'NUKE EM BEFORE THEY NUKE US!' and 'SAVE OUR PLANET!' were just a few.

The hypocrisy of those suddenly being desperate to protect the planet didn't strike me until much later.

I think Shelley and I had expected the visitors to be arriving within days, but it turned out there were still lots of processes to be gone through. Along with everything else I was learning, I was getting an insight into this aspect of adult life; nothing was simple. Every step taken had to be thought about carefully, analysed and approved. Being a grown up looked like hard work, and I made a pact with myself not to complain about my school work and the chores around the house anymore, for at least a week anyway.

The next step for the politicians and scientists was to work out the logistics of getting the aliens down to Earth, and the safety measures to protect both us and them once they were here. Mum was sitting in with some of the space engineers to try to work out how to use the technology in the visitor's pods along with our own to help them land. Mum admitted to us that the technicalities were all way too complex for her to fully understand (feelings shared, if not openly, by most of the top experts on our planet), but that she was there to keep the communications clear and friendly, as she had been all along.

Even when they were here, the next obstacle was to work out how to keep them alive, and avoid any cross contamination that could harm them or us. Mum – and then the news reporters – told us that they had requested to send down a probe to test the Earth's atmospheric conditions compared to those of the pods, to check that the levels of chemicals like oxygen and carbon dioxide weren't going to kill them outright as soon as they stepped out into our world. In an attempt to calm fractious factions, much was made of the fact the visitors had asked permission, rather than simply sending the probes down anyway. So far their politeness was approved of, and so was their request. If the levels of certain gases were to prove deadly to the visitors then they would make the necessary adaptions, whatever they may be.

For the first time ever we were able to see the mysterious pods that had caused such fear, excitement and unrest among us. The sending of the probe was to be televised using satellite technology, and it was said that over half the population of the world watched it live.

This time we really were staying up. The operation began at 10pm UK time, and we all curled up on the sofa in our pyjamas, with blankets and snacks, hot chocolate and wine (for Mum), and most of Shelley's teddies, as she hadn't been able to decide which one to share this momentous occasion with. It reminded me a little of when we stayed up to watch two astronauts launch off towards one of the space stations; there was a similar feeling of excitement and tension, but magnified beyond anything we had known before. We were about to see a real spacecraft, something that had been made billions of miles away, on a distant planet whose existence we could barely comprehend.

The cameras were showing us our planet, quiet and calm and beautiful in the vast darkness. The angle turned slightly and there it was. At first I didn't know what we were looking at, but it was a bright silver object floating in the near distance. Perfectly curved, almost egg-shaped. It was impossible to tell how big it was, but it had no windows, or visible breaks in the smooth surface. The camera stayed on it for a while, letting the humans back on Earth study it, scour its surface for any clues or insights into what was within. Kind or cruel? Innocent or evil? Who had been right, the Welcomers or the Protectors? But we wouldn't be finding that out yet.

After several minutes of staring, transfixed, we saw a tiny movement in the base of the pod. A small, previously invisible hatch was opening, very slowly. From it emerged a capsule, cylindrical, edging out of the hatch bit by minute bit. I realised I was holding my breath and sneaked a brief glimpse of my mother and sister who were poised, hardly moving, like waxworks frozen in place. Shelley held a piece of popcorn, forgotten in mid-air. The capsule had fully emerged and we could see it was slowly moving. Now it was free of the pod it gained momentum, faster and then faster still, shooting towards our planet. The camera angles changed several times as the different satellite cameras tried to keep up with it, then we could see it drifting away from us, getting closer to the surface of the Earth. It took some time and everyone let out the breaths we had been holding and shifted to more comfy positions.

"This is so cool," Shelley breathed.

"It doesn't look real," I said.

"Isn't it fascinating," agreed Mum. Further and further away the capsule flew, getting closer to us with every second.

"I wonder where it's going to appear." I said, looking up involuntarily as though expecting it to burst through our ceiling.

"This particular pod is currently over India, I think," answered Mum. "But you wouldn't be able to see anything from there. The probe is only going to go just inside our atmosphere, and then somehow it will fly back up."

After the excitement of seeing the pod for the first time, there wasn't a lot to actually watch. The capsule was taking over an hour to descend, even at the speed it was going, and once it was far enough into the atmosphere it was going to suspend there for around another hour, collecting data and measuring levels, before being brought back up. Shelley drifted off to sleep and soon after I felt my own eyes grow heavy as I stretched out under my blanket. I fought to stay awake, but before I knew it I was opening my eyes to the morning sun reaching through the blinds.

Stretching and rubbing my eyes, I saw Shelley was waking up too. Mum was in the kitchen getting coffee.

"Did I miss much?"

"Not really," Mum answered. "You saw the most exciting part. It was after one by the time the probe returned to the craft. I was quite curious about how that bit was going to work, but it was just the same in reverse. Somehow it just started shooting back up into the atmosphere again. Goodness knows how they controlled it. It really is a signifier of how much we have to learn from them."

"So what happens now?"

"Now we wait."

Chapter 9

And it felt like quite a wait. Now a decision had been reached to allow the visitors to actually visit us, there were weeks' worth of checks to do, calculations to make and procedures to decide upon before they could actually touch down.

While I had a sense that there had been a giant shift, and that nothing would ever be quite the same again, it did feel as though some sort of normality had returned. There were still items on the news about pockets of unrest; protests turning violent or Protectors going to extreme measures to defend themselves or show resistance to what they saw as an imminent attack. Gun sales in parts of the world where they were easily acquired had apparently rocketed. Also there were stories of entire families moving into underground bunkers, or people building fortresses around their homes. And it wasn't just those who feared the visitors; on the other side of the argument, some Welcomers were seen dancing around dressed in odd costumes, or even in alien fancy dress, shouting or singing welcome messages. It felt like some people were going quite mad. But, on the whole, much of the discussion I experienced was calm and rational. I once caught the end of an interview between a well-known TV presenter and someone – I wasn't sure who it was – discussing the recent increase in large protests.

"…and while no one wants to deny people their democratic right to protest, surely we still need to remember the threat of another global pandemic, or another strain of the virus, is still as real as ever, and people need to maintain social distancing–"

"So, what we're being told is: it's okay to allow these aliens to land here, with God knows what diseases and pathogens they might be carrying, but we don't want a few humans to gather together? That doesn't seem reasonable to me."

"Well, it's my understanding there will be rigorous checks to make sure no harm comes to them or us through this operation. Are you saying you're against their arrival in principle?"

"Not at all. I recognise the potential for huge leaps of knowledge and understanding, both about our own planet and way, way beyond it. However, I feel we're concerning ourselves with the wrong issues here. We need to be extremely careful…"

Around this time there was another address to the nation by the Prime Minister, along with the video footage of the atmospheric probe and various charts and diagrams mapping out the proposed next steps.

"We are living through the most exciting time in the history of space exploration since mankind stepped onto the moon, almost eighty years ago, and more recently on Mars. For centuries the question has been asked 'is there life out there?', and at last it has been answered in the most definite manner. Without even leaving our own planet, we are going to be able to discover and share information with beings from far beyond our own solar system. This unprecedented experience is bound to strike some fear and trepidation in our hearts; it is the very definition of the unknown, and we have all watched those thrilling science fiction films and read the books depicting hostile invasions from extra-terrestrials. However, this is not fiction. This is real life, and my colleagues around the world and I have full confidence in the positive intentions of our visitors.

"I would like to praise you, the British public, for your resounding support and acceptance of these gestures of peace that have gone both ways, and I would like to share with you the suggested procedures for welcoming them here.

"Only the occupants of one pod will be joining us initially, so this will be two – er – beings, if you like. I would like to pass you to Defence Secretary Geoffrey Gregson with further details." He turned to his left, where a tall, rather skinny man was standing.

"Thank you, Mr Prime Minister. As you can see from these images, the pod that will be joining us is projected to land here, in the Atlantic Ocean, around a thousand miles south-east of Newfoundland. Here it will be met by both British and Canadian aircraft carriers and other military fleet. A temporary base will be set up aboard a classified vessel, where the visitors will be quarantined and receive the relevant medical attention. Having been monitored there for three weeks it will be decided what the next steps will be, whether to return them to their pod or consider a longer stay. This will depend upon many different factors throughout these three weeks. The craft in which they will be travelling will also undergo rigorous checks and be kept in a secure facility."

"Thank you Mr Gregson. So, the timescale of these events will depend on when the results of the probe test are communicated, and then we will take our lead from the visitors, as it will mostly be their technology used to ensure a safe landing, and of course currently we have limited knowledge of this technology. Thank you."

The news reporter appeared back on screen to tell us when the next update was likely to be, and also began to read a statement from Buckingham Palace echoing that of the Prime Minister.

I went through to the kitchen where Mum was preparing dinner.

"Oh, good timing, can you chop these carrots, please?"

I wandered over to the holochef.

"Did you hear all that just then?" I asked.

"Yes, a lot of it I knew as we've been discussing it at work. It really is all up to them now, everything is more or less in place for their arrival. We're as prepared as we can be, considering we know nothing about their anatomy, or their nutritional and atmospheric needs." I stared ahead of me. She was right. Despite all the time I had spent mulling it over, it only really struck me then just how little we knew of the basics about these beings. For all we knew they were akin to sea creatures and needed to be submerged in water, or blobs of slime that would dry up in the heat of the sun.

"Don't you need to find all that out before they get here?"

"As much as possible, yes. It's what we're working on with them."

"Do you think it's strange that we don't really know what to call them? I mean, they're either aliens, extra-terrestrials or visitors. They can call us humans, or people, but we don't really have a proper name for them."

She put down the garlic powder and looked at me.

"Do you know, I've been wondering the same thing. Perhaps I should ask them what they'd like to be referred to. It would make things a lot less awkward wouldn't it! Not that I think you can be awkward with species from a different planet. I hardly think they've got customs or traditions that are in any way similar to ours!"

Her watch rang shrilly, making me jump. She glanced at the screen and frowned a little.

"Oh... sorry darling, I need to take this. Are you happy to take over?"

"Sure, it's only spaghetti bolognese."

Mum was on the phone for a long time, shut inside her study. At one point I pressed my ear to the door to try and listen in, but I couldn't make out what she was saying beyond a few 'No's and 'well of course, but...'. Something in the tone of Mum's voice, though, suggested she was worried, or arguing with the person on the phone. I held off dinner for as long as I could but Shelley was complaining she was hungry and the pasta was starting to stick together, so we ate without Mum. It felt strange, the two of us alone at the table, as though we were playing at being adults.

She came to find us straight after the phone call. We were both in Shelley's room, I was trying to negotiate her into her pyjamas with the promise I would read her a bedtime story.

"Oh girls, you are good. Thank you for helping out, Faye. I can't believe how late it is suddenly."

"It's okay. I covered up your dinner and put it in the oven to keep warm, but I'm not sure it's going to be very nice, sorry."

"It will be perfect, thank you." Mum sat down on the edge of the bed and stared at us both for a bit with a strange half-smile on her face, absently smoothing Shelley's hair.

"I'm sorry I was so long."

"Who was it?"

"It was Rishi, from my department. He's been contacted by some people quite high up in the government. They know about the work we've been doing with the visitors, of course." She looked down, patting the bed covers, and swallowed. Something was up. Shelley, absently arranging her soft toys, didn't seem to notice. When Mum sighed and met my eyes again I noticed with a shock that hers were shining, as though she was trying to fight tears.

"Mum?"

She let out a little laugh and wiped a hand across her face. "Sorry, I'm being silly. There's really nothing for you to worry about. There's just something very important I need to talk to you both about."

"You'll need to go and see them." My sister spoke in that sudden way of hers; just when it appeared she wasn't paying any attention, she would say the most perceptive thing in the room. She had done it so many times already in her short life that I had learned not to dismiss or ignore her. My eyes flitted between them both.

"What? Who?"

"The visitors, of course. Mum's been the one talking to them, so she's going to need to go and see them when they land. Otherwise they won't know anyone and they might be frightened."

Mum laughed through her tears.

"Yes! Yes, darling, that's exactly right." She looked at me, I staring at her wide-eyed.

"Is that what they were asking you about on the phone?"

She nodded.

"It was. A lot needs to be finalised yet, all the different things they were talking about on the news earlier, so it won't be straight away. But yes, they'll need me to go out there, preferably a week or so before the landing for medical checks and to be quarantined, then be there ready to greet them. It won't just be me, of course, there'll be all sorts of other officials and scientists, but they feel there needs to be a friendly face, as it were."

"Can't they just carry on talking to you the way they are now? They could even use the wall, have video calls."

"Darling, while that makes perfect sense and – actually – was a point I made myself, they've travelled trillions of miles from home on this hugely brave mission. They're taking such risks approaching us like this. A lot of talk has gone on about whether it's safe to let them in but, really, *they're* the ones who are in the most precarious position. They're hugely outnumbered, have no knowledge about us beyond the very basic. For all they know we're going to blast them to oblivion the moment they set foot – or whatever – on our planet. This will hopefully be seen as a reassuring gesture of peace and harmony. Which is the most important message to get across right now."

It all made sense, of course.

"But… what about us? What will we do?"

Mum hugged me. "Like I said, a lot needs to be finalised, but I'm sure Frankie will be happy for you to stay with her, or she could move in here." She gave me an extra squeeze. "It wouldn't be for long. A few weeks at the most."

The three of us sat on the bed like that for a few minutes, hugging each other tightly as though Mum was leaving there and then. It was perfectly clear that she needed to go away; I was even a little annoyed at myself for not working it out as quickly as Shelley had. But it didn't make it any easier. We were a team, the three of us. Beyond the small pocket of people at my school I barely saw anyone else. There was rarely tension between us beyond the odd moment when Shelley was an annoying little sister or Mum got me to do things I didn't particularly want to; life at home was easy, it ran smoothly. I didn't want anything to disrupt it. The world outside was changing faster than I could keep up with it, there were dangers and hostilities, and life forms from other planets hovering expectantly above. But at home, things were safe and secure. Ordinary. Just how I liked it. I couldn't shake the feeling that Mum going away marked some momentous change. She'd been away from home before plenty of times on work-related missions and projects, but this was nothing like that. I was afraid. Afraid for her, going off into the unknown, but afraid for us too. What if she never came back?

Chapter 10

Around this time, and most likely because of Mum's new mission (not a parenting one, this time, I couldn't help but think), her role in the negotiations so far was made public. She warned us one morning at breakfast that a local reporter had got hold of the information and called her, so it was inevitable that more would follow. Her department no longer saw the need to keep her association secret, so were going to release a statement that evening.

Even I knew what this meant, or would probably mean. The news coverage had been non-stop since the signals were first detected. Which, of course was hardly surprising with such a story. But anything else hardly got a look in: worldwide elections, the possible threat of another pandemic. The floods, hurricanes, forest fires and latest extinctions were also overshadowed. So I knew the press would latch on to this new development and our part in it. And I was right. When Shelley and I left for school the following day there were reporters waiting for us outside the gates, recording devices thrust into our faces. While there were only five or six of them and not quite the crowd I might have expected from various news reports and TV programmes I'd watched, it was still intimidating, walking along the path while they fired questions at us.

"How do you feel about your mother speaking to the aliens?"

"Was it a shock when she decided to get involved?"

"Can you look this way for a photo? Girls, over here?"

I grabbed for Shelley's hand and we started to run. As we reached the road I could hear Mum's voice.

"Hey, leave my children alone! Please. I'm giving an interview today for EBC, and I'll say everything I have to say then, so you're wasting your time." The cluster of reporters had the grace to look sheepish. "Sam!" Mum called over to the security guard who did the early morning shift. "Sam, isn't there anything you can do?"

"Sorry Helen, they're technically outside the gate." But by now they had seemingly though better of harassing us, and slowly drifted back to their various vehicles.

On the way to school Daisy and Aaron bombarded me with questions about how long I had been hiding things from them, and what exactly I knew. I could see Shelley in front of us on the bus, being interrogated by her friends, too. I didn't mind too much – in fact, hiding the truth from Daisy and Aaron had been incredibly tough. I hadn't been able to talk to them freely about any of it. In ordinary circumstances Mum would be the one I would confide in about anything that was worrying me. But how could I tell her that her job – the one thing outside her role as a parent which gave her great pride and was hugely important – was giving me nightmares, and causing me such anxiety? So in effect I had been hiding not just from my friends, but from her too. To be able to finally talk about it without fear of slipping up and getting Mum sacked or arrested, and to be met with such curiosity and unexpected empathy from Daisy and Aaron, felt like a huge burden being lifted. The attention from everyone else at school, on the other hand, was a bit harder to cope with.

I considered myself a happy introvert. This reticence had rarely been a problem for me – I had been raised knowing it was an asset rather than a flaw. Apart from, that is, in situations when I somehow became the unwilling subject of everyone's attention. I spent an agonising day having kids I didn't know from the other zones shout things at me in the corridor. None of it was insulting or even remotely cruel, but I didn't know how to respond. I simply smiled, went red and ducked my head. I was grateful that inside the classroom there were only ten of us, and that I had known the others for so many years that it didn't really matter. In fact, most of their questions and comments had dried up by first break. But at lunch time, in our section of the playing field, I felt like a reluctant celebrity.

"That's her, that's that girl!"

"Hey, what's your mum been saying to the aliens?"

"Has she seen what they look like?"

Those who didn't call out simply stared. I was glad when the final bell sounded and we could get back onto the school bus.

Preparations – both for the arrival of the visitors and, closer to home, for my mother's departure – took weeks, but the time felt like it was rocketing by. The results from the probe test proved that our atmospheric conditions were suitable for them if they took certain precautions at their end (I wasn't completely sure what these were, but they involved something to do with supplementary oxygen). I was gratified to know Mum had put my question to them about how best to address them, although it had been met with some confusion, I think because they didn't really use names or titles in the same sense as humans.

The aircraft carriers and military personnel from several nations began creating the base in the middle of the Atlantic Ocean where the visitors would be kept throughout their stay. Footage, albeit restricted, showed it to be quite advanced, with a small hospital, sleeping accommodation for humans and non-humans (if indeed they needed to sleep) and several air locks between the compartments to avoid any cross contamination. The humans would be wearing full protective equipment when dealing with the extra-terrestrials. I wondered what their first impressions of us would be. Would they think the baggy silicone was our skin, the goggles our eyes? There had been no way discovered yet to transmit anything but decrypted messages between Earth and their crafts, so we had no film, no photos or even audio to tell us what to expect. And neither, of course, did they. There was huge speculation around the globe, theories put forward and wild guesses made. It was as though the world was holding its breath, steeling itself for some sort of impact.

Mum's TV interview was well received. It was recorded on the wall and it was slightly surreal to see her on TV in her study, lined with the familiar books and files of paperwork. She had decided only to give one interview, and chose EBC because the interviewer had been very pleasant on the phone and supportive of her intentions. This came across on screen, and so largely achieved what she had set out to do. Those who watched it would have been reassured that the visitors meant no ill-will, although those who were still adamant their intentions were to eliminate us would probably not have watched anyway. I had already learned that many people disliked having their viewpoints challenged logically, especially when those viewpoints were extreme.

The three of us watched the interview together. It was part of a weekly show about items that had been in the news, and the presenter was well-known for supporting various charities – specifically environmental and anti-poverty – and generally for being a nice person. Mum was on edge before the programme began. She may have commanded great respect and authority within her daily role, but she hated the idea of being watched by – potentially – millions of people, as she surely would be, now and in the future. I could not say I envied her for it, either.

"I'm talking to Helen Sanders now, the woman behind the scenes of peace talks and negotiations around the world for some years. But more recently she has been involved in the very different, very high-profile project ComET. Helen, welcome to the show and thank you for talking to me."

"Thank you, it's my pleasure."

Shelley and I giggled with excitement at seeing Mum on the TV whilst simultaneously sitting next to her. We had helped her pick out the outfit, her smart shirt with the stripes, and I felt a rush of pride that brought a surprising lump to my throat.

"I'm referring of course to your communications with the extra-terrestrials, which are set to visit us in the next few weeks."

"Yes. And you're right that it's a very different project; obviously we have huge language and, indeed, species barriers. But it's different in many other ways too."

"What ways are those?"

"It's simply about being friendly. Of striking up a rapport and a feeling of mutual trust, which of course is very difficult when you have no prior knowledge of the communicant's culture or customs, background… anything. Usually I would do a great deal of research, but of course this time that was impossible. We came into it completely blind."

"So with that in mind, how *did* you approach it?"

"By remembering that they are in the same position as we are. In fact, if anything their position is more vulnerable than ours. They have limited information about us too; our attitude, our intentions. And they are simply here on a fact-finding mission which I sense is vitally important to them."

"And you're a passionate advocate for the opinion that that is all they're here for."

"Absolutely. They're a very inquisitive species. We already know they're hugely intelligent simply by the fact they have developed the technology to find us and reach us, but I also feel they are excited – if indeed they feel such emotions – at finding life here, and very motivated by the prospect of meeting us and discovering more about us and the planet on which we live. From what I can gather – and it's difficult, because time and distance are difficult to translate when we have no idea how they measure it, and vice versa – but I think they've been on this mission for a huge chunk of their lives already."

"You sound like you're also very passionate and excited."

"Of course, yes. I don't see how we can fail to be. Not only is it a huge honour for me personally, but as a species we too have been searching for evidence of life outside our own planet. So it's a wonderful opportunity for us here on Earth as well."

"In fact, isn't it true that you're going to be amongst the welcoming party when they finally arrive on Earth?"

"That's right. It's a giant understatement I know, but it really is a unique opportunity." She laughed a little. "I've been finding it hard to find the appropriate words to express it all, but I'm very proud to have been selected, and am looking forward to it hugely. We felt it was important I be there as I've

69

spent so long – along with my very hard working team, of course – building up this relationship and more or less being the spokesperson for our species. It makes sense that I should be there to welcome them. Especially as they will be subject to many different tests during their first weeks here, it will more than likely be very overwhelming for them."

"Of course. That's something I think we all need to remember. Now, is it true you will need to be quarantined alongside them?"

"Sort of, yes. I will be in isolation at the base for a week leading up to their arrival, as much for their protection as for ours. And we will all be wearing protective gear when interacting with them."

"Just one final question that I know many viewers will want me to ask, although I think we've covered it already. I suppose I'd just like you to confirm it: do you trust them?"

The camera zoomed in a little closer, possibly for some kind of dramatic effect. Next to us Mum muttered an embarrassed "ugh!" On screen she met the gaze of the interviewer along with that of several million viewers.

"Yes. Completely."

The day before Mum was due to leave, Frankie moved in with us. It was strange; we loved her like she was family, but would have much preferred for Mum to stay home instead. Frankie was used to her own space; she lived alone and was perfectly content. According to Mum she had owned her own law firm a few years back but had sold up and taken early retirement in order to live her life more freely. She clearly had enough to live on, owning a home as large as ours outright, and she spent her time writing for various websites and tending her beautiful garden.

Now she had to share her space with two young girls – not only that, she had to be solely responsible for us. She had no children of her own or, as far as we knew, any childcare experience with any nieces or nephews, but she had looked after us before – albeit only for a few days at a time – and it had always worked out very well. She was always kind and fair, and lots of fun, and I had sometimes thought she would have made a great mum. I knew it wasn't something you could ask someone about. We had learned at school about the birth rates dropping, partly due to a drop in fertility rates, but largely as the popular opinion became more widespread and in-built: the planet was full. It wouldn't have surprised me very much if Frankie had been of the latter opinion, and had simply made the decision not to have children based on that. Or, possibly, she simply relished her independence.

Mum buzzed about, showing her how things worked and chattering about our routines in a way that betrayed that she was anxious about leaving, too. Frankie, who already knew most of the things Mum was telling her, sensed this, and allowed herself to be led from room to room, nodding and reassuring. I felt a tug of gratitude towards her for it.

Shelley had been unusually quiet, despite being more pragmatic than me when Mum first told us she was going away. I made the decision to step up and be the big sister for once, and make sure I was nice to her and try not to get annoyed with her too much over the next few weeks. My mother had already taken me aside to ask me to help out as much as possible.

"Can you please make sure you brush your sister's hair now and then? I don't want her going to school looking like an abandoned child."

"Well, effectively, she is, isn't she?" I teased.

"Ouch!" Mum put her hand to her heart in mock horror. But she was right about Shelley's hair – it had a life of its own and looked like it had been growing for far longer than five years. Left for more than a day or so it became wild and tangled, and I was the only person she ever allowed to brush it, even then often under duress.

Then, suddenly, the preparations were over and the morning arrived when Mum had to leave. The driver arrived early – or so it felt to us – and took her cases out to the car. All that was left was to give her a gigantic hug and then let her go. There was a moment, as she stood there on the threshold looking at us, when I thought she might be about to change her mind. But she didn't, and I knew that I was glad, really. We stood forlornly at the end of the driveway until the car turned the corner and went out of sight.

It wasn't an in-school day for us that day, and so Frankie called in sick for us both and gave us a movie, snacks and pyjama day (although she made it clear it was a one off occurrence). It was just like her to know exactly what we needed: some escapism, combined with too much salt and sugar. I let out a breath I didn't realise I had been holding, and decided maybe this wouldn't be so difficult after all.

The days drifted by and we found a new routine for ourselves. Not a lot changed; I still had my online learning and my days at school. But in between I felt myself a little lost. I wasn't able to settle to anything for very long. The book I was reading didn't hold my attention, Shelley's pleas to play her various games didn't appeal, and I certainly didn't want to sit watching television. The news channel had finally been turned off, perhaps because Frankie felt it wasn't the healthiest thing to have commentating constantly in the background, so for the first few days I searched on Newsquest for developments, not admitting to myself I was looking for a glimpse of Mum. Maybe she'd be in the background, arriving on board the ship and walking past into her quarters.

We spoke to her on the holowall every day, and she had told us about her journey. After a long flight she had been choppered out to the aircraft carrier as though she was in some film. It had sounded thrilling, and we relived it through her eyes as she described it to us. Seeing the huge craft as they emerged from the clouds, surrounded by the stark grey battleships. Landing and getting out onto the vast flight deck, wide and flat and exposed to the elements. The combined force of the wind and the helicopter rotors meant she could hardly think or hear at first, but then the rotors had slowed and been silenced and she had been led to the elevator, a giant platform that took her down to the aircraft hangar. Everything was on a huge scale, made more so by the fact that the ship was mostly empty. The hangar, home usually to planes and other craft, held only a few helicopters. One end, completely inaccessible, had been cordoned off and was hidden behind sheets of a white, plasticky material. This would be the biosecure living quarters for the visitors, and there was room inside for everything they would need, including the pod that would act as their life support vessel.

Mum had been desperate to explore but that would have to wait. For the time being she was sequestered alone in her cabin, a dorm with ten bunks, having meals delivered to her. She had taken her e-book loaded with plenty of reading material, and kept abreast of the news either from the other crew members who made deliveries (shouted conversations through a metal door, which made it sound as though she were imprisoned), or online. But other than that she was quite isolated. Once a day a masked, plastic-aproned doctor came to take her blood pressure and temperature, and, along with chatting to us, that was her only contact with other humans.

Chapter 11

So, after my initial interest in the events of the world, I switched it off, as though I, too was hiding away. Curled up one afternoon on the sofa in the living room I persisted again with the book I was meant to be reading for school, but after ten minutes of reading the same paragraph over and over I let it fall from my hand. I couldn't even focus on any of the games I usually played, and instead lay there thinking. Wondering what Mum was doing right then.

This was how Frankie found me, staring at the ceiling and looking rather downcast, it would seem. She paused in the doorway, hands on her hips, and observed me for a bit.

"Nope. We can't have this," she said suddenly, as though reaching a decision. "Come on, let's go out."

"*Out*? Where?"

"Fetch your sister, get your boots. You do have walking boots, don't you? Or wellies at least?"

"Not really…"

"Trainers, then! Get yourself ready and help Shelley. Don't forget the sunblock and hats. I'll see you at the front door in five."

I didn't feel like there was any point in arguing, but was also pleased to have a distraction, so meekly did what she asked.

Frankie ordered a car for the day and, after switching over to autodrive, she turned up the radio and we sang along to some of the songs.

"Where are we actually going?" Shelley asked.

"I don't really know, I haven't made an exact plan. Just seeing you two mooching about, I thought we should head to the place I always go when I'm feeling... moochy."

The place was the coast, only about twenty minutes' drive from our house. A place of craggy clifftops battered by the wild ocean. She parked in a car park in a place I'd never been before, although I had recognised some of the sights on the way there. A broken castle jutting drunkenly on a tall hill, narrow lanes that wound around improbable corners, abandoned stone houses with once-thatched roofs that had caved in, ivy creeping up the walls. It felt like going back in time in more ways than one – Mum had brought us to the area once or twice when we were younger. I tried to think how old Shelley had been last time we came, but she insisted she remembered it so it couldn't have been as long ago as I thought.

The car park was in woodland, and it was difficult to get my bearings and remember which direction the sea was, or how far away. Ours was the only vehicle there.

"This way," said Frankie decisively, checking her watch, and we followed her as she marched ahead.

The path led us out of the woods and along a more exposed grassy area, where we clambered over stiles and up a hill to be met with the sight of the sea, far below on the other side. We all found ourselves taking deep breaths, inhaling the ocean air. It felt like the cleanest, freshest air I had ever breathed.

"Yes. That's better now, isn't it?"

I smiled at Frankie and nodded.

We walked for a while. Much of the old cliff path had eroded and fallen into the sea, and a new route had been carved out. I spotted some steps leading down that had been blocked with wire fencing; it was clear to see why, they fell away a few steps down into nowhere, a sheer drop into the ocean.

"I'm sure we used to walk down those as a child," mused Frankie.

After some time we found a flat bit of ground covered in thick grass, and sat down to take in the view.

"Wonderful isn't it, girls? I'm surprised you haven't been here more often, I really am."

I was filled with the urge to defend my mother.

"We have been here before. Well, maybe not this spot, but to the coast."

"Of course, I'm sorry. It certainly wasn't a criticism. I know your mother is very busy doing extremely important work. I admire her hugely, and often wonder how she does it. Work so hard, while being such a good parent to you girls. All on her own."

"You help us though," said Shelley.

She smiled. "And it's my absolute pleasure."

"Maybe you can bring us here. More often, I mean."

"I'd love to."

We sat there, taking in the unfamiliar sounds. Gulls crying overhead; the ocean's constant breath as it whooshed up to assault the cliffs, time after time. It was a beautiful day, spring was in full swing but the breeze meant it wasn't unbearably hot – yet there wasn't another person to be seen. The sun shone proudly out of the improbably blue sky. I looked up and thought of the visitors, waiting up there, seeing that same blueness from the other side with its wisps of cloud. Our planet stretched out below them like a giant marble. I wondered what they would make of it when they finally saw it from down here.

Closing my eyes and letting the warmth bathe my face, I made a pact with myself to go out in the open more. Even if it was just into the garden – I had spent so much time, especially recently, indoors, I had almost forgotten the great outdoors existed. It was too easy to do; too easy to get caught up with day to day routines and school work and silly videos online posted by strangers. And it made me realise that the manufactured air inside the house was really no substitute for the real thing. Shelley was right – we would ask Frankie to bring us out here more regularly and, when Mum was home, ask her too.

Frankie sighed.

"I'm sure I remember sitting here as a child and seeing quite large beaches down below."

"Really?"

"Yes. I mean, they had already shrunk quite a bit by then. There were once huge stretches of sand all the way along the coast, and families would sit on them…"

"Yuck!" Cried Shelley.

"Oh no, they were cleaner then. And people would paddle or even swim in the sea, build castles out of the sand."

"Castles?"

"Miniature ones, with buckets and spades."

I thought of the beaches closer to home. It was easy to forget they were even there; even if we'd wanted to visit them, they were closed off to the public. Unsafe to walk along, let alone to think of paddling in the ocean itself, unless you wished to be exposed to the hazardous sewage and rubbish that floated on the surface and spat itself out. It occurred to me that they, too, must have been like the beaches Frankie was describing, once.

"Where are they disappearing to? The beaches?"

"They're still there. Hidden under the sea."

"Oh, I know why! Because of the ice melting." Shelley interjected proudly. She had recently had a school project about the weather, and liked to tell us everything she had learnt in her earnest way, as though she was the first to discover it. But she wasn't, of course. Humans had known about it for years and years.

"Yes," she continued now. "In the North Pole, where the polar bears used to live."

Chapter 12

As the time approached for the landing of the visitors' pod, anticipation – and tension – grew further. It was palpable; every time I left the house, walking to the bus stop, at school. Strangely, the protests seemed to have died down, although it may just have been that I heard less about them now I wasn't watching the news all the time. We certainly didn't see any from the bus windows any more – the odd sign pinned to a gatepost or window, maybe, but I wondered where those angry people had gone. Aaron said they were all hiding out in their bunkers, biding their time. It filled me with a strange sense of foreboding and I couldn't pinpoint quite why.

Speaking to Mum the day before the landing, the distance between us felt larger than ever. She had finally been allowed out of quarantine and given a tour of the huge ship, which had lasted over an hour. It had been exciting – it was her first experience of life on board an aircraft carrier after all, and her description had been fascinating, with the cafeterias and shops, the TV lounge and the huge gym and the new science labs. But it was all eclipsed by the excitement of the imminent arrival of the honoured guests for whom all these preparations had been made.

Frankie had promised we could sit and watch from the sofa together, with snacks and blankets, but she didn't realise how reminiscent it was of watching the other milestones, with Mum there. It was appreciated, however, and of course I wanted to watch it: yet another moment in history unfolding before us.

Plus it was hardly Frankie's fault she was there in place of of our mother.

"Enjoy it girls, I'll be watching it with you in spirit on my little screen here."

"But Mum! You're going to be right there!" Laughed Shelley. "Just look out of your window!"

"I wish I could, sweetie! But it's happening a couple of miles away – they couldn't station the base too close to the impact site in case of miscalculations. A lot of work has been done to check they're entering at the correct speed and angle, but because we don't really know how their technology works a lot of it is being left to them, which is a bit nerve-racking. We've passed on all the data we can about the Earth's atmosphere and everything, so hopefully they will be safe."

"And they won't burn up?"

"Well... let's hope not, darling."

"Are they scared?" I asked, the thought occurring to me, not for the first time, that they were risking everything to come here. I hoped it would be worth it for them.

"It's hard to know. I haven't been involved that much in the communications since I've been here because it's been more about the technical side, so I've left it mostly to the scientists and engineers. But they don't appear, so far, to show the same emotions as humans. It'll be an interesting thing to find out when they get here. One of the many. I'm really excited to finally be meeting them."

"Tell us all about them, won't you Mummy?"

"Of course, darling!"

We were in our usual spots on the sofa that evening, me to the left and Shelley to the right with Frankie in the middle where Mum usually sat. The weather had been checked and re-checked, and the mission was set to go ahead. This time it was all happening a bit earlier in the day; the school had closed to everyone so that we could all watch it at home. I imagined people around the world, grown-ups and children, watching the same images at the same time, all transfixed together. Just as we had been throughout, whatever our thoughts and leanings may be.

The timing had to be just right, according to the commentary on the EBC broadcast we watched. The pods were in orbit around the globe, and this particular one needed to make its entry at the agreed position. The satellite image of the bright silver pod came into view in the darkness of space. It was the same pod that had released the probe, the voiceover told us. It looked as it had before – there were no openings or windows that we could see, it was like a bright, round mirror.

For a while nothing happened, we were just watching the pod floating there, apparently motionless but actually travelling thousands of miles per hour. It felt like the human race was holding its collective breath as we watched. And then, almost imperceptibly, it began to move. With no visible thrusters or jets it was impossible to see at first, but then suddenly it was whizzing through space. The first camera went out of range and another picked it up, it had simply changed direction and slipped out of orbit to begin hurtling towards the Earth's surface. The next view was from the Earth, filmed by the crew of one of the ships out at sea waiting for the pod. First there was a cloudless blue sky, and then a tiny dot appeared, glinting in the sunlight as it grew and grew. It was travelling at an impossible speed, still.

"Is it going to crash land?" Shelley whispered, peeping out from behind a cushion. No one could answer. We just watched, wide-eyed.

And then, a few hundred metres from the surface of the ocean, the pod slowed down. Again there were no visible thrusters, no parachute, to explain how, it just stopped plummeting and began to drift downwards, like a skydiver, seemingly in total control of its descent. The impact when it hit was still huge: it caused a splash so large it was momentarily hidden from view. As it bobbed about on the resulting wave there was no way of telling which way was upright, and I could imagine the creatures inside being tossed about. Had they even survived the impact?

Cheering could be heard from the crew of the ship filming the footage, but I wasn't sure if it was too early to rejoice. The commentator was telling us that the capsule had entered the atmosphere travelling several thousand miles per hour and had slowed down to fifty in less than thirty seconds. He was marvelling at the advanced knowledge of physics and engineering required, speculating on all that we could be taught. To me it had looked like some sort of magic, or trickery. Some special effects in a film that couldn't possibly be real.

Several boats had raced towards the pod and we watched as one of them anchored alongside it before a special crane was used to bring it on board. It was strange to be seeing this craft, created in another world, another part of the universe, bobbing about on our ocean. Watching it floating in space had been fascinating, but it had sort of fitted up there. That seemed to be where it was supposed to be. And now here it was, on Earth, about to be opened to reveal who knew what inside. I had heard many tales of UFO sightings and reported alien abductions, especially recently. In fact, I had seen a group of people on a social media video a few days before, who claimed to be descendants of the visitors; they believed their family was returning to Earth to take them home after impregnating a human many years before. It was easy to laugh these stories off, put them down to madness or delusion, but here, on my TV screen in my home, was the real thing. No one could argue or dismiss it as fantastical: there they were.

The pod lifted onto the vessel, it was hidden from view under a large silver tarpaulin. The whole thing, from the first movement to impact, had taken less than five minutes. In fact, the crane had taken longer than that to pick it up out of the ocean, as the cumbersome grabbers tried to get a purchase on the featureless surface.

"And so, there we have it," the man on the EBC was saying as the footage continued. "A real moment in history; one none of us will ever forget, I'm sure. For now the capsule will stay aboard the ship as it goes out to the carrier back at the temporary base that has been prepared. How it will be opened is unclear; I believe the extra-terrestrials themselves will do that from the inside. This will of course be filmed for posterity but will be aired at a later time, to allow for any… mishaps, and I think also to give our visitors some time and some privacy. They will need to have a period in isolation, they have special adaptations they have mentioned to allow them to breathe in our atmosphere, which will need to be tested, and doctors are on standby at the base to run tests and checks to ensure they are healthy and, equally, to ensure they don't pose any health risk to humans…."

As he spoke, the footage changed to a view from above, filmed from a helicopter following the boat as it sailed to join the others at the base. Soon the giant aircraft carrier came into view, grey and still on the thrashing waves. The collection boat carrying the unique cargo drew up alongside, looking dwarfed by the larger vessel, and there was a delay while the alignments were checked and the crane moved into position. Crew members started to unveil the pod and the crane arms grabbed it from each side. It seemed to take a long time, but I supposed, again, they were ensuring the grip was secure before the pod could be moved. Eventually, though, the pod could be seen being gradually lifted off the deck of the smaller boat and raised up towards the flight deck of the carrier. It was a painstaking manoeuvre and I had that nervous feeling yet again of watching with the rest of the world, in case the grip on the smooth sides of the pod slipped and sent it rolling into the sea. But the transfer was successful; it landed safely on the deck, and the huge elevator Mum had told us about lowered it down to the hangar and safely out of sight. Nothing more of the visitors could be seen for now.

Chapter 13

Our first sight of the aliens was tantalisingly close, and everyone had an opinion about what they would look like. Some thought they would be just like humans, others felt they would have blue or green skin, perhaps with scales, perhaps with several eyes or eyes on stalks. But none of this could prepare us for what we would really see when the first photographs and footage were released, because it was all pure speculation. We had to bide our time.

The base's location in the Atlantic, and the armed ships surrounding it, provided substantial protection. Nevertheless, security was tight. There was a risk from news reporters desperate for a first glimpse – and, better still, a photo – of the visitors. But, more alarming than that, was the threat posed by vigilantes attempting to 'destroy the aliens, before they destroy us,' as several people had been shouting since they were first detected. I had been hearing a lot of conspiracy theories in those weeks, one of which involved a wide-eyed woman shouting intently that the world's leaders were plotting with the aliens to take over planet Earth, kill off its occupants, and start a comfy new life on their distant planet. As far-fetched and ridiculous as they were, these stories were capable of whipping some people into a dangerous frenzy. But a no-fly zone had been created about the ComET base, and without helicopters or drones they had no chance; with them, they would be spotted before they got anywhere near.

And Mum was right there, in the coveted – or unenviable, depending on which way your opinion swayed – position of being one of the first humans to lay eyes on the extra-terrestrials. It happened the very day after their arrival. The visitors had been given time to acclimatise and asked what they would need to make them comfortable. There were two of them, and communications were still via the same software used when they were in orbit, mainly because they hadn't yet mastered actually speaking any of our languages. And it was through this that they requested a meeting with my mother.

For the few hours they had been on Earth, the visitors' limited contact with humans had been with all parties in full protective equipment. The doctors at the base that were going to deal directly with them – and there were as few as possible so that contact could be kept to a minimum at first – had been issued with full body suits, white plastic-looking things with a bulky head covering and a window to see out of. Mum had practised wearing hers for a few hours and hated it, but the rules were clear and the reasoning behind them unarguable. The result, though, was probably that the first encounter was more intimidating than it had needed to be.

Mum's request that she and the visitors 'meet' face to face, with no strange looking disguises, was therefore ruled out as impossible at first. But she was persistent, and eventually it was arranged for there to be a thick layer of perspex screening between them, acting as an airlock but also as a window. After that, it became the preferred way of interacting.

On the day the meeting was due to take place, we couldn't wait to talk to Mum on the wall. We had asked Frankie to join us, knowing that she too would be eager to hear all about it. Fortunately, due to the fact that it was known our main guardian was not around, the press had been ordered by law to stay away from us. If this hadn't been the case, I was certain there would have been a crowd from every news channel in the world camped outside. Hearing Mum's first hand descriptions of day-to-day life on ComET base would have given them the biggest news sensation in history. And we had a front-row seat.

"Hi girls! It's so good to see you. I miss you so much. And you of course, Frankie! I hear you're spoiling them rotten and being generally wonderful as always. I hope they're not giving you any trouble?"

"Not at all Hels, they're lovely. And you're looking very well, I think this confinement suits you! I hope you're getting some sleep in amongst all this excitement."

"Well – some. I must admit it's quite difficult, with everything that's going on."

Shelley was almost bursting. "Come on then! What are they like? Tell us!"

Mum and Frankie laughed.

"Sorry darling, I know you're desperate to know."

"Along with the rest of the world, Mum!" I said. "Did you do the plastic screen thing you were telling us about?"

"Yes, it worked very well. We still can't actually talk to each other because of the language difference. I'm still not even sure how, or even if, they speak, or if so whether it's in the same way that we do. So we used the tablets, and I typed my words to them like I've been doing from the start."

"And what did they do? Did they type too?"

"Do they have fingers? Or hands?"

"Well, we've given them the equipment needed of course, the tablets and things, and the words appeared on my screen but I didn't actually see them typing."

"Wow, they really are magic aren't they!"

"I doubt it Shelley, I think you'll find it's just really advanced technology," I told her.

"How do you know? Maybe that's what magic is!"

"Okay, girls, let's not argue. You're probably both right, in a sense."

I ignored Shelley as she stuck out her tongue at me.

"So... what do they *look* like?"

"Not all that different to humans, anatomy-wise. A head, two arms and two legs. They have hands, as you asked, and fingers, but no thumbs that I could make out. They're quite tall, and very slender. Their faces are quite remarkable, I mean – bear in mind I was seeing them through two layers of plastic – their faces are arranged in much the same way, but I couldn't see ears. Not like ours, anyway. But no, what was amazing was their eyes. They're incredibly large, compared to their noses and mouths, and so... bright. I could see that, even through the screens."

"Did they smile at you?"

"Not that I noticed, but they certainly didn't look unfriendly. I tried to smile at them but... it's so strange, not knowing if a smile even means anything to them. Or thinking it could be a sign of aggression! I found myself so painfully aware of every twitch of my face and body, just in case it was misunderstood."

"What did you say to each other?"

"I welcomed them, and told them how delighted we are to have them here. I asked them if they were comfortable and had everything they needed."

"What do they eat? And drink?" Shelley wanted to know.

"They had supplies on the pod – actually, they haven't ventured far out of it yet. I suppose it feels safe to them, and familiar. Our scientists have taken samples to analyse in the lab so we can replicate what they eat, somehow, or find something similar here. We've provided water and they seem to be getting through it. They also have special vials of something they need to ingest or inject – we're not sure which, yet – to allow them to breathe outside. At the moment their environment is being controlled, they're letting us know which levels need adjusting. We've taken some of those to be analysed too so that we can manufacture it for them. Sorry! I'm going on and on, I think I'm on rather a high from it all."

"That's understandable, Helen!" Frankie laughed.

"Please don't stop talking, Mummy, you did say you'd tell us everything."

"Gosh Shelley, I really do think you're going to be a scientist one day."

"That's what Frankie said the other day, wasn't it Frankie? I told you Mummy says it lots too."

"You did, dear!"

"So what happens next, Mum?" I asked.

"The visitors have agreed to a physical examination by a doctor to get a clearer picture. X-Rays, blood tests if that's possible, various samples taken. It's all going to be very thorough, to see if they have DNA and if we can get an understanding of their genetic makeup. But because we need to be so thorough we have to be very careful to protect their dignity, and to make sure we don't offend them in any way. So I'll be there with them, to explain exactly what's happening and check they agree to every procedure. And to reassure them, I hope."

"That's going to be amazing, Mum. I can't believe you've actually *met* extra-terrestrials."

"I know darling, neither can I. I'd think I was dreaming, but I doubt that my brain could conjure something up quite like this."

"Did you find out their names?"

"No, Shelley. I don't think they have names, as such. We need to try and find out more from them about their home planet too, what it's called and how far they've travelled. There really is so much to discover."

It sounded like she, and the scientists researching them, would be there forever finding everything out.

"When will you come home, do you think?"

"I have to be here while they're quarantining. And then after that, I don't see any further need to stay here. Once they're acclimatised I can either go back to communicating with them from home, or... maybe they'll go home themselves."

"I hope not, Not yet," Shelley said, through a sudden and very huge yawn.

"Oh my goodness, look what time it is!" Frankie cried. "It's nearly ten! Come on you, we need to say goodnight."

"Absolutely – sorry to keep you all talking so long."

"Are you kidding Mum? I could chat all night about this. I mean, it's actual people from an actual different planet!"

Mum laughed and wished us goodnight. Shelley was practically asleep before she got to her room, but I lay awake for a long time, thinking about everything Mum had told us.

Chapter 14

Daisy and Aaron grilled me relentlessly about it the following day, and I was happy to provide details. Aaron, who was really good at art, sketched a picture of them based on Mum's description.

"That's really good, Aaron."

"Keep it," he handed it to me.

It was strange to be sharing such momentous information with my school friends before most of the rest of the world knew about it. Mrs Gibson, my teacher, invited me to speak in front of the rest of the class but I preferred to just hand Aaron's drawing around. Shelley informed me later that she did a whole presentation, with a Q&A session at the end.

But the first photos appeared on the news sites anyway, later that day. Aaron's drawing was uncannily accurate.

Both of the beings were standing side by side in a small, bare room on board the ship. Mum was right: their eyes were the most unusual thing about them, and the first thing you looked at. Very large and blue-grey in colour, they looked similar to human eyes but for the black pupils, which were elongated and went from top to bottom, a little like a cat's. Their noses were very small, more like two nostril holes set into their heads, and their mouths were thin and wide. Their heads were completely hairless, their skin a sort of grey colour. They both looked very alike, except that one was slightly taller. The photo was surprisingly clear and I thought the camera must have had a clearer view than my mother had through the screens. I stared at them for a long time, as though hypnotised. It was hard to believe I was looking into the eyes of creatures that had evolved on another planet. Just a matter of months ago we hadn't even known they existed, and could hardly have believed they were real.

After the scientists at the base had completed their examination, the news channels clamoured to be the first to report on it. It was so strange how we awaited updates on the extra-terrestrials, how we talked about it among ourselves. It was becoming everyday conversation in the way that the weather had been before. It had become a normal, integral part of our lives and every now and then I would hear people stop, mid conversation, to say 'have you heard…' and 'isn't this just so surreal'.

I watched the video on the report from the laboratory as soon as I saw it pop up on my news app. There was the chief doctor on the base, an American (or so I gathered from her accent when she spoke) woman, perhaps in her early fifties, with shoulder-length black hair streaked with grey, and a slightly gangly, young-ish man with owlish glasses who was a professor of anthropology. They sat side by side to explain their findings so far. The doctor spoke first, a caption reading 'Dr Ling'.

"The extra-terrestrials are, on first sight, very similar to humans in that they have four limbs and stand upright," the doctor told us. "Facially they also resemble us. Today with their permission we carried out an examination, which included X-Rays to examine bone structure and organ placement, more detailed scans, plus internal and external exams, along with blood tests, breath tests etc. This examination took place with the zoologists on board, also, to get a better picture of these beings.

"Our findings tell us they are very hard to classify according to the systems used on Earth, for example if a new species were discovered. This is not surprising as they do not originate here, and their climate etcetera could be very different. Their DNA is not recognisable to us. However, we do know how they breathe, reproduce and what they eat. This is both through today's examinations and from talking to them.

"So, let us begin." She tapped the screen of her tablet and scrolled though the notes she had made. Diagrams and pictures appeared to accompany her report. "Their skin is completely hairless; they have no eyelashes or eyebrows. The skin is quite rough, the only comparison we can make to give an idea of its texture and make-up is to that of a shark's. It is grey/blue in colour, but this has faded from a dark green when they first arrived. Colouration does therefore seem to change slightly in different lights, or perhaps to communicate different emotions; more needs to be discovered about this.

"Their eyes are disproportionately large, and hyper-sensitive to the light levels on Earth. Their eyes function in much the same way as humans' do; scans show retinas and optic nerves which are recognisably similar. However, their pupils are slits rather than circular, and vision tests suggest their sight is excellent, particularly long-distance and when it is dark. It is thought that the pupils are usually wider, but as I've explained they are affected by our light and so are likely to be narrower than they would be ordinarily. They have two sets of eyelids, with an inner membrane similar to a feline's.

"Their nostrils are very small and their noses barely protrude from the face. While they do breathe through the nose, there are also some curious gill-like openings on either side of the neck, which I will come back to in a moment. The mouth is very wide, with no lips. Inside the mouth is a tongue much like ours, but no teeth as such, rather a sort of rough corrugation on very tough gums, used for grinding food. They produce saliva of a similar make up to a mammal's. On either side of the head, around the temples, are ears, which are small holes with no outer section. Their hearing is very good, although not much more advanced than an average human's.

"On to the gills on the side of the neck – we are unsure exactly what purpose these serve, but unlike a fish we think they assist with breathing alongside the nose and mouth, probably providing some sort of filter. Again, more work needs to be done on this." She took a sip of water. She had been speaking for some time and had hardly begun. But it was fascinating. There were no further photographs of the beings themselves, probably to protect the visitors' dignity, as Mum had said, but diagrams and drawings gave a picture of what she was describing. It was clear already that the creatures, visitors, whatever they were, were going to give us a huge insight into life on their home planet. And that was before they had even spoken.

"X-Rays show a very similar skeleton to a human's, with a skull and backbone, rib cage and pelvis. The arms and legs are far longer in proportion to the rest of the body, the fingers and toes longer still than ours. There are four fingers on each hand, with no thumb, and four toes on each foot. There are no finger or toenails.

"So, onto the organs of the beings. Scans show the brain is similar to a human brain, but the EEG graph analysis showed a huge amount of activity between the different brain networks. Our neuroscientists are analysing these further.

"The heart and lungs are like those of a mammal, although the lungs are perhaps smaller than would be expected on a being of this size. The stomach is like a human's but with a much shorter intestine. I think this is a good time for Ernst here to tell us a little about their diet."

I had almost forgotten the man sitting beside her, the anthropologist. He looked a bit unprepared for the sudden attention, and took some time clearing his throat and looking through his notes.

"Er, yes, thank you Doctor Ling. So, their diet – so far we have discovered the ETs are non-meat eaters, in fact they seem herbivorous. The closest food we have found to their diet is seaweed; they had several canisters of dried food stuff on board the pod which resembled this in make-up and nutritional value. They have been drinking the same water as the crew on the base, so far with no adverse effects."

He continued, his voice sounding stronger and more confident now, with a hint of an accent which I thought could have been German or Dutch. "As an aside, the ETs sleep between four and five hours at a time, and they have informed us that days on their planet are around half as long as days on Earth. Also," he was getting into his stride now. It was clear he was passionate about his work, even if he had seemed hesitant at first. "Also, it is very interesting that we have observed a specific greeting between the ETs, also directed at us when communicating. It is kind of like this," he put his fingertips together and held his elbows out, almost elbowing the doctor beside him. "And there is a bow of the head, like this. It seems to be both a greeting and a farewell."

He paused, and looked at the doctor expectantly. She took over without hesitation.

97

"Back to their anatomy: there are no nipples and no umbilicus, or belly button. We believe so far that reproduction is asexual, or even parthenogenetic (where the female can reproduce with no male), but more needs to be learned about this. And, to answer one of the questions we have probably been asked the most: both these beings are female; they have wombs and other reproductive organs similar to humans, although not obvious externally. In fact, Doctor Bauer may have more to add here."

"Ah, yes. We have learnt from our communications that the ETs' young are born more or less self sufficient, and can live independently very quickly after birth."

Doctor Ling continued. "Excretion we think is via the anus, but it's thought also that some waste gases may leave via the skin, rather like a plant's, but again we need to learn more before we can fully understand. We would rather come to understand about these aspects when the language barrier has been improved, for reasons I am sure are clear.

"Blood flows through veins and arteries, and initial tests show it is similar in composition to ours, but more analysis will take place. One thing that was noticeable was the colour and consistency: it is far darker and more viscous than human blood.

"And that sums up our anatomical findings so far. Anything to add, Ernst?"

"Er, yes. More will be of course be discovered as further tests are done, but also as we communicate more. And the zoological or anthropological aspect of our knowledge will increase with time. The ETs have been heard to 'speak' to each other, a sound which is like a series of high pitched notes. Some attempts have been made by them to speak in the languages they learned to write so rapidly, and progress has already been made with this. We are in fact drafting in a speech and language specialist to work alongside our communications team to teach the ETs to vocalise like humans. If successful – and early signs suggest it will be, as they are clearly highly intelligent and fast learners – this will be a very significant step forward. Thank you."

With a brief nod, Dr Ling stood up and left the room, leaving the younger man to scrabble up his tablet and glasses case and awkwardly scurry after her.

"Thank you to the chief doctor on project ComET, Doctor Amy Ling, and Doctor Ernst Bauer, anthropologist, for that truly fascinating report."

I watched as the clip ended, and was lot in thought as another one quickly loaded. A wild-looking man with long matted hair was shouting into the camera, which was swinging around erratically.

"...first of all they try to control us with all the pandemic hoaxes, telling us who we can or can't get close to, saying we're not allowed to even hug our own mothers. Wear plastic to protect you, inject these unknown chemicals into your bodies, blah blah. Even after a so-called vaccine is found and the sheep all queue up to have it, a year, two years later there's another virus? And then another! It's been going on as long as most of us can remember. And now this! They've known about these aliens for years, my friends. I know someone who saw a secret government report that mentioned them, like, ten years ago. The vaccines were taking samples of DNA, and it's not a coincidence they're doing the same with the aliens. It's all about control, and now they're gonna use it to manipulate us and tell us what to do?" His high-pitched voice trailed off and there was shouting in the background.

"What is that you're watching?"

I spun round on my bed where I had been lying on my stomach in front of my tablet.

"Oh, hi Frankie."

"Sorry, I didn't mean to make you jump. That was one of those conspiracy theorists, right?"

"Yeah I suppose so. I wasn't really watching it, it just came on after the other thing I was watching."

"Does your mum mind you watching things like that? It's just that you have to be really careful, there's all kinds of stuff online you shouldn't be seeing. Especially in these strange times."

"It's okay, really. Mum's given us the talk loads of times. We're only allowed to search on Newsquest or the other kid-friendly sites and she's got about a million filters even on those. I know that guy on the video was a bit crazy. It just came on after the medical report I was watching about the ETs."

Frankie relaxed and came to sit down on the bed next to me. "So you saw that? What did you think? Amazing, right?"

I sat up. "It really is. It's so cool to be able to find out so much about them."

"We are very lucky."

"I wish I could actually meet them, like Mum has."

"You and me both, girl. I know it's strange without her here. But I hope you feel you can talk to me about worries you have or… anything like that."

I nodded and smiled, and must have seemed a bit awkward.

"Not that there is anything, I'm sure, just... you know, if anything comes up."

"I will. Thank you, Frankie."

"Now come on, dinner is served. No seaweed tonight, I'm afraid."

Every night now when we spoke to Mum, she had more news about the ETs. Even across the miles and with the sometimes dodgy connection, I could tell she was more excited by the ComET project than by anything else she had worked on. There was a light in her eyes and a sort of glow about her skin. It was hardly surprising of course; she was in the midst of the most exciting era in human history. Even back at home there was a certain buzz, which could be attributed both to the same excitement and, paradoxically, to a tension in the air as though we were waiting for something to happen. It gave me a peculiar sense in my stomach, like a constant fluttering or both nerves and anticipation. I wondered if those around me were feeling the same, but couldn't quite find the words to ask them. I had difficulty describing the feeling to myself.

The next big information breakthrough was about the ETs' home planet. Working alongside the earthbound scientists, they calculated they had travelled around 5.8 light years from their sun, which amounted to around 34.2 trillion miles. These were figures no ordinary being could quite comprehend – the significance of it was certainly out of my grasp. The very existence of these ETs, appearing in our orbit, was causing impenetrable puzzles and head-scratching among the most intelligent minds on our planet. Some of the questions, surely, would never be truly answered, at least not to the satisfaction of those astrophysicists and cosmologists, not to mention the rest of us. To a child like me it was like standing on a precipice, peering over into the blackness of space, knowing I could never understand it, but wanting to tip forward and be immersed in all its wonder.

We had a name, at last, for both the mysterious planet and for the ETs themselves who had originated there. I wasn't sure who had originally thought of it, perhaps a scholar somewhere in an old-fashioned library, but suddenly it was everywhere. Planet Thule: meaning something or other to do with a distant far-off land, I think in Latin. Pronounced 'too-lee'. And so, instead of 'ETs', or 'visitors', or the term 'aliens', which had become somehow slightly offensive, having been spat out of the mouths of angry people for so many weeks, we had the Thulians. There were a few jokes at school at the expense of some kid whose grandad was called Julian, but aside from that I liked the new name. It felt right to finally have something to call them. Mum told us one evening they seemed to like it too, or as much someone could who came from somewhere that had no real concept of names for places or beings.

And the Thulians were able to tell us more about their home. Much of the information emerged over time as more and more features of our own planet were revealed to them for comparison. While they couldn't travel – or even really look out of a window – to see much for themselves yet, Mum said they were fascinated by film and webcam footage of mountains and deserts, forests and oceans, but especially wildlife of all types.

We had already been told that the days on Thule were shorter, due to the speed at which the planet rotated. But now we were told the planet orbited further away from their sun, so that the years were longer and the climate cooler – explaining the need for the ambient temperature in their quarters on the

102

ComET base, replicating those of their pod, to be several degrees lower than completely comfortable for the average human. At first it seemed strange that they didn't need clothing to stay warm, but then it was put forward that humans were the only animals on *our* planet to wear it, while other creatures had adapted and evolved to suit their surroundings, just like the Thulians had. They had no sense of nakedness, no impulse or need to protect their modesty.

As well as the colder temperatures, the light was dimmer – again an explanation for their light-sensitive eyes and advanced ability to see in weaker light. The sky, like ours, was blue but often obscured by clouds of ash from a multitude of active volcanoes. One scientist on the base suggested this may be why the Thulians had evolved with those curious gills: to filter out chemicals in the air given off by the constant eruptions. This theory, in fact, was later proven accurate.

On this chilly, dim planet there were no oceans or rivers, the only bodies of water being lakes of varying sizes. The water in these was murky, stagnant and undrinkable, if not poisonous, but water from abundant underground springs gave life the water it needed. There were no trees – nothing grew higher than a few inches from the ground – but the vegetation was plentiful, and provided the Thulians with their main food source. This all grew from soil that had a strange red tinge, much like the rust-coloured sand in outback Australia.

Not much was known yet about other species on planet Thule. Other creatures lived there, we were told, but not nearly the variety we had here on Earth, even after some of the mass extinctions we had seen in recent years.

And though the Thulians willingly told us about their home and answered endless questions from our scientists, it was nothing compared to their hunger for information and craving for knowledge about Earth.

Chapter 15

The three-week quarantine period was almost at an end, and lots of work had been done to prepare the Thulians for the next phase of their time here. Tests had been carried out to ensure they could be exposed to longer and longer periods outside their quarters. The levels of oxygen and carbon dioxide in the metallic vials they absorbed through their skin were carefully adjusted – these meant they could breathe our air and get the correct levels of oxygen and CO_2 their bodies needed to survive. Humans coming into contact with the Thulians still wore protective clothing, albeit scaled back since the first encounter, and strict hygiene procedures were enforced.

Even with all these precautions, it was with huge trepidation that our visitors were first let out onto the deck of the aircraft carrier. Doctors and scientists lingered nervously, as close to them as they felt they could risk, watching for any signs of imminent collapse, any change in skin tone, anything that could signal that a miscalculation had been made. A mistake in the levels, perhaps, or anything missed in their meticulous planning and preparation. Each Thulian had been given a device to wear around their wrists which constantly measured their heart rates and other levels, and a specially-prepared biosecure tent had been brought up on the elevator with them, mimicking the conditions in their quarters enough to provide a short-term safe area for them in an emergency.

These beings were simply too precious to risk – they were the gateway to more knowledge than these professors could have hoped to have had in their lifetimes. Scientists around the world were clamouring to be a part of Project ComET; they couldn't hope to actually win a place on board the base itself, but demand was high even for a five-minute interview on the wall. Mum told us that the research team had been inundated with requests and questions to support long-running PhDs and theses. Imagine, therefore, being partly responsible for the death – or even serious illness – of one of these invaluable creatures. The world would be aware within minutes, and no career or reputation could recover from such a disaster.

Fortunately the careful monitoring paid off and no mishaps took place. The Thulians stepped out through the plastic sheeting into the airlock, and beyond, breathing our air for the first time, looking out over a grey, choppy ocean. They were too far away to glimpse land, but still they stood, side by side, staring out intently. Mum went with them, keeping her distance like all the others, keen to get some air herself after all those weeks spent cooped up inside. And she noted how the pair of them looked out, barely moving, as though hypnotised by the movement of the waves. Coming from a planet with no oceans, I tried to imagine how they must feel. I knew there were people on our planet who had never seen the sea. Even where we lived, close to the coast, I had heard of children who had never visited it. But they had grown up knowing of its existence; would have seen film and photographs of it. I could hardly imagine looking at the sea through the Thulians' eyes at that moment. It was no wonder they were reluctant to return to their cramped, windowless quarters with the piped-in air. But they had had their first taste of Earth's wonders, and would be able to increase their time outside more and more as the days passed.

As time had gone by, the Thulians had shown themselves proficient at learning to speak and understand the languages of Earth – given how quickly they had mastered the written, or typed, word it perhaps shouldn't have come as a surprise, but it really was a marvel. It had been decided the focus should be on Mandarin, Spanish and English, and the language experts taught them the nuances and pronunciations as best they could. And so, it wasn't too long before Mum was able to converse with them properly.

"I didn't realise just how wonderful it would be," she told us. "I've been communicating with them for months, and even on a normal project a lot of the comms are through the wall, rather than face to face. But to actually speak to them! And now I can see their faces too, and sit beside them."

"What do they sound like? Their voices, I mean?" I wanted to know.

"Well, one of them talks a lot more than the other because they've mastered the language a bit better. The taller one – we call them Thulian A and Thulian B, imaginatively, so it's Thulian A I speak to the most. Her voice is quite high-pitched, but I think if I closed my eyes I doubt I'd know it wasn't a human I was speaking to. There's a slight – accent, I suppose you'd call it, but it's so amazing how quickly they've learnt to speak. It would be impressive enough for a human to do that. I think they're finding the Chinese language a little harder because it's so different to the others, but even with that they've made huge progress."

She told us about the endless questions the Thulians had asked – via the tablets still – on their first encounter with the outside world. It had been, to the human mind, an unexceptional day. The sky and sea merged together in a foggy grey haze, and the sea lurched them from side to side as it rose and fell. But to them it was awe-inspiring.

"So there is also dry land? But the water covers most of the planet? And is there life in the ocean? What sort of creatures live there? Are you able to use the water for drinking? And how long does it take to travel to land? How deep does it get?"

They stood and they stared, and then one of them looked up at the sky and so they wanted to know about that; about our aircraft and flying creatures, the clouds and climate and the sun rising and setting. It had been a challenge to usher them back down into the safety of their quarters. Their hosts felt keenly the need to share everything they could about our planet, and felt the responsibility of the sheer scale of such an undertaking, and so vowed that, the next time the conditions were right, and the Thulians' body clocks allowed it (for they were still not quite in tune with the rotations of our planet), they would bring the visitors out on deck to experience the drama and majesty of the rising or setting of the sun.

The other silver capsules suspended in space had not been forgotten, and while on board the ComET base the visitors had been communicating with their fellow Thulians, using technology not yet fully understood by our scientists. Human nature being as it is, this raised suspicion in the minds of some. The already wary groups: the conspiracy theorists and the Protectors and those that already hated and feared anyone that was different to them. But, also, among even some of the more reasonable inhabitants of our planet. Arguments were made: of course they should be able to send messages back to their kind; they must tell them they are alive, and are being treated well and provided with everything they needed. And of course they must share all they are learning about our strange world. But the doubts lingered; the shouts from the more extreme groups wormed their way in to the consciousness of the rational. What if they were planning something? What if those creatures were poised, waiting? What if it wasn't wise, after all, to put so much trust in these beings whose temperament we knew nothing about? There was no way of knowing exactly what was being transmitted in those communications. The everlasting fear of the unknown crept in, and began to grow tiny roots.

Chapter 16

Mum had been away now for several weeks and, while we had settled into a routine and were speaking to her every day, I was really missing her and could tell that Shelley was too. Neither of us spoke about it out loud, out of loyalty to Frankie. We both loved her, but even so she could be no substitute in the long term. I also couldn't help feeling a little sorry for her. Used to living an independent life, with her own space and freedom to come and go, here she was stuck in someone else's home, being responsible for someone else's kids – even if we had practically grown up knowing her. To her credit, she never showed any sign that she regretted agreeing to mind us. In fact, she continued to be enthusiastic about her role, spending the time to cook healthy, delicious meals and listening patiently as we prattled on about things that must have been of very little interest. She had also taken us out on several more walks by the coast and in the forest, and we had explored a fair few places we hadn't been to before. So life certainly wasn't worse for us with Mum away: we just missed her.

And so, on that early summer evening when Mum first put her idea to us, I had a confused mix of feelings. Shelley had asked (yet again) how long she thought it would be before she came home, and Mum had paused and stared at us for a few moments. A giveaway that she was about to share something that she had been considering carefully.

"Actually girls, that's what I need to talk to you about. It's looking like the project will be going on for some time yet – we've barely started really. There's just so much they want to know, and us too of course. There are no plans yet for them to leave. I think that will be a long way off, in fact."

"But why do they still need you?" I asked. "They can all speak to each other now, can't they?"

"It's a bit more complicated than that. They've always been able to talk to each other in one way or another, that wasn't really why I was brought in. It's more about the possibility of misunderstandings and decisions about what is said and how... I'm still very busy here."

I looked at her and knew what it was she wasn't saying. She would only hide the truth from us to protect us, or in case it caused hurt in any way. She didn't *want* to leave the project yet.

"So you're not coming home for ages?" asked Shelley.

"I really want to, because I miss you both so much. But I also really want to be a part of this, and the head of the operation has actually asked me to stay on. I love it, I feel like I'm still needed even as they do learn to communicate more. But I love you girls far, far more than any of it. This is just a job, and you are more important to me than anything."

"So what is it you're saying?" I asked nervously, but I think I betrayed my impatience.

"I've got a solution, but I just want you to think about it for now as a possibility. And you both have to agree one way or the other. If either or both of you don't like my idea you need to say so and I'll just come home, and I will be very happy to do so. I promise."

We nodded, waiting to hear what she had to say – again, I think I already knew, but it's always hard to tell for certain after the event. Perhaps I just wanted to think of myself as the more perceptive of the two sisters, for once.

111

"How would you feel about coming out to stay with me for a bit?"

"Yes yes yes! Yes please!" cried Shelley, bouncing up and down. I nudged her irritably and stayed looking at Mum.

"Okay, okay!" She was smiling. "Just listen for a bit though, because you really need to think it through. I've had to clear it with everyone here, and emailed Frankie to sound her out. There's your schooling to think about. We'd need to keep it secret, just until you get here, and we'd need to make arrangements for your journey. Actually, there's something else I haven't said, which is also top secret. You need to promise you won't tell anyone outside our household. No one at school, none of your friends."

We solemnly promised.

"They're moving the ComET base. It's no longer practical to be out in the middle of the Atlantic, so they're going to find somewhere on dry land, although we haven't been told where yet. Somewhere secure though, like an army barracks I should think. So of course that would affect everything too – your journey, for one. I have been assured it will be safe for you; I would never have considered this otherwise. Of course, it has to be secure, for the Thulians."

"Well I want to come and stay with you, wherever you are," Shelley said earnestly.

"That's lovely darling – I want you here too, but as I said, either way we will be together. If it means me coming back home in a couple of weeks instead, that's fine with me. And you both need to take time to really think about it. Okay, Faye? I don't want you to feel any pressure at all, even though Shelley seems so keen."

We nodded, already deep in thought. Shelley probably imagining herself there already, wherever 'there' was going to be.

"If either of you would like to ask me anything, together or separately, just message me for a call."

We signed off. It had certainly given me a lot to think about. My gut feeling was the same as my sister's; I couldn't actually come up with a valid reason not to go. But there was something in the pit of my stomach that made me hesitant, and I wasn't sure why. Mum was wrong about one thing for certain though: with Shelley so eager to join her wherever it was she ended up, how could I possibly feel anything but pressure to agree?

Chapter 17

As it was, though, it didn't take me long to decide. My instincts were telling me to go, simply because I didn't want Mum's part in the project to come to a premature end and ruin her chances. It was all very well hearing her say that she wouldn't mind, and that we came first. I knew that we did, but how could I be the one responsible for that? Shelley's mind was already made up. In fact, I found it very difficult to think of a real reason for staying. I wouldn't particularly miss my friends – we could still email and chat. Most of my schooling was remote anyway. And on top of all that, it would be a huge adventure. If I had any trepidation it was because I didn't know where in the world we would be going. I knew this should have added to the excitement, but I was a planner; I liked to know what to expect and prepare myself for it.

One afternoon, right in the middle of a remote lesson, my smart speaker let out a loud 'ping'. I paused my video so the teacher couldn't see me.

"Yes."

My sister's voice floated into the room.

"What are you doing?"

"I'm in the middle of a lesson, Shelley."

"Oh. Sorry."

"Hang on – shouldn't you be too?"

"I've finished my work. It's break time."

"Okay… was there something you wanted to say?"

"Faye?"

"Yes. Still here."

There was a long pause.

"What are you going to tell Mummy?"

"About what?"

"About going to stay with her. Are you going to say yes?"

"I think so. Probably." There was another pause. "You still there, Shell?"

I heard her sniff and her voice sounded funny when she answered. Then there was a noise and the sound of her thumping feet just before she burst into my bedroom. She ran across the room and threw her arms around me before I could speak.

"Thank you! You're the best sister." I hugged her back, bemused.

"Why?"

"I thought you were going to say no!"

I untangled her arms and looked at her. Her face was red from trying not to cry and I felt a lurch of love, perhaps triggered by my conscience.

"Really? Have you been worrying about this?"

"A bit. Even though I know we're going to see Mummy anyway."

"So why are you so desperate to go?"

She looked at me solemnly. "I want to meet the extra-terrestrials."

I couldn't help but smile.

"You've even learnt how to say it properly. But, you know, we might not actually get to see them. They'll be hidden away in some protected bubble thing."

She shrugged. "I know. But it'll be like going on holiday! We never go anywhere. Not to sleep over, anyway."

And I stopped over-thinking it and trying to find reasons not to go. We let Mum know our decision later that day.

Arrangements were set in motion very quickly once we had told Mum. She called the school to let them know we'd be learning entirely remotely for at least a few weeks, for 'family reasons'. She had to sign lots of paperwork to say she would find us suitable tutors, who could keep an eye on us and make sure we didn't fall behind. She agreed to this rather hastily, but I wasn't sure who she had in mind. Everyone at the base would surely be too busy. In fact, I was to learn, it was a condition of us being there that we didn't disrupt the project or cause a distraction in any way. Mum had made a lot of promises on our behalf, I just hoped she'd be able to keep them without compromising her place on the ComET project.

She also felt that she had to tell Dad. He hadn't called since our last chat when he'd asked us to go over to live with him; apart from the odd email with a few photos, we hadn't heard from him at all. But Mum said he had emailed her and didn't sound very happy about the idea of us going off into unknown territory, so I shouldn't have been surprised when my wall screen started pinging at me while I was doing my homework one night, and his picture popped up in the contacts.

"Hi Dad."

"Faye – your mum tells me she's out there on the ComET base?"

"Yeah, exciting isn't it? Hadn't you heard about it?"

"I guess I missed it. I've been off-grid for a while. It sounds pretty reckless to me and I told her so. I'm not sure what she's thinking going off there and leaving you girls alone." His chat with Mum had left him irate, but I wasn't sure what he wanted me to tell him. I felt a stab of irritation at his criticism of her; it didn't seem fair that he felt justified in leaving us to work on the other side of the Earth but didn't think the same could be allowed of Mum. But in the face of someone else's anger or irritation I always shied away from confrontation. Not because I was afraid of it, but because I just never saw the point. If someone disagreed with you it was pointless to try and change their mind. In fact, whenever I found myself in such a situation – and it was, admittedly, rare – I tended to find myself becoming calmer to counteract the other's exasperation.

"We're not alone, Dad. We've got Frankie."

"Frankie's just some neighbour."

"She's Mum's best friend, we see her most days." Unlike you, an unkind part of me added silently.

"Still. Look, I don't like the idea of you going off to be with her."

"But you just said she shouldn't have gone in the first place. Isn't this the best solution?"

"She should be home with you girls. Look," he seemed to realise he was sounding hypocritical – or perhaps he remembered he wasn't talking to an adult but his ten-year-old daughter. His voice calmed. "I'm just worried you don't know what you're getting into. What are these… Thulians actually like? Why are they really here? We don't know for sure. I know your Mum is certain everything is fine, but she always sees the best in people. And... aliens, I guess."

I smiled. "It's okay, Dad, we'll be careful. Mum just misses us, that's all. But she really loves being there and learning about them. She's talked to them more than anyone, and she wouldn't put us in danger."

By the time we ended the call he seemed placated, and I wondered if some of Mum's negotiating skills had rubbed off on me after all. It was hard to be annoyed with my Dad for long. I think some people expected the three of us to resent him or feel abandoned, but we ticked along very well without him. Shelley and I were too young to really remember him being around, let alone miss him, and Mum didn't seem lonely or sad with him gone. I remembered asking once why he'd left, purely out of curiosity rather than anything else. Her answer had stuck with me.

"He loves you girls, don't ever doubt that. But he's always been so passionate about his work. He was already away more often than he was home, and so when this job came up there wasn't even a question about whether he'd take it; it was like a calling. He wanted to dedicate his life to trying to save some of the last of the endangered species and patches of the wild, and that meant leaving us behind. I'm proud of him, we all should be. But he wasn't an easy man to live with. He knows he's fighting a losing – or lost – battle, and it's made him bitter. Understandably, of course. He once said fighting the damage mankind has done was like trying to clear up an avalanche with a dustpan and brush. Futile. But he can't stop; he won't give up."

The media had somehow got hold of the fact that the ComET base was being moved, but the location was still a secret from all but those involved. Mum told us a suitable spot had been found, and she now knew where, but couldn't tell us yet. So, until it came to the time when we had to leave home, we didn't even know how we were getting there. Shelley was bubbling with excitement, adamant that we were going to be travelling on a plane or even a helicopter. We had been on neither, worldwide travel being restricted and very expensive due both to the viruses and the climate devastation. I found her squealing enthusiasm irritating and endearing at the same time, which pretty accurately summed up my feelings towards her generally.

Frankie had helped us both pack our things. Mum had confided in her for practical reasons, but none of the items or the clothing she selected seemed to give away many clues (not for want of Shelley analysing them). There were clothes for all seasons, which if anything confused us more as, surely, we were only going to be away for a few weeks. What we also didn't yet know was that there was a more immediate reason for Frankie being aware of our destination. She was going to be taking us there herself.

Chapter 18

Frankie left it until the morning of our departure to give us the news. We were to travel to Scotland; the new base was in the Highlands, just north of Inverness. So Shelley didn't get her plane or helicopter ride, but she didn't mind in the end. We travelled in the rented car, a journey of twelve hours, and on the way we each entertained ourselves separately. In a nod to the amount of hours we were going to spend in it, Frankie had arranged for a more luxurious car than we had been used to hiring. This one had the individual entertainment systems, so that we could switch between movies, gaming or audiobooks on our own screens. Shelley opted to watch a movie she'd already seen again and again, and Frankie settled back to read an ebook. It felt strange to be on such a long drive. We had travelled by train to London with Mum a couple of years before and this felt similar to being on a train, the difference being we had to stay in our seats, but had a personalised carriage just for us.

After several hours we stopped at the charging station and were able to get out to stretch our legs. Frankie drove the car up to the battery exchange before going inside to buy us some food. I hadn't paid much attention to the outside world on our journey so far; when I had glanced out of the window it had just been miles of grey road and industrial units, with hardly any other traffic. It was noticeably chillier here – we were probably about three hundred miles north of home – but there was still a slight warmth in the breeze. I had an excitement at the pit of my stomach that I had felt on our rare holidays. I tried to recall when the last time had been – maybe when Shelley was a toddler, not long after Dad had left. We had taken a trip to Devon and stayed on a pod park; I remembered Mum telling us the whole place had been painstakingly relocated further back from the cliff side a few years before after it had started eroding into the sea. I hadn't slept well, lying there at night imagining our pod perched on the edge, and then suddenly falling as the ground beneath us crumbled away.

"Are you coming, dreamer, or do you want to stay here?" I hadn't noticed Frankie had returned, holding a greasy bag of delicious smelling pastries and several assorted cans of drink. She led the way to a table and we demolished our food, suddenly ravenous despite our inactivity for the last few hours.

"How far now?" Shelley asked, yet again.

"I'd say we're about half way, so at least five more hours or so of driving I'm afraid."

"Oh goody, I can watch my film again, then!"

Frankie and I shared an amused glance at Shelley's unshakable enthusiasm.

"What will you do when we get there?" I asked her, slightly ashamed for not having put much thought into it before now. I had been so preoccupied with the trip: the thought of seeing Mum again, the nearly impossible task of keeping secrets from Daisy and Aaron, not to mention the very real possibility that we were set to be in very close proximity to two beings from another planet. There had been a lot going around my head in the past couple of weeks. But Frankie had been our substitute mother for over a month. Her kindness and patience had made my mother's absence a great deal easier for both of us during that time.

121

"I'll stay the night tonight – I've got a room booked nearby. Then it's back home tomorrow. It'll be strange to be back in my own home. But I'm looking forward to it, even though I'll miss having you girls take care of me!"

We were all keen to set off again. With the fresh battery in and connected up, Frankie climbed into the driver's seat and steered the car back onto the motorway, before switching it to automatic drive, stowing the wheel and relaxing back into her seat again.

I watched out of the window for a bit and thought about my farewell with my friends. I hadn't been able to tell them why we were going so it had all felt very strange. In the end I had made something up about Dad working on a new project nearer to us and going to visit him, which had only encouraged more excited questions about where and for how long. I panicked a bit and said Norway; I think Scotland and New Zealand somehow became confused in my mind, and that was the result. They had even gifted me some of my favourite chocolate and snacks in case I couldn't get them in Norway. Daisy, in particular, expressed concern about how it might feel to see Dad after all this time, so that by the end I was keen to get away if only to leave behind the guilt at misleading her. I hoped that she would understand, and forgive me, when she inevitably discovered the truth. I resolved to call them when I had settled in, and own up myself.

The landscape had changed quite dramatically from the uniform grey of earlier. We were still on a fast, wide road, but now huge hills reared up on either side of us, with abandoned windfarms rusting on the slopes like the carcasses of giant defeated robots. I stared out, not having ever seen a landscape so vast. I nudged Shelley with excitement when we saw a sign for the Scottish border, but Frankie warned us there was still a great deal of the journey to go yet.

"It's a good job we're making this journey in the summer time," she told us. "These roads often become impassable in the colder months because of flooding and landslides."

It was getting dark when I woke up. The others were still fast asleep in their seats. I peered out of the window to try and work out how close we were. There wasn't much to see; the headlights picked out a narrow road that looked like a forest track, tall trees loomed up either side of us against the grey-blue sky. Ahead were large structures – they looked like the walls of a building. The car was rumbling along the bumpy track, and Frankie stirred and woke up as the sat nav quietly spoke:

"You have reached your destination."

Frankie had called Mum an hour or so before to let her know when we were scheduled to arrive. I felt an odd sort of nervousness and anticipation as I saw her now, running out to greet us, her outline unmistakable. As soon as the car drew to a stop she opened the door. My sister, who had still been asleep, stared at her groggily for a few moments before realisation crept in and she leaped out of the car and into Mum's arms. My greeting was only slightly more reserved. I had been eager to see her and had missed her, and could feel tears brewing and the tell-tale ache behind my nose I always got when I tried not to cry. It was the longest time we'd ever been apart from her, and seeing her now, looking exactly the same even in the dark and bundled up in a coat – which she was removing to drape around our shoulders – It occurred to me that I had been afraid we might never see her again. It was a strange realisation and didn't even know why that should be the case. Perhaps it was a childish sense in me that when people were out of sight they disappeared into an unknown void.

As Frankie drove the car through the gates I could see several guards – soldiers in camouflage uniform, many of them armed. We followed on foot and Mum led the way into a gatehouse where more guards waited. The brick walls were bare and strip lighting glared overhead, making my eyes water. Mum had to scan a pass that was hanging around her neck, and she tapped something on the tablet they handed her. Then Shelley and I had our pictures taken and scanned, before we too were handed electronic passes.

"Don't lose these," one of the guards told us in a stern tone edged by a strong Scottish accent. I stared up at him; the expression on his face was as severe as his voice.

Mum smiled and put an arm around Shelley and me. "You'll get to know everyone pretty quickly. This is Ben. He's friendlier than he looks!"

After all the security checks someone took our bags to our new living quarters, and we went for something to eat. It wasn't that late – around 8pm – but we felt the strange exhaustion that comes from long journeys; even those largely spent lying about and reading or watching films. It had been a long day. I sleepwalked my way through the meal, served in a large room with several tables scattered around. Frankie was invited to join us and I was glad when she accepted the offer. I was dimly aware there were other people in the room who smiled at me – a man asked me a question but I just smiled back at him and nodded, and Mum answered for me instead. I was awkward around strangers at the best of times, and couldn't find the energy it took to interact now. Mum and Frankie walked us across the compound to the house we would be staying in. I was alert enough to register that it was a small house in a long row of identical others, with a rather old-fashioned looking front door. The entrance hall felt slightly cramped compared to our wide, open plan spaces at home, with a staircase directly in front of us Before we went up the stairs, Shelley and I hugged Frankie goodbye.

"Oh, wait! Mummy, where is my rucksack?"

Frankie wasn't allowed to go anywhere until Mum had found it, which took several minutes, as someone else had brought our things to the house. Eventually it was located in an upstairs room, and Shelley rummaged about before carefully extracting a slightly battered homemade model. She was keen on making odd things out of various bits of cardboard and old packets, and it wasn't always clear what they were meant to be. Fortunately she didn't leave Frankie guessing.

"It's a bird feeder. For your garden. See, the food goes in here and the birds can perch there. I know you love gardening and you're looking forward to living back at home because *your* garden is nice and tidy."

"Oh! I didn't say that…" she glanced shiftily at Mum, who was frowning in mock outrage. "It's beautiful, Shelley, thank you. I'll send some pictures of the birds enjoying it. There was really no need for a gift though, it's been a wonderful couple of months."

It was partly the fatigue, but also a genuine feeling of loss, that made the farewell an emotional one. We both clung to her. Mum tried to insist Frankie stay the night on the sofa.

"I can clear it with the guards, just for one night?"

"No, really – I've got a place booked, and I'd like to start the journey back nice and early. I'd disturb the girls, and they need a lie in."

We all had tears in our eyes as we waved Frankie off at the door.

Mum showed us up to our shared room. It was small and plain, but cosy, with two camp beds and a large rug-type thing that covered the whole floor. But that was all I took in before falling into a vast sleep. Tomorrow, we would explore.

Chapter 19

Our first day at ComET Base mark two dawned bright and blue. It was a fort – one that had stood in that spot for hundreds of years. Its position on a jutting peninsula had in more recent years, however, seen the once grand garrison shrink to less than half its original size. But it served a purpose now, one that none of those who built it three hundred years before could ever have foreseen. Its earlier scale and magnificence was still apparent, but the sea had encroached upon it greatly, wearing away much of the strong stone outer walls that had stood for so many years, in less than ten. But the inner section was still secure, and rose high enough above the ocean to provide protection and security for the precious guests inside.

Stepping outside our home for the foreseeable future on that first morning was invigorating in more ways than one. Tiredness and the encroaching night had meant I had paid little attention to the surroundings the night before. But now, refreshed by the sleep and the wind blowing off the Firth which surrounded us on three sides, I was struck by the magnificence of it all.

We breakfasted in the same large circular room we had dined in the night before. Shelley was back to her gregarious self, and she chattered away to the perfect strangers beside her as I took in our new surroundings. The huge dining room was in the oldest building in the fortress, and the bare stone walls looked ancient, each stone roughly cut and secured in place. And yet they were solid, and probably over a metre thick if my history project on castles had taught me anything. It felt as though a medieval king and queen would be quite at home there presiding over a banquet, and I imagined tapestries hung around the walls depicting battle scenes. But instead the walls were bare, apart from a row of high windows, and rows of heated stations stood on one side of the room containing all the elements of a delicious cooked breakfast (most of which Shelley and I had greedily loaded onto our plates). The tables, dotted around the room, were almost all occupied with people chatting, some seriously, some laughing, some uniformed and some not. This was more people than I had seen together in one place for as long as I could remember.

Mum explained that this was because a few of the people at Fort Leigh – as it was called – had been aboard the carrier in the Atlantic, so had effectively quarantined together. In fact, looking around now, I recognised with some awe a few of the scientists and doctors who had been interviewed on the news. Although there was no immediate virus threat presently, precautions had to be taken as though there was. My sister and I had been tested for the latest strain – which was still rumbling about with isolated cases here and there, but had been declassified as a pandemic – and had also remained at home for several days before we left, so were considered safe. Some of the team had been replaced to relieve those jaded from weeks on a remote base, or who simply wanted to get back to their families. I could tell there was camaraderie between the adults in the room, stemming not just from spending so many weeks at sea, but from being a part of such a world-changing, life-defining phenomenon.

Mum took us for a tour of the areas that we were allowed to go to unaccompanied. It turned out these were limited to our own living quarters and most of the outside space. The former was clearer to see now, one of a series of modest little terrace houses standing in two angular horseshoe shapes facing each other in the centre of the compound, each of which contained a small lounge and kitchen with two bedrooms and a bathroom upstairs. We were used to living in our sprawling house down in the south, and yet I was already beginning to feel at home here. Our house was safe and compact, with that warm, welcoming feeling of a hotel, albeit with the slight barrenness of one too; no personal effects or pictures decorated the walls, and the simplest and most minimal furniture occupied the rooms. It was similar to the way I had felt in that camp pod in Devon; the novelty of everything, from the unfamiliar beds to the carpeted floors. And it was old-fashioned in quite an appealing way, not just the beautiful stone architecture around us but the interior of the simple house, with its manual light switches and twist-on water taps. There were some aspects that took a little getting used to – there was no robovac or laundrybot, so we had to do stuff ourselves, like operate the dishwasher and load the washing machine. We even had to get to grips with an ancient push-along vac.

The house was built at a time when there had been little or no need for air conditioning, and so sometimes became quite stuffy. In fact, as the weather warmed up during our time there, we often had the front door propped wide open to allow air to circulate. There was also the fact I was sharing a room with my little sister – it was something I would have baulked at in most circumstances, but it was a novelty here, and also strangely comforting. We were together in encountering these strange new surroundings.

As we wandered around that first morning – in the few sections that weren't out of bounds to us – it was hard not to stare at the camouflaged soldiers walking about, or stationed around the edges and guarding entrances. The only route to the fort by road was the single track we had driven along the night before. Access by sea was possible but hazardous, the original small harbour that served the fort having been washed away years before. There was no room for doubt that we were in a fortress.

We had more freedom of the outside spaces, but still there were many areas restricted to us. The houses were arranged around a central courtyard area, while the main buildings were a short walk away, housing the offices, labs and the 'mess' area, as well as the buildings only accessible to certain adults with the correct clearance – one of which had a large helipad on the roof, Mum told us. And beyond that, towards the tip of the peninsula but bordered by smaller brick huts with corrugated roofs, stood the most forbidding-looking of all: a large dome-like structure made of stark, rough concrete. And forbidden was the right word – guarded day and night, we had been directed to stay away. We knew why, of course. Everyone from the Atlantic base had been gradually choppered in by Chinook a couple of weeks before our arrival, to join the professors and military personnel already isolating within. And the final helicopter had contained the precious cargo: the Thulians themselves. They were now safely stowed inside the concrete building, the strongest part of the fortress, where they were to stay for at least another week, getting acclimatised to their new home like they had done on the ship.

Shelley and I felt a little sorry for them, confined once again in a windowless vault. The two of us stood outside that day, as close as we were allowed to get to the dome, and tried to picture the creatures inside. We – and they, we were sure, as our mother would have explained it to them – knew though that they were there for their own safety and protection. Their ability to breathe outside their quarters on ComET Base One for longer and longer periods had been a huge breakthrough, which was why it had been decided to brave them on dry land. It had the benefit of being more accessible, but also allowed them to see more features of our planet for themselves.

And what features they were. Buffeted by the wind, we climbed up the steps of the stone walls to take in the views. It became a daily habit, and it was never the same. Although always beautiful, the sky varied from day to day – hour to hour – from watery blue to moody, rippled grey to dazzling white. Across the water the hills rolled, in colours I had hardly seen in nature before. Brownish golds, yellows and greens, bright pinkish-purple flowers standing in tall clusters. In the distance, tall majestic fir trees marched over the hills in dark, military rows. We could see from our spot where the old walls had crumbled away beneath us, claimed by the ever-rising sea, the remains of a white turret sticking up defiantly.

Mum had warned us about the storms here, and told us never to climb the walls when there was one forecast. It was unlikely in this, the early summer, but the weather was unpredictable even in the calmest of places, less so here. As it was, we found it hard to believe the wind could be stronger than it was up there on our perch, as we stood with feet planted in a warrior's pose, letting our hair flap and whip our faces. We were quite a sight on those days as we re-entered the house: wild, tangled hair (Shelley's even more so than usual) and red, wind-kissed skin. Storms were a part of life everywhere – even our home in the south had to be storm-proofed, like all the others. In this exposed position, though, they hit worse than most. When the weather turned on us there would be no hiding from the persistent lashing rain and violent wind.

On wet days we stayed indoors and caught up on the schoolwork we had missed while roaming around the fort. Shelley had initially complained about the lack of technology.

"How are we supposed to do our home learning without a smart speaker?" She'd whined. Mum had pointed out that she should be finding information out for herself anyway, and she soon got used to using just her tablet.

Mum had a bit more time than usual to spend helping us, because while the Thulians were kept hidden indoors there wasn't much they needed to communicate. The pod they had travelled in had been carefully transported with them so that they could still access the equipment and supplies from it, and so they were self-contained in their bunker, perhaps not exactly content there, but provided for in the short term. So it became my mother's rule that we spent at least two hours on our studies before we were unleashed into the great outdoors, when the weather allowed, and onto our screens when it didn't. We argued that just being there was more education than we could ever have gained elsewhere, but Mum was immovable. Probably because she had made a lot of promises to the school to get them to agree to us taking so much time off.

And so the days passed. Shelley and I became used to our new surroundings very quickly, and fell happily into our routine. Although supplies could be ordered and delivered to the main gate, on most evenings we ate in the mess room, or grand hall as we preferred to call it, with the other members of the ComET team who were in there, and we got to know a few of them very well. They seemed to enjoy hearing Shelley chatter away, and I became more confident with them too. I was slightly awestruck one day to meet Doctor Bauer, the anthropologist who had been at one of the press announcements talking about the Thulians' medical examination. But he was very kind to us, and I found him easy to talk to. Perhaps because he himself had seemed a little awkward on TV – he even admitted, when I brought up the interview, to being terrified of having to speak with the whole world listening.

"No one would have noticed," I told him kindly.

But neither he, nor Dr Ling (the chief doctor, who had also stayed on for the next phase of the project, and who aroused similar feelings of awe when I met her) were anything like they had been in that presentation. I suppose that wasn't too strange, as there they had been professionals who clearly took their jobs – and their vital part in this unique project – very seriously. In normal life, though, they were easy going and friendly, not seeming to mind having two young kids tagging along. No one else had brought any of their family, choosing to go home to their families instead and give up their place on the project to another eager researcher. I guessed Mum's expertise in negotiating and persuading had been called into use when she sought permission for us to be there. I never found out exactly *how* she had achieved it, but put it down to her being very good at her job.

Ernst Bauer, or Ernie as Shelley decided to call him (he never objected), was tall and thin and slightly gangly, with round glasses that were a little too large for his face and seemed to accentuate his long thin nose. He was German, but spoke very good English – as did most of the team members, in fact, regardless of nationality. He patiently answered all of our questions, of which we had many. He often took his time answering, as though our questions were the most intelligent he had ever been asked. They were far from it, of course, but we grew very fond of him and his way of making us feel like we belonged there, and the little squint he'd make as he looked up and considered his answers. Amy Ling was born in China but grew up in America and was a little older – perhaps around Frankie's age – and she and Mum became firm friends. She too would seek us out to sit with during those mealtimes, and we started to look forward to it very much, never running out of new questions to pester them both with.

One exchange with Ernst has always stood out in my mind. I can't remember who else was there, or how the conversation began, but I do remember him pointing out the strange paradox with the ETs. On the one hand, they were so far advanced, their knowledge and skills far surpassing ours. Yet on the other, it could be said they were rather primitive; they were used to neither the comforts or the conveniences we had derived for ourselves, or – from what we had learned – the society or infrastructure. But then, they also seemed to have no desire to own, expand or rule.

Not all the members of the team were quite as patient or accommodating. While everyone took the job seriously, even reverently, there were a few who felt – perhaps rightly – that us children had no place there, running about and getting under their feet. Not that we did of course – Mum had warned us about doing just that on our first morning.

"Right you two, time for a serious chat," she'd said, and we knew whenever she said that to stop playing about and listen, because she was true to her word and it was usually in our own interests to listen when she was being serious.

"This project is important – really important. Not just to me, but to all the people here, and to the whole world. I think you both know that. It was really difficult to convince everyone to let me bring you both here. In fact, there are a few in the team who feel it's very inappropriate for you to be here at all. And they're right, in a way. Or they would be, if you were the kind of kids who didn't do as you were told or didn't follow the rules when the rules are important. What I'm saying is: please do as you are told, and keep away from the places and people you are asked to keep away from. Otherwise we will have to go home. Okay?"

We had both nodded solemnly and made our promises, and we both meant it. Young as we were – well, as Shelley was – we were mature enough to understand what she was saying.

Still, some of the professors and soldiers either ignored us or gave us disapproving glances now and then. But that was fine by us – as Mum had said, it was rather incongruous for us to be there. And we learned very quickly who was accommodating, who would smile at us or talk to us, or even sneakily hand us sweets when no one else was looking.

It was only probably our second or third day when the world press discovered the ComET base had been relocated to Scotland. It was remarkable really that it was kept secret for that long, although I suppose the people in charge of keeping it so were very experienced at it. I believed MI5 had been involved, although I couldn't remember where I had first heard that. Anyway, discover us they did. Not that they could do much about it – we were protected by international law (I'm not sure which one exactly, as I doubt there were any specific laws for such a thing), and also by the remoteness and inaccessibility of our location. Still the odd helicopter circled, hoping for more than just an ordinary aerial shot of the fort – a glimpse of a grey-blue being wandering about, perhaps. It made us feel very cut off from the real world, and very ensconced in this secret one, all at the same time. My life at home; school, my friends, even Frankie, seemed more than far away – it was as if they no longer existed in real terms.

During our evening mealtime chats with our new friends Shelley, with her characteristic innocence and determination, asked over and over when we would get to meet the Thulians.

135

"Lots of us in the room have not met them yet," answered Ernst. "You will have to get in a queue."

"So there's a queue? Where?"

"He's joking, silly," I replied. I found myself smiling knowingly at the adults at my sister's naiveté, as though I were a grown-up too. But I was secretly pleased she was asking, because I was hoping for the same thing.

I remembered when I had been terrified of the very thought of ETs finding our planet, let alone stepping foot on it. The fears that had plagued me night and day still seemed very real, but since Mum had been speaking to them they had slowly become people, rather than monsters. It had been the mystery I had been afraid of, just like all the so-called Protectors and conspiracy theorists and demonstrators. But Mum had seen these beings, actually spoken to them, and judged them to be safe. Now all I wanted was to meet them for myself. But, Ernst was right, so did everyone in the room – not to mention half the world – who hadn't been fortunate enough to meet them already.

So it was a great, but delightful, shock when, two weeks after our arrival and just before the Thulians were set to venture out of their confinement, Amy came to find us with some news. It was the morning, so we had been sitting at the kitchen table with our tablets trying to concentrate on our lessons. Mum was out – she had been working a lot more lately, in the lead up to the release. Part of the deal of having us there was that it wouldn't impact on her work. A consequence of that was that we were sometimes left alone in the house, if the weather was too bad to spend much time outside or we had schoolwork to do. She wasn't happy about it and had given us another serious talk about not trying to cook or use knives or do anything remotely risky. And so we weren't sure at first whether to answer the knock at the door.

"We don't even know who it could be," I whispered, always the more wary of us both.

"It's not going to be a baddy, we know all the people who are here!"

I sighed and rolled my eyes at her practicality.

"Okay, well stay here, I'd better answer it."

Of course she followed me, and we both peered warily around the door, letting out a breath of relief when we saw Amy.

"Hello Dr Ling!"

"Do you want to come in for a cup of tea?" Chimed Shelley.

"You don't know how to make tea," I hissed unkindly. Shelley just gave me a look and stepped back to let the doctor in.

"Hello girls, I'm sorry to bother you, your mother said you were home working so I won't keep you long."

"No really, it's fine!" we both said hastily. We hadn't had any visitors since we had arrived, and it felt rather grown up to have a house guest. Amy came in and sat with us in the kitchen after politely declining the tea (probably aware we weren't allowed to touch the kettle anyway). She asked us about the school work we were doing and showed great interest, even though she couldn't possibly have been as interested in Shelley's spellings as she was in my history project.

"So, I'd better tell you why I'm here. I've been talking to Alek Ivanov, the professor in charge here. He's the one who gave the go ahead for you to stay here for a bit."

"Right." My heart had suddenly sped up a bit and I felt a bit sick. We hadn't met Alek yet, and I couldn't think why he would want to talk about us unless it was bad. We had been careful to follow the rules, but only the day before I had been running away from Shelley when she was pretending to be a zombie, and rounded a corner crashing straight into Ben, the slightly scary guard we had met on the first night. He hadn't seemed very impressed – in fact, he had frowned at us and shaken his head. This was it – we were being sent home. Mum would go mad. And, worse than that, she would be devastated to have to leave the project.

Shelley was still leaning forward, elbows on the table with her chin on her fists, looking excited. She hadn't realised yet. But then a voice inside reminded me that Amy had asked Mum where to find us. Surely she would have told Mum first that we were in trouble, and if so wouldn't both of them be here? All these thoughts must have gone through my head in less than a couple of seconds.

"Is he the one with the shiny bald head? Or the bushy moustache?"

I frowned at my sister questioningly. She shrugged, "I saw Mummy talking to some people the other day."

Amy smiled. "Bald head. Anyway, I told him about how excited you both were about the project, and how many questions you've been asking. I said I really thought you'd both be scientists yourselves one day."

"Really?" I'd heard people say this about Shelley all the time, but never about me. I wasn't sure I even wanted to be a scientist when I was older, but her words still gave me a bit of a glow.

"And he said, in that case, you should be able to come in one day and see for yourselves what it is we do. Sort of like a school project. Or work experience, even."

"With the Thulians?" Shelley always pronounced it 'chewlians', but Amy was nice and pretended not to notice.

"Well, we're not sure when that might be, a little way off, but until then you can have a tour of the lab and then maybe see them from one of the other rooms."

For once my sister was speechless. She stared open mouthed at us both, looking backwards and forwards. It didn't last long: she jumped off her chair and danced around squealing. I looked at Amy and laughed.

"Thank you, that would be amazing," was my more restrained response, although my heart was hammering inside my chest.

She leaned forward and spoke theatrically behind her hand. "Don't tell your little sister, but we may be able to work it so you get a proper meeting." She winked and put her finger to her nose conspiratorially. I could only stare, my mouth hanging open stupidly. Busy celebrating, Shelley hadn't heard or noticed a thing.

"Right girls, I'll leave you to it. Back to studying kings and queens, and spelling words with 'ee'!" And off she went.

Chapter 20

A few days later, we went into work with my mother. Even though I had spent all those hours listening in on her meetings, fantasising that I too was solving world problems and getting important people to listen to me, this was different. At home she was still just 'Mum'; we had never actually accompanied her on work trips before.

That day she was to oversee the arrangements for the Thulians' 'breakout', as it was jokingly referred to by some of the staff involved. Different measures had been put into place to make sure they weren't in any danger – or not too grave danger, as it was a risky operation no matter what. Although they had already breathed fresh air on board ComET Base one, they had only ever been outside for short bursts and there was still the risk of something going wrong. The aim eventually was for them both to be able to walk among us without needing to keep retreating to the capsule for top-ups of air. The daily dose they were absorbing from their vials had also been adjusted – but there was the risk that the adjustment could have the opposite effect. Although calculations had been carefully made in the labs, these were unfamiliar beings they were dealing with. Mum was there to explain all this and decide with the team and the visitors if the arrangements put in place would work for them.

Only the people really essential to the well-being of the Thulians were being allowed close, and so Mum was communicating through the wall from one of the nearby labs. We walked with her to the building that had been commandeered for research, with the pop-up labs and offices set up inside. This building had been strictly out of bounds to us up until now. At the door, where Mum had to swipe her security card and speak into the camera to announce herself, we exchanged our own masks for hospital-grade ones, and daubed our hands with antibacterial gel that smelt far stronger than the stuff we were used to. Dr Ling was there to greet us, and even presented us with two white lab coats, I suspected just to make us feel a part of things than out of necessity, as Mum didn't put one on. We had to roll up the sleeves, and Shelley especially looked comically swamped, the coat almost trailing on the floor.

As we followed them along the corridor I had the strange sense of the old meeting the new, passing clear glass walls with sliding doors locked with combination pads, contrasted with the heavy brick external walls visible behind. Inside these glass boxes were strange machines with complicated buttons and wall-mounted tablets and various pieces of unfathomable equipment on the surfaces. There were people working in the sterile labs, looking through microscopes or operating the machines or tapping on the tablets. At one point I did a double-take as two white-coated staff members stood in a room seemingly with our visitors, tall and silent in front of them with no-one wearing protective gear or masks. But the illusion was shattered when one scientist reached over to grab something, passing his hand directly through a Thulian. A hologram of some sort. I turned to Shelley and saw her watching, the same wide-eyed expression on her face as mine.

At last we came to a room that wasn't see-through – it had what looked like plasterboard walls, which gave it a temporary feel. Amy tapped a code into the keypad and the door swooshed open, revealing an ordinary-looking office with a large desk, a couple of chairs and not much else. There wasn't

141

even a window. I wasn't sure what I had been expecting, but felt a little disappointed after all the interesting-looking rooms we had passed. We could have been anywhere, about to speak to someone quite mundane. Mum sat down at the desk, tapped a code into a keypad on the table and logged on to the wall.

Shelley and I pulled one of the large chairs into the corner and both sat in it, watching as the researchers in the central lab appeared on the large screen on the wall. After a short chat they turned the camera and we saw two greyish figures. I thought at first they were in shadow, but quickly realised my mistake. One of the Thulians was standing, tall and poised, the other sitting on the floor, back straight and head upright. They had a proud, dignified air. I felt my skin prickle at the thought of them being so close; in a room somewhere not far beneath us.

"Hello. I hope you are both comfortable and well." Mum spoke clearly and steadily, but not slowly or condescendingly.

"Yes we are. Thank you."

It was the first time I had heard them speak. It was difficult at first to work out which one had spoken, but the voice was strange, as though two voices spoke at once with slightly varying tones, high pitched and musical. When they spoke again I realised it was the one that was standing, but I only saw the mouth move slightly.

"We aim to get you outside in the next one or two days, when preparations are finished."

"Yes."

"This is the plan: your dosage has been calculated to allow two hours outside, but we will try thirty minutes to start."

"Yes," the figure said again, simply. I wondered why she wasn't saying more, and thought perhaps it was because their language was still quite limited.

"Ten people – two guards and three researchers for each one of you – will walk with you around the perimeter of the area to give you an idea of the size of it, and so you can see the views over the land."

"Yes."

"Have you been shown maps and photos, so you know where on the planet we are?"

"We have."

"This is my home island, I live in a country to the south. I will point it out on your map."

"That is interesting to know. We will have questions for you."

"We will be able to answer them." My mother paused, as though allowing them to process the information before she moved on. "After the thirty minutes, we will ask you to return to your pod so the doctors can assess your levels."

"Yes."

"Do you want a time piece so you can see how long you are out?"

"Yes, that will be useful to us."

"Can I confirm it will be both of you going outside?"

"Yes, it will be both of us."

"Thank you for waiting for so long and letting us do our tests, I hope you understand they are to help you to acclimatise to our atmosphere."

"Yes, this is clear to us."

"Do you have any more questions for me about the arrangements?"

"No." The seated Thulian had not said anything, and the one that spoke did not seem to confer with her. I wondered if this was because the standing one was in charge, or if they communicated in some other, telepathic way.

"My colleague, Doctor Ling, will talk to you now to decide the details of the dosage and the tests she will do."

"Thank you and goodbye."

Mum got up and ushered us out of the room as the doctor moved from her place in the other corner of the room and sat down to continue the briefing. We followed Mum outside and walked across to the mess building where she bought herself a coffee and a hot chocolate each for us. It was around ten o'clock and only a couple of tables were occupied. Shelley had been bombarding Mum with questions all the way there, but Mum had insisted she needed a coffee first.

"Ah, that's better! I always feel so tense when I'm talking to them. It's just so important to get it right."

"You did an amazing job, Mum."

"Thank you darling," she smiled at me and squeezed my hand. I felt a little breathless, as though I had been sharing the tension my mother felt. It was strange because we had only seen them on a screen. It wasn't all that different from watching them on TV at home. But I had a sense that I, too had conversed with them.

"Do they both talk, Mummy?"

"I've only ever heard one of them speak – the same one each time, which is the slightly taller one with the darker eyes. I'm not sure why, but it was only that one that worked with the speech and language specialist. I get the feeling they both understand what's being said, though."

"I loved the sound of the voice… is it a girl or a boy?"

"They are both female."

"And do they have babies like us?" Shelley asked, a bit louder than we would have liked. A guard at one of the other tables turned around – I saw it was Ben again, the one I'd nearly got into trouble with. When he saw us he gave a wry smile and rolled his eyes slightly, as if to say 'those bloody kids again.'

"Shelley! You don't need to shout!" I scolded, embarrassed on her behalf. But Mum just went on to answer her.

"Yes. They have wombs, so give birth to live young like mammals. But the really interesting bit is how: they can reproduce without a male. It's called parthenogenesis, and it's also been observed on Earth in some snakes and sharks."

We both stared at Mum. "Wow."

"Do they ever speak more than that?" I asked. "Like, to say more than just 'yes'?"

"Sometimes, if they're answering a specific question about their home. I have to be very careful when I speak to them. I have a sort of list of rules: no contractions, so 'it is', not 'it's'; never be vague, always direct, so there's no room for crossed wires; make sure they answer after each statement, or acknowledge they've understood it; don't overwhelm with information, but keep statements short and simple, and don't refer to emotions, such as 'I'm happy to answer you', or 'I'm so glad you're here', in case of ambiguity," she looked at Shelley "not making myself clear enough to them."

"That's a lot to remember."

"It's very similar to the way I negotiate in other situations too, so it comes quite naturally to me now. Oh, I forgot one more important thing: don't tell them how things are going to be, but allow them to have a say and decide for themselves. It gives them autonomy, rather than feeling we're deciding everything for them. It's all about empathy too – I'm trying to imagine how I would feel if I was more or less alone on a strange planet where nothing and no one is familiar."

"How can you do that, though?"

"It's not easy. I just try to compare it to other situations I've been in where I've felt vulnerable or out of place. But you're right Shelley – I can't really completely understand what it must be like for them. Not even in my wildest imagination."

Chapter 21

Since arriving at Fort Leigh I hadn't been paying nearly as much attention to the news. There hardly seemed any point when we were right there, at the heart of it all. What could possibly be reported that we hadn't heard about, or already seen for ourselves? It was a heady feeling, one of unreality. Like being detached from it all and completely immersed at the same time.

I did find out that the giant space telescope that orbited Earth had been able to pick up the craft the Thulians had arrived on, positioned some mind-boggling amount of millions of miles away. It had only been spotted after the Thulians themselves had given the necessary information to the astronomers. Co-ordinates, or whatever you have in space. It was significant in that it backed up their story, but also meant the craft was looming there, ready to creep closer, depending on which side you listened to these days.

More and more footage was being released to the press of the Thulians, speaking to the camera as we had seen them. This was in a bid to satisfy the continuing and ever growing hunger for information. Once a week a helicopter or boat arrived with supplies for the occupants of the fort – food, medicine scientific equipment – but recently, more and more helicopters were seen circling in the skies, which had no official business related to the ComET project. Also, marine traffic had increased on the Firth to one side (there was no access for them into the Bay, to our left) with, if we looked carefully, people on board hunched behind cameras and filming the base.

There was another reason for the release of the footage too, though. The demonstrators and activists who were against the Thulians coming here seemed to have quietened down a bit, but now there was concern that fear and suspicion was growing among those that had at first been relatively open minded. Since the base had been moved to Scotland, there had been less new coverage – all the initial discoveries had been revealed; there wasn't much more to say while we waited for them to quarantine there. But that stream of information had been reassuring – it humanised the ETs, gave them faces and characteristics. So now they had a voice, and were speaking our languages, it made sense to share that with the outside world. To quell the slowly growing disquiet.

We went into the control building – known as the 'Hub' – with Mum a few more times over the next couple of days; I assumed Alek – or Professor Ivanov, as we were told to call him should our paths cross – had been pleased with our behaviour that first time. I hadn't seen him to say thank you; I still hadn't even met him. He didn't ever seem to be around when we went into the dining room. I guessed, as boss of this part of the show, he must be pretty busy.

Sometimes we listened in again on Mum's interactions with the ETs, but on a few occasions Amy took us into one of the labs. We had to wear special gloves when we went in there, and full helmets with clear bits that we could see out of, on top of our masks. All the researchers in there wore the same. It was to cover our hair as well as to stop us breathing germs or getting fingerprints on any of the samples and contaminating them. She showed us the blood samples that had been taken – almost black in colour – and the scan and X-Ray pictures, the magnified skin cells. I had taken in every word on her original report about the examination of the Thulians, but to see it all for myself was truly fascinating.

Even so, a lot of what went on in the labs was too complex for us to fully grasp, despite Amy's patient explanations. So we both preferred listening in and watching the interactions with the Thulians. Even these were quite technical, but that didn't matter. I had the same desire as the media and everyone else in the world outside: to know and see and try to understand these remarkable beings.

A week or so after our first venture into the control building we were in the room again with Mum. It had been decided to postpone the Thulians' trip outside because heavy rain had been forecast for the next day or so. Although there was nothing to suggest that rain would cause any definitive harm, the medical team still wanted to wait until it was dry. We sat in the same corner, on the same chairs, but this time it was just the three of us. Mum was explaining the reasons for the delay. I had felt frustrated myself when I had first learned of it because it felt like we had been there, waiting for this moment, forever. So I could only imagine how the news had been received by the Thulians themselves. The researchers must have felt the same way too – so much preparation was going into such a seemingly simple operation, just for it to be affected by the weather.

But it seemed the Thulians seemed to share none of this disappointment; they accepted it without question. I wondered if it was true that they didn't feel emotions, and how that would affect the perception of them by the rest of the human race. For me it just added to the mystery; it was just one more thing I wanted to understand.

"It is forecast to be dry in two days," my mother was saying, as we perched in the corner, the very example of flies on the wall.

"We have communicated with the other pods in orbit. Their weather data confirms this," answered the taller one, who always did the talking. At least, that was what I assumed, because today they were both seated on a wooden bench and it was impossible to tell which one was taller. I hadn't seen them enough times yet to know them apart any other way. I searched the background for clues to their personalities, their preferences. There was nothing, although their quarters looked very comfortable, with a well-cushioned sofa just to the side of them, and I wondered why they had chosen to sit on the hard bench.

"Our weather is hard to predict, but it is good that you have data from space too. We also use this – our satellites help us to forecast storms and rain."

"On our planet it is also hard to predict, but we have a thicker atmosphere so the temperature does not vary as much as it does here. We also have more rain – it is something we need to know; why there is less rain here but you have large oceans. Has it always been so?"

"Well... no. It's to do with the water cycle. Plus, the weather and climate on Earth has changed a lot in the last few years. We get a lot of rain in the winters. But this is something you can discuss with our meteorologists and environmentalists in more detail." I was impressed by Mum's answer, as she had seemed a bit caught out by the question. Maybe because it was outside her area of expertise. But also she was slightly distracted, typing something quickly onto her tablet. I thought it was the information about the planet that they had given her; perhaps it was new. This didn't occur to me as strange at the time, even though the conversations were recorded and so there was no need to write anything down. I was just finding it hard to believe they were discussing something as mundane as the weather.

"These are them? The meteorologist and environmentalist?"

Mum looked up. She hadn't been paying full attention. "Please can you repeat that?

"The people in the room with you. They have been here before. Are they the scientists you refer to?" I caught my breath.

Mum looked round at us as though she had forgotten we were there.

"Oh... no! These are... my children. They wanted to learn more about you and so are here, listening. I hope that is okay for you?"

Sitting in the corner of the room, we were out of sight of the holowall camera. Even to this day I have no idea how they knew we were there, or how they had seen us there the other times too.

I felt tense, as though picking up signals from Mum, although she was showing no outward signs. Something wasn't right – no one had discussed this with us; the possibility of the Thulians minding us being there silently observing, or of even knowing of our presence. But it seemed a huge oversight now – surely their permission should have been sought? We were just innocent, curious kids, but it must have looked very strange for us to be there, lurking in the background like spies. If the situation had been reversed there would have been huge wariness and suspicion on the part of us humans. A lot had been made of our acceptance of them, the possible danger they might pose to us, but what about the other way around? There were just two of them, their position was far more risky than ours right now.

"Hello," said Shelley, jumping up from her seat. I urged my limbs to move – to grab her and stop her – but I wasn't quick enough and she was already standing beside our mother.

"Children? This is what you call young humans."

"Y-yes. This is my youngest daughter – female child – her name is Shelley."

"And the other one is slightly larger."

Mum turned around to me and motioned with her head for me to stand up. I forced myself out of the chair and stood on the other side of her.

"Yes, she is five years older. This daughter is named Faye."

"H...hello." My voice sounded thin and weak.

"What is your name?" asked Shelley, chirpy as ever, with no idea that this could go – or possibly already had gone – terribly wrong.

"We do not have names in the same way as you do here."

"Oh. Well then, can I give you a name, please?"

I stared at her, marvelling at the audacity of a five-year-old. But the Thulian seemed unfazed.

"I know this is your custom. So yes."

"I know that you're a girl," she chattered on, as though simply talking to another child at school. "Even though it's quite hard to tell."

Watching her felt like seeing an awful accident about to unfold, but being powerless to stop it. I looked at Mum, wondering why she wasn't trying to take charge of the situation, but to my surprise she had a strange half smile on her face as though she was amused and slightly wary all at once. Possibly she was just curious as to what might happen.

"And I think you would suit the name Seraphina. It's the name of one of my favourite dolls." The Thulian looked at her for a moment, as though considering. Although, possibly, she was simply as baffled as we were.

"Seraphina. Yes."

"And what about your friend?"

The Thulian, or 'Seraphina', as I suppose she was now called, looked at her companion. To my amazement she, too, stood up and moved closer. Although we hadn't seen or heard them communicate, she seemed to understand the question, and moved her head slightly in what I took to be a very human nod.

"You should be Sylvian. My other favourite doll's name."

The newly-named being gave that strange ghost of a nod again, and sat back down. As I stood there I wondered if I was in fact asleep – it did seem like the sort of strange dream I would have. Had my little sister really just given names – dolls' names, no less – to two of the most advanced beings in the universe?

"Thank you, Shelley," Mum interjected. "I think that's enough for now."

"I would like to ask more questions," said Seraphina (I knew I would have to get used to it). "I wish to know more about your young."

"Of course. What would you like to know?"

"Many things. I will ask some things now, and then we will prepare some more questions for you."

Then a remarkable thing happened. If indeed you can say that when you're conversing for the first time with an extra-terrestrial being from several light years away (who has just been given a stupid name by a five-year-old). I suppose it would be more accurate to say something *else* remarkable happened. The Thulians began communicating together, audibly this time, but not in English or any language I had ever heard. Or even with any sounds I was familiar with. The sounds they made were wavering, high pitched notes that merged together into one sound. I couldn't tell which one was making them, but thought that both could have been, at the same time. The three of us watched, transfixed. Mum had her chin on one hand and her eyes were wider than usual and shining a little, a bit like the look she got when she saw Shelley do something for the first time like walk or chat to her toys.

After a few seconds it was over, and it was like a spell had been broken. The sounds had been strangely soothing, lulling. Seraphina turned to face us.

"We would like to ask how you reproduce."

Mum gave them a detailed answer. There was nothing new to learn for us – due to her characteristic openness we had always known everything we needed to. And I was too young yet to feel any embarrassment about her practical descriptions.

"So your young are born much smaller, like ours, but completely helpless and dependant."

"That is correct. I have some footage here on my device if you would like me to email it over later on. It is of my two when they were babies. Parents – usually one or two adults – take care of and teach the child until they are fully grown and independent. Actually, it usually goes beyond that and there is a level of nurturing that takes place throughout the parents' life."

"Until the parent dies?"

"Well… yes. The child is independent by the time they reach adulthood, and will usually live elsewhere, but – yes, they are still cared for in some ways."

"What are baby Thulians like, Seraphina?" asked Shelley.

"I will give a detailed answer after I have asked my questions. Shelley."

"Okay! Thank you." Shelley beamed. The Thulian – Seraphina – had just used her name: they were friends now, as far as she saw it. I couldn't help smiling too. It seemed that they had no fear of us, or suspicion of the way we had been listening in. They were just curious. Perhaps they didn't ever harbour suspicions of things or beings that were different to them, like so many of the human race seemed to.

"So, humans live around ninety to one hundred Earth years, as we have already learned. At what age does reproduction occur?"

"It is complicated because many choose not to have children, or are unable. Plus there are so many variables, but it is any time from sexual maturity to… well, around forty-five, fifty… it can be later. I suppose most females that give birth are between thirty and forty-five, but I would have to look up some proper statistics for you to be sure. I could do it now but it will take several minutes."

"It can wait until next time we talk. What number is the human population at now?"

Mum clicked on her tablet and tapped the screen.

155

"Around nine point two billion, it says here. We have a population expert you can speak to..."

There was a tiny 'ping' sound and I saw a message banner pop up on Mum's screen. She hastily swiped it away before I could read it properly, but I was sure I saw Alek's name, and caught the word 'dangerous'. I looked quickly at her.

"Apologies to you both but I am going to need to stop there. Could we continue this conversation tomorrow? And I will ask some of the experts to join us who will be able to answer your questions in more detail."

Seraphina didn't answer for a second or two. Then, again, I was sure I saw the slightest of nods.

"Yes."

After signing off, there was none of the usual awed analysis between us. Instead, Mum hastily grabbed her bag and strode to the door, gesturing for us to hurry up and follow. We almost crashed into an imposing figure standing just outside. I looked up so see a smartly dressed, stocky man with a bald head.

"Professor!"

"Helen," he spoke with a deep voice, the hint of an accent making him sound gruff and serious. Or perhaps that was just the way he was. For this was the Professor in charge of the whole operation here at Fort Leigh, Ivanov himself. "We need to have a chat."

They strode briskly towards the main exit. Apart from a quick backwards glance from Mum to check we were following, it was as though we had been forgotten. The professor hadn't acknowledged us at all. He was a big bear of a man, his suit, although impeccably fitted, somehow looking out of place on his large frame.

"Yes, the conversation took a bit of an unexpected turn." Mum was striding to keep up with him as she spoke. "We need to ask some of the others to be there next time so their questions can be answered a bit more satisfactorily. It really isn't my area…"

"What do you think…?" Shelley hissed. "Is he cross that I gave them names?"

I shushed my sister, trying to listen in. She never took this well, and started to protest.

"Sssh!" I hissed again. "I want to hear what they're saying, then we'll know what's going on."

"…really could have gone either way," Alek was saying.

"I felt the same way. Actually Alek, there's something I wanted to ask you." Mum took her tablet out of her bag. "When they asked me about the climate, I wasn't quite sure what stance we're taking. How we tell them, I mean."

The professor stopped abruptly, meaning we had to, as well, or risk colliding with him. He turned to face her and I saw dark, heavy eyebrows above intent, almost black eyes.

"Tell them?"

"Yes. About the state of things."

"There's no need for that, Helen. If any more questions of that nature are asked we can answer more generically." He waved his hand as though to dismiss her concerns. Mum paused, considering her response.

"I'm not sure they'll accept that, they seem to prefer specific data."

"They're here on a fact-finding mission, this is true, but not to check up on our treatment of the planet."

157

"That's why I don't think we should hide information from them."

"I really don't think it will be an issue."

"I disagree," she said firmly.

The professor suddenly looked at us, standing there trying not to be seen and witnessing every word.

"Right, well, let's have that chat in my office shall we. I've got Amy and Tony in there, plus a couple of the team from climatology."

Mum looked at us, "I'll see you both at home."

We waited back at the house for her. Shelley was still excited and set to work compiling a list of questions to ask at the next meeting, trying to write it in her wobbly handwriting and pestering me for the spellings before I took out her tablet and started to help her type it out. I too still had the remnants of nervous energy from the encounter, but also couldn't stop thinking about what the professor had said. My mind replayed the conversation over and over, so I was quite glad of the distraction of Shelley's list and the TV comedy playing in the background. In fact, I looked up and was shocked that it had grown dark already. Mum still wasn't back.

"I'm hungry."

"Right. I'll see what we've got." I searched the fridge and cupboards to see if there was anything I could make that didn't involve cooking, and settled on a sandwich. I had just started buttering the bread when Mum walked in.

"I'm so sorry girls, I completely lost track of time. Have you been all right? Here, let me cook us something. I think I'd rather eat here this evening."

She banged some cupboards open and shut, looking frustrated. I wasn't sure if it was simply because she couldn't find what she was looking for, or if something else was bothering her.

"I hate leaving you two alone. I almost think you'd be better off at home with Frankie."

"No!" we both said. Mum smiled, but it didn't reach her eyes like a proper smile.

"Poor Frankie!"

"We love her. We just prefer being here with you."

"And Seraphina!" added Shelley.

As Mum put some pasta on to boil I sat at the table and watched her, waiting for her to start telling us what was happening. Shelley was desperate to show her the list she had made.

"Let's have a look while we're eating, shall we? It was exciting today, wasn't it. I still can't believe you got to speak to them."

"I know! We made friends!"

"At first I thought they might be angry that we were there, though," I said.

"I must admit I was a bit nervous too. I don't know why we didn't just introduce you at the start, really. It doesn't do to keep secrets…"

159

Mum stopped, and busied herself getting things out for the meal, taking extra time to straighten the cutlery and select the dishes.

"So what was your meeting about?" I asked.

"Just trying to decide the next steps. Finalise everything for Wednesday." She didn't meet my eye. It was an unpleasant feeling, having her hide something, let alone lie to me. I knew many of her operations were secret and she wasn't able to discuss them with us; whenever she shut the door to her office I understood it meant we weren't to disturb her or ask questions. But this project felt different – we were practically involved now. And it wasn't just that. The operation affected the whole human race – the entire planet. Something important had been said, and secrets were being kept, not just in this room tonight, but from the visitors. I knew Mum didn't like it, from what she had said to the Professor, and I couldn't help agreeing with her. Even though I hadn't understood what was being hidden or the significance of it, instinct told me it would be a bad idea to be deceptive. Earlier on that day we had been sitting in a room out of sight, and those Thulians had known we were there. Surely it followed, then, that they would be aware when they were being misled.

Chapter 22

'Breakout Day' – as it came to be known (I thought it made it sound as though they had been imprisoned. Which, I suppose, they had, albeit with their own consent) – was, fortunately, as clear as had been forecast. We were heading towards midsummer now, and the days were getting warmer and longer. While we had experienced two fierce storms, where the wind had whipped the sea up into a bright white froth and hammered the rain against the windows, we had been told that the proper storm season was still a few months away. That day, the sea was blue and calm, the sky showing patches of paler blue through the wispy white clouds.

All the arrangements had been made. The staff who were to accompany them were inside the bunker compound, the medication had been adjusted to help them breathe. A polytunnel had been put up, creating a corridor from the door of their building to a large open tented area, to allow them to walk without being too exposed to the sun, or indeed to the hovering helicopters above. News – along with footage – of the release was not going to be given out until after the event, but there were always hopeful reporters in the vicinity, and the sight of the white tents must have raised speculation that something was about to happen. Shelley and I had been allowed to stand at the edge of the tent to watch them come outside, along with most of the other staff, soldiers and scientists and doctors together, trying to catch a glimpse.

At eight am exactly, the heavy metal doors slid open, and we all edged forward as one to get a better look. I recognised some of the guards and researchers, including my own mother, who stood just outside the doors and momentarily blocked the Thulians from sight. But then, there they were. They couldn't be hidden for long because they stood taller than the tallest human there – they must have been almost seven feet. I spotted Seraphina – slightly taller still – striding just in front of her companion, Sylvian. Their limbs were long and thin; their legs didn't look like they should be strong enough to support them. Their extraordinary fingers stretched out beside them, finishing just beside their knees. Their fingertips had no nails, but looked sort of bulbous, reminding me a little of the toes of a gecko. I looked at their feet and saw their toes were indeed the same.

As they got closer I could get an idea of the colour and texture of their skin. It was remarkable – whether it was the quality of the light or not I couldn't be sure, but it was not simply grey. It was a colour I had never seen before, and seemed to change even as I was looking. A blue-grey, getting slightly darker and then lighter as they walked. And it looked smooth and rough all at once, the colour tricking my eyes into thinking it had a sheen to it, but then showing, as they moved closer, tiny bumps and grooves that I imagined gave it a roughness. I took all this in very quickly – it couldn't have taken them longer than a few seconds to walk towards me – but then it was Seraphina's face that I stared at. More specifically, her eyes. I knew they were unusual because I had looked into them across a wall screen, but nothing could have prepared me for the face-to-face encounter. They were mesmerising. Huge – taking up probably a third of the face – the irises neither blue nor grey nor green, but a strange mix of all three, with tiny black and silver flecks. They were somehow luminous, shining out at us and seeming to me to reveal all the intelligence of the universe. And those pupils, black vertical lines, slightly wider today than I had seen in photographs and on screen.

The wide line of Seraphina's mouth opened slightly and I thought she might speak, but then she just looked around and stood aside to check her companion was there. They were just an arm's length away from me: I found it so hard to keep myself from reaching out and touching them, but we were under strict instructions to keep a distance. It was for their safety more than anything: one gloveless touch or airborne germ could prove catastrophic to them.

If seeing these beings in the flesh was a miraculous experience for me, I couldn't imagine what it must have been like for them, standing there, being stared at by all those humans. They had been outside before of course, on board the first ComET base. But there, human interaction had been kept to a minimum. Here were fifty pairs of eyes all focusing on them. If they felt unnerved they didn't show it, but looked boldly around, meeting each gaze.

And then, Seraphina's eyes met my own, and stayed there for a bit, and I had the strangest sensation. It was as though an electric current were running from my heels to the base of my neck. The hairs on my body stood on end, and I felt a sort of shiver, but not a chill. It was probably only a few seconds, but as she looked into my eyes I felt again that awareness of the immense depths of her knowledge and understanding that went way beyond the perimeters of my own. Or, indeed, anyone's on this Earth. It's difficult to put into words, because it wasn't a feeling I had ever had before. And I felt as though she smiled at me, even though her mouth didn't move. I was sure that from somewhere came a glimmer, some sort of recognition. And then I blinked, and she was looking elsewhere. I came to, as though I had been under hypnosis,

163

and I looked at the people around me; no one else seemed to have had the same feeling.

It had been agreed that the Thulians would be escorted on a tour of the fort, and someone produced some large golfing umbrellas that looked comically out of place. But they were the best measure to keep out both the sun's rays and the prying eyes of the outside world, at least temporarily. For the whole morning so far, there had been the constant beat of helicopter blades and the tiny buzzing of drones in the sky above. To shield them from the cameras on the water, the guards and researchers – my mother, as their main contact and go-between, being a part of the group – formed a protective circle around the two figures. In time it would be arranged for representatives of the world's nations and their press to visit the base, but not yet. For now, we could keep them to ourselves.

Shelley and I stood back and watched the strange group as it made its way around the different areas.

"Did you see them? Aren't they amazing?"

I wasn't sure why, but I didn't feel like sharing my feelings with my sister right then. I wanted to contemplate it all quietly. She didn't seem to mind or notice my lack of response, but chattered on anyway.

The tour took a bit longer than the scheduled half an hour because Seraphina was asking so many questions. I could see the scientists hovering nearby were getting a bit edgy, worried about the effects the prolonged exposure might have. The group was at the far edge of the old walls, the higher section that hadn't crumbled away. They seemed to be standing there a while and I wondered what it was they could have been talking about. Perhaps seals or dolphins had been spotted, although they were rare now. Shelley and I had spent many hours scouring the waters for fins or little black heads bobbing about, with no luck.

Eventually the nervous scientists were able to usher the Thulians back into their concrete dome, and a short time later Mum made her way back over to us.

"Mummy that was ama-a-zing!" Shelley bounced up and down on each syllable and Mum laughed and hugged her.

"Yes it was! I'm so glad you could both be here to see this. That's one of the reasons I pushed so hard to have you here. I was missing you, obviously, but also I was desperate for you to be here to see moments like this."

"Well I'm really glad you did, Mum."

"Seraphina is sooo cool."

"Mum, what were they saying? When you had the tour."

She looked at me as though trying to decide if she should tell me something.

"Well, actually there was something pretty exciting. Seraphina has asked to see you both again, but properly this time. Not on the holowall, but inside their quarters."

I stopped and stared at her. "Wait, what? Why?"

"They'd just like to chat to you. You're the only human children they've seen, so I can imagine they have questions for you."

Shelley was bouncing again. "Can I show them my list? Please?"

"I don't see why they wouldn't answer some of your questions too. Of course."

She ran back towards the house to find it and see if she could add to it.

"Mum what else were they saying, when you were on the battlements over there? You seemed to be standing there ages."

She put her arm across my shoulders.

"They were asking about the ruins of the walls, wanted to know why they had broken away. So I told them about the sea levels rising all the time. Of course, that led to more questions and – well – you know me, Faye. I don't like to lie, or hold important things back."

"Why would you have lied?"

Mum stopped and sighed.

"Because I've been asked to. Specifically where issues around human-inflicted global damage are concerned."

Of course. The urgent – and so far secret – meeting the other day.

"By Professor Ivanov?"

"Yes. And I'm not really sure why. At least, I don't like to think why it might be."

"And what did you tell them?"

Mum looked ahead at the row of houses.

"The truth. That it was because the polar ice caps are melting. And I told them that was because of irreparable damage done to our climate," she looked at me, "by humans."

"Oh."

"Oh, indeed."

"Will you get into trouble?"

"I doubt Alek will be too happy. I did go against direct instructions. But we're both professionals; I can argue my point very calmly and convincingly when I need to. And I happen to really believe that directness and honesty is vital – not in every situation, maybe, but certainly this time."

Chapter 23

It wasn't long after we got back to the house that Mum was called into another meeting. The Thulians, inquisitive as always, had asked further questions about her revelations, and so Alek held a 'briefing' to discuss the best approach. It didn't seem very brief to me – she was gone for the rest of the day.

I was torn between concern for her and residual excitement. Shelley, who didn't know that Mum was potentially in trouble, was simply excited. I passed the time helping her to refine her list, which now read:

Do you live in houses on your planet?

Do you sleep in beds?

Do you have pets?

What do you eat?

How do you eat?

What creatures do you have on Thule?

Do they live in the water or on land?

Do you have cars?

Unfortunately our meeting would have to wait, because the Thulians would be occupied for the time being. A group of aerospace engineers was arriving the following day, having travelled from the United States and spent their time in quarantine, to study and examine the Thulians' technology and try to uncover some of the mystery about how they could travel such distances and at such speeds. The engineers already at the base who had been studying the same thing would be sharing their findings too, so there would be at least a day – probably longer – dedicated to it. They were one group of a number of visitors who came to the base during the project, including theologians, astronomers, meteorologists – even the PM had been there briefly to greet them on arrival. The Thulians had apparently shown the astronomers their home planet using a powerful telescope, and I wondered how they had felt, seeing their home as a tiny, unattainable speck.

Mum came back around dinner time, and we went to the mess to eat so she wouldn't have to cook. She looked tired, but not as stressed as I thought she would be.

"It was fine," she said under her breath, while helping herself to a plateful of lasagne. We went to sit down at the table furthest away from other people, which I sensed was deliberate on her part.

"Was he cross?"

Mum smiled. "No. Like I said, we're all grown-ups, and he saw my point of view. We respect each other a lot and so were able to reach a compromise. We can share information, but anything that seems sensitive needs to be discussed first, and maybe taken higher."

"But I thought *he* was the chief?"

"Not of the world! No, I mean to the chief scientific advisers that work with the government."

"Wow."

"Who *is* the chief of the world?" mused my sister.

"No one person, thankfully."

"So don't they have to check things like that with the other countries? Not just our government?"

"That's a good question Faye. I'm not really sure. Officially, while the Thulians are on our soil, it's up to the UK government to make decisions about their welfare and how we communicate. We actually have to report any findings to them every day. But if certain things are considered planetary security issues, they may have to be taken to the other world leaders to decide."

"Planetary security? Like what?"

"Anything that affects the world's safety, I suppose. It's very difficult though because everything about this situation is completely new, so we don't have any protocol to draw on."

A couple of the researchers she worked with came to sit nearby, and she gave me a look that said the conversation was over. I knew she wasn't supposed to discuss sensitive things with us – for obvious reasons – but I didn't feel she had given anything away that she shouldn't have. She wouldn't have had the conversation with us at all if it had been inappropriate because Shelley, although rather precocious, was still only five, and, frankly, a little blabbermouth, so it wasn't fair or practical to expect her to keep quiet about anything.

Meanwhile, the footage of the ETs' first proper encounter with dry land had been shown around the world, and the Thulian-fever – as Mum called it – was more intense than ever. The sky was buzzing with drones, like giant insects hovering in the sky. Shelley and I would watch them from the battlements, and she thought it was the funniest thing she had seen when two crashed into each other and went spiralling into the sea.

Journalists were desperate for a direct interview with the Thulians, even if only via the wall, but everyone on the base agreed that it was too much to ask of our visitors just yet. However, as a compromise, an interview was recorded with them and broadcast later, with some of the questions that had been asked in the press. We watched when it went out, which felt very strange; all the previous interviews and events had been seen from the distance of home. And now here we were, very much involved ourselves. Shelley wasn't particularly impressed with the quality of the questions asked, compared to her own ever-growing list. There were some that were of a technical nature prompted by the visit from the aerospace engineers, but it still made interesting viewing. Of course, any interview with alien beings, regardless of the questions asked, would have been pretty riveting.

The majority of the world's population had no idea about what it took to travel 34.2 trillion miles – apart from that it was deemed impossible by Earth-dwelling experts, unless astronauts had a few million years to spare. But when those experts released their verdict, albeit in somewhat simplified language, it was basically to say that they were stumped by it too. The physics behind it, and behind the landing that we had all witnessed around the world, was simply too advanced. This proved what we had already guessed, from the very fact that they had found us and were here: the Thulians were of far superior intelligence to humans.

So the majority of the interview was more viewer-friendly.

"I'm sitting here in the living quarters of the most famous beings on our planet." It was Faiza, the press officer, who I had spoken to once or twice, who led the interview, rather than my mother. Mum had been offered to sit in on it, but had turned it down. She confided to us that she hadn't been keen on her first experience of being in front of a camera, and I could certainly relate to that.

"They have very generously agreed to answer some of the millions of questions we have been sent on our blog."

For the first time, only Seraphina was in view, although I was sure Sylvian wasn't far away.

Faiza turned to her. "Before I begin, is it all right if I refer to you as Seraphina?"

"It is."

My sister was, of course, delighted by this. But not as much as she was a few seconds later. Faiza turned back to address the audience of several billion around the world.

"I must explain. It is of course us humans' custom to name each other, and the Thulians are aware of this. With this in mind, one of the children of a staff member here chose names for them: Seraphina, who you see here, and Sylvian."

Shelley was speechless, and I had to laugh at her wide-eyed, wide-mouthed expression.

"So, I will begin the questions. I have selected them at random from, as I said, a huge amount." She turned to Seraphina. "I would like to thank you for agreeing to this interview, on behalf of the whole human population, who are truly fascinated by your story... more than that, by your mere presence!."

Seraphina inclined her head slightly in response.

"So. First up. How long do your species live, on average?"

"Our days and years differ in length to yours." Seraphina spoke in her hypnotising multitone, and I was aware it was probably the first time many were hearing her voice. "Our days

172

are about half as long, and our years two times as long. But we calculate that I have lived around two hundred and seventeen of your Earth years. Our species live for much longer than this. Around three to four hundred of your years."

Faiza paused to allow this information to be processed by the viewers, if indeed it ever could be.

"Gosh. And how do you explain your long lifespan? In relation to a human's?"

"The doctors here are working on finding this out. But I feel our cold climate and size in relation to other species may explain it. And we have developed filters to adapt to the airborne chemicals."

"Could you explain that a bit more?"

"Yes. The filters here," she touched her neck where the strange little gills rippled slightly as she breathed. "On our planet there is a large amount of volcanoes. They release chemicals that can be harmful to living things."

"So when you say you 'developed' those filters..." Faiza paused, and Seraphina gazed back at her with those expressive eyes, and I wondered again what it was they were actually expressing. The pause stretched on, and Faiza seemed to realise that she needed to ask a question. "What do you mean by that?"

"I think on your planet it is known as evolution."

"Yes, that's right. But here on Earth it can take millions of years, in more complex creatures."

"Correct. On our planet my species adapts to changes faster."

Faiza paused again as she consulted her tablet.

"We could discuss that for weeks, I'm sure. But that's what the scientists' jobs are! So I'll move on. The next question I have for you is this: how long did it take to get here from your planet?"

"Around twenty-three of your years. When we set off our mission was to discover and then communicate with life on other planets. We knew this solar system was similar to ours, and so this was where we began our mission."

"How many planets are in your own solar system?"

"Six. These were examined long ago and found to be uninhabited by any form of life."

"How many of you are on the mission?"

"There are twenty-five pods orbiting Earth, each with two occupants. Then a further ten beings on board the craft we travelled here in."

"Yes, our Webb telescope has identified it using the co-ordinates you have provided. Are you hoping for any of your fellow Thulians – I hope you don't mind me using the name we have given you and your planet – to join you?"

"That is not our plan. It is enough to have two of us here. We are in constant contact with the others and are giving information to them about our findings here."

"And what do you think of planet Earth so far? Do you like it?" Mum did comment here, later on, that Faiza had mistakenly tried to endow the ETs with emotions, or opinions based on feelings. But Seraphina didn't hesitate or react.

"It is a large and varied planet. We still need lots of information. We want to know more about your climate and how it is changing, all the habitats that exist around the planet, and the many and varied species that live in them."

"Lots to keep you occupied, then!" Faiza consulted her tablet again. "Ah, yes. There are questions that have been asked over and over again, and this one stood out for me. Over the course of our history, there have been reports of strange sightings: lights in the sky, unexplained objects flying around, even claims people have been taken away by... er... aliens. The questions is: was any of this to do with you, or other beings from your planet?"

I listened to this with a mixture of feelings: outrage that Faiza would ask such a question, effectively linking those eerie mysteries to the Thulians in everyone's mind (if the connection had not already been made); but also interest. What would Seraphina's response be?

She paused. "No. This is our first visit to Earth. We could have arrived and landed, with no invitation, but this is not our preferred way. We decided to seek permission and co-operation instead."

I wasn't sure how convinced the likes of the Protectors would be by this. But I hoped the more open-minded among us would be reassured.

Chapter 24

Having been monitored even more closely than usual since their outing, and seemingly suffered no side effects from their journey into the Highland air, it was deemed safe for the Thulians to venture out more often. For the first time, they were able to enter the control building, which proved useful to the scientists there who could share aspects of their research in the labs. And of course, their sheer intelligence was invaluable. They had brought samples from Thule – rock, sand, water. I remembered the sheer excitement about these at the beginning, from the fortunate scientists given the job of analysing them. Some of the samples had been shipped out to labs elsewhere in the world, but the visitors were able to help our researchers analyse what had been kept at the ComET base, and compare them to rocks and soil on Earth.

Rather than be jaded by all the questions and interviews, as I'm sure many Earthlings would have been by then, the Thulians seemed inexhaustible. Then, to our delight, they requested the audience with Shelley and me. We didn't get much notice – even though we had known it was coming, I don't think either of us really believed it would happen – and therefore didn't have time to get too nervous or excited. I had asked that my mother could be there too, partly for maternal reassurance, but also out of concern about saying or doing the wrong thing. Although the beings had, up until then, been nothing but courteous and patient, I was still in fear of somehow offending them. I worried about this enough in my dealings with fellow humans, not to mention the prospect of talking to people about whose culture and customs I knew zero.

Instead of meeting in their quarters, it was decided (I wasn't sure by whom) that we meet in a room in the main building. It was off the same corridor we had walked along when we had first accompanied Mum, but this we took some twists and turns, climbed steps and went through a series of double doors until I was quite disorientated. So I was surprised, when we entered, not the usual featureless room, but one that was bright and airy, with a large window overlooking the Firth and the hills on the other side. All the buildings at the Fort, although built at different time periods, had some historic significance – even the concrete dome in the centre had, I believed, started life as a World War II bunker. But this meant they all had character: archways and details around the windows, which had pretty white leading. Even the fairly plain houses which were lined up uniformly had a charm about them. And this room was no different. I could see why it might have been selected as an alternative to the windowless, probably rather dingy interior the Thulians were used to. A great effort had been made to ensure their quarters were comfortable, but when it was completely unknown what they were used to either back home or on board their spacecraft, this had proved a tricky task.

Unfortunately, very soon after we arrived the windows were checked to make sure there were no drafts, and the blinds were pulled firmly down. Anywhere the Thulians were to spend any length of time had to be protected from the sun and wind. The heating always had to be adjusted too, to mirror the lower temperatures they were used to and were more comfortable with.

We didn't have long to wait before Amy came in, followed by the imposing figure of Seraphina, who had to bend low to fit through the doorway. We hadn't met her face-to-face indoors before, and it felt incongruous to see her here, in an ordinary setting. I wasn't sure I would ever get used to it. We were surprised today to see that she was alone.

We greeted her in our awkward way – even Shelley didn't quite seem to know whether to smile, wave or curtsey, so she did an odd mixture of the three. Of course we couldn't shake hands; even though we were wearing masks and gloves we had to keep a cautious distance. Amy nodded at Mum and left the room. I wondered if this encounter was to be recorded by some invisible listening device, like all the others.

We all sat down: it seemed Seraphina had become used to sitting on chairs.

"Thank you for meeting the children," said Mum. "They are very happy to be here."

Seraphina turned to each of us. "Thank you for seeing me."

"Could they ask you some questions, please?"

"Yes."

Shelley worked her way enthusiastically through her prepared list. In her lulling voice Seraphina calmly and patiently answered, adding details that were thrilling to us. Sometimes Mum would intervene to clarify something, for instance if Seraphina didn't yet have the word to name or describe something, or if Shelley didn't quite understand. Seraphina explained that yes, they lived in houses but not like ours. Theirs were oval structures, similar to the pod they had travelled in but with openings very like our windows. No, they weren't glass as such but a similar semi-transparent material they manufactured. Each house was quite small, really just a shelter in which to sleep. They slept directly on the floor, which was lined with a material similar to felt.

They ate a green plant which grew abundantly on their planet, and could be picked and eaten raw. Seaweed on our planet was very similar, but the doctors had recorded a slight spike in the Thulians' salt levels since they had been eating it daily, so had given them a supplement to take alongside it. They ate and digested food in a similar way to us, but excreted it differently (here my sister needed an explanation of the process of excretion. "Oh! You mean poo!" she called out happily when she understood). Their way of removing waste products from their bodies had been compared to that of plants on Earth – they sort of gave off gases through their skin. Shelley and I both wrinkled our noses involuntarily, imagining a nasty smell – although there was actually nothing of the sort.

When it came to the question about pets, it was Seraphina who needed an explanation.

"What is 'pets'?"

"Well it's when you have an animal in your house that you look after. I want a cat but Mummy won't let me."

"A cat… like the tiger or the lion? I have seen pictures."

"Oh no! They only live in the zoo or in a special park. I mean little cats, they're very friendly."

"What do they do?"

"They sort of just sit on your lap and purr."

For the first time since I had seen her being questioned, Seraphina seemed flummoxed. Mum stepped in to try and explain.

179

"They don't do anything as such, they just live there, and become a part of the family in many cases."

"And the creatures choose to do this?"

"Well, they can't talk, so no. It is us who chooses it for them. But when treated well they are very happy. There are other animals we take into our homes as pets too."

"How is this happiness communicated?"

"Various ways. Cats will purr, like Shelley mentioned. A sort of low rumbling noise. But... I think we're getting a bit off topic here."

But Seraphina wanted to know more.

"So you have many species on Earth, and humans are in charge of them all?"

"Well, yes and no. We are the dominant species."

"And how is this decided?"

"We can walk and use complex language, and have intelligent thoughts..."

"And the other species cannot do this?"

"Well, they walk. And they communicate with each other."

"But are they not intelligent?"

"Well... not in the way we are."

I watched the back and forth with interest. Mum was simply explaining the way things were – had always been. It made sense, and yet under Seraphina's scrutiny it sounded flawed. Wrong.

"Is it not the same on your planet?" Mum asked. "Are you not also the dominant species?"

"No."

We all looked at Seraphina.

"I mean, we know you do *have* other species on your planet..."

"Correct."

"But it is your kind that has developed the technology, and who has travelled all this way..."

"Incorrect."

"I... Sorry, could you clarify that?"

"Life on our planet is not as varied as yours. This is true. But there is no dominant species. On this mission are many different species. All have worked towards getting us here."

We stared for a bit while we took this in. All this time we had assumed all the Thulians were alike; not just the two visiting our planet, but those in the pods in orbit and those in the main craft in deep space.

"So the rest of you, up there...?" Mum began.

"There are many different creatures."

"But who is in charge?" She asked.

"No one."

"You have no captain? Or chief or... commander?"

"We do not use these terms."

"And what about all the other species?" Mum pressed. "Back on your planet? Are they as intelligent as you?"

"We do not categorise according to levels of intelligence. Every creature works together in an important way to help the planet survive." I had a sudden and absurd vision of groups of

181

dogs and cats scurrying around building houses and tending to gardens. But then I remembered how ants worked, and other insects I had read about.

"Like in our ecosystem!" I blurted. Seraphina turned her intense gaze on me.

"So all of your creatures have a job to do also?"

"Well… yes," I replied softly.

She held my gaze. "And yet many of them are dying?"

Chapter 25

Over the next few days I had a lot on my mind. I went over our conversation, again and again. It wasn't that I had never thought about any of it before, it had just never been brought up in such a way. Or made so obvious. I knew from what Mum, Frankie and the teachers at school had told me, that they grew up in a world that was under threat. Not from external powers, or from the forces of nature acting alone, but from the actions of humans. Their parents' generation had first heard the stark warnings and were told the changes we all, collectively, had to make if we were to reverse the damage. And they all lived through the moment (right around the time I was born – I had been told that), when it was realised – or admitted, anyway – that it had been left too late. The politicians and offending companies around the world made promises to change, to cut carbon emissions, use alternative sources of power, protect the fragile places and wildlife… but it had all come too late. They hadn't believed, or perhaps cared, that the situation was so drastic.

After the great realisation that there was nothing left to do, anger, bitterness and blame were thrown around. But rather than carry on trying to make things better anyway, for the sake of the future generations; rather than trying to reduce the pollution and continue cleaning the plastic out of the seas and save what was left of the wilderness, they simply gave up. 'What is the point? We tried and it made no difference', was the widespread opinion. And it was true, to a point – the decline was accelerating and nothing could be changed about that now. So collectively we just continued as before, and made it worse and worse. And more animals faced extinction, more forests disappeared. And the wildfires burned and the rains fell and the winds blew, and the crops failed. And famine and drought became a way of life all over the world. This is the world that I know.

I had heard all of this from my father too, of course. It was his life's work to try and correct what damage he could. I was ashamed to admit to myself now that his words had washed over me a little. I had been of the same mind as everyone else: if it's too late, why bother? I knew his work was important, I felt pride when people asked me what he did. And as a household we were as careful as we could be. But still, perhaps I was as much a part of the problem too. We all were, of course. It had taken the insight of an outsider to wake me up, more so than anything my own father had said.

All I could do now was keep asking, why? And I couldn't understand how I had lived on this broken planet for so long without asking it before. I too had closed my eyes to it, and now it was as though they had been opened for the first time.

I began to understand more of how my father must feel, why he was so sad and felt so helpless. For the first time his analogy about the dustpan and brush made sense to me. It expressed his sheer frustration in his lonely quest. And yet, *he* hadn't given up. He had gone away, left his family behind, to travel the world and try to put things right, or to salvage what he could. While I had never resented him for not being around, I had also never truly appreciated his work before.

Mum tried her best to answer all the questions I suddenly had, but really there were no satisfactory answers. And likewise, in that room confronted by Seraphina's stark questions, there was nothing *we* could say.

I searched for answers online and came across some old nature documentaries, showing parts of the world that were now lost forever. The beauty and the majesty of it all. It was true that I hadn't travelled very much, and I knew that tiny pockets of wilderness were protected even now, but it was unfathomable to me that I wouldn't ever be able to see it as it was in those beautiful films. The jungles and the rainforests, plains and rivers, oceans and skies, teeming with life. I thought about the cliff tops and the sea back home, the kind of blue it has that I hadn't seen anywhere else. That had been the same for millions of years, long before humans placed their footprints on the Earth, and it had hardly changed, despite us. And yet, there was really no hope. It was so hard to believe it, and to realise these films had been made relatively recently. Some of them just a few years before I had been born.

I was watching one of these in the living room, probably for the third or fourth time. It had become a favourite, one of the hundreds filmed by a famous naturalist that had spent a lifetime travelling the world bringing new footage and images to delight and amaze. Seeing the destruction gradually unfold before him. This one had been filmed during the window: the time when humans were fully aware of what was happening, and had time to solve it.

In fact, documentaries aired after the window made for bleak viewing. Much of the Amazon rainforest was reduced to dust now, the animals that remained clinging on to life. Some of the islands that had held the most diverse creatures were gone, swallowed up by the sea. The steep decline in plankton, caused by pollution and a drop in oxygen, meant larger animals starved. The ocean was expelling its creatures at a quickening pace, they rose like bubbles that burst on the surface, lying beached and rotting on the shores. It was no wonder that these films weren't as popular as they had once been.

The presenter was there, looking earnestly at the camera, telling us what we needed to do. Giving solid, practical solutions.

Mum came past and, seeing me there hunched over my tablet yet again, came to sit by me and put her arm around my shoulders. I paused the film.

"That's a good one, isn't it," she said. "I used to love watching his programs."

"Why does he look so sad?" Shelley asked. I hadn't realised she was looking over my shoulder; she had been occupied with one of her complicated games on the floor.

"Because no one was listening," I answered. Mum kissed the top of my head.

"But I don't get it!" I pulled back and looked at her. "You all *knew*! Couldn't you have done something?"

My voice sounded harsher than I had meant it to. I knew I was hitting out at the wrong person – it was hardly my mother's fault. But I didn't know who else to blame. Mum sighed, and thought before answering.

"I remember feeling the same, when we thought we had more time. My mum told me about the first time she heard about any of it. It was when she was a child, and there was talk of a hole discovered in the Earth's protective layer." I listened. Both of Mum's parents – my grandparents – had succumbed to the SARS35 outbreak before I was born, and Mum hardly ever spoke about them.

"Many of us did do our bit," She continued. "We tried to create less waste and use less energy, save water and do beach cleans where we could." She smiled and did a little laugh, "I

186

actually went on a protest march a couple of times. In London, with your father. But we were seen as a nuisance; a bit crazy.

"And it just wasn't enough. I suppose everyone thought we had longer, although that's no excuse of course. It's easy to blame the governments, and they played their part, certainly, but not enough people took it seriously. Or, maybe it was easier to ignore it and hope the problem would go away on its own. Lots of people denied it was happening at all."

"But how could they? Wasn't it all over the news?"

"It was mentioned, of course. But people don't know what to believe. And the truth is, no one likes being lectured, and told their way of doing things is wrong. And there were so many things – everywhere we turned, every aspect of our lives had something that was bad in some way. From putting the heating on to having a shower, washing your clothes... even which breakfast cereals you ate. I suppose it was overwhelming."

"But surely that meant there were lots of things you *could* change, to make it better?"

"Yes, that's true. And we *did* make lots of changes..."

"But not enough."

I lay awake one night, struggling to get to sleep as I had for days. Going over my conversations with Mum, I knew it hadn't been fair to take out my frustration on her. With an irritable sigh I got out of bed, thinking an aimless walk around the house might help to reset my mind in some way. As I went down the stairs I heard something and stopped, remembering that Mum was bound to still be up. Sure enough it was her voice I heard in the living room, talking to someone. I sat down on the stairs and listened, wondering who it could be.

187

"...I know, it's just so hard. I don't know what to say to her, she's devastated. But what can I do?"

"Be honest." It was my father's voice; for some reason it surprised me that they should call each other for a wall chat. "That's the best you can do."

"I *am* being honest, Mark, of course I am. I just wish there was a way I could reassure her and make it all better."

"Well there isn't. That's the frank truth – we're way past all that. We knew that when we had them."

"Oh, please, don't bring that up now. It's too late for 'I told you so'."

"I would never say that. I'm sorry, it's just that... we did discuss all this at the time, if you remember."

"Funnily enough, Mark, yes – I remember."

"We knew this would be a conversation we would have to have, and that there was no way of justifying it."

"I have *tried* to justify it to her though... and I've been honest, like you said. But I hate that I can't make it better."

"I wasn't talking about justifying climate change, Helen. I was talking about having kids in the first place. Just one of the many mistakes we made."

I suddenly felt very cold. I wanted to run back to bed, to not hear any more, but I couldn't will my body to move. And a self-destructive part of me wanted to hear more – or to be reassured I was mistaken and had misheard my dad tell my mum they hadn't wanted us.

"Again, this isn't the time for that talk." Mum was saying. "We went over and over it, you agreed, and it happened. It's too late to change things now."

"Exactly. Which is why now is exactly the time for the talk. You called *me* remember? I'm not sure what you were hoping I'd say."

I felt sick. I started creeping back up the stairs.

"I was hoping you'd talk to Faye for me…" Mum's voice trailed off as I quietly shut my bedroom door. Shelley murmured in her sleep and rolled over as I crept back to bed.

As soon as dawn started to pale the sky I quietly grabbed my coat and boots and went outside. For the first time since our arrival I cursed the fact that we were on such an enclosed, protected base. It had never felt claustrophobic because Shelley and I had more or less had the run of the place, and despite its depleted size it was still impressive. But that morning, as I sat on the battlements, I wished I could be a million miles away. Through a rent in the grey clouds gleamed a sunrise like a gigantic fire. The hills across the Firth took on more colours than I thought possible: vivid greens and browns, oranges and reds, the colours changing and merging as the light grew and cast its shadows on the land. Nature was putting on quite a show and it was breathtakingly beautiful. Ordinarily, it would have filled me with a sense of calm, and awe. But that day I stared at the sea, throwing itself repeatedly at the remaining walls, and I felt its anger.

While I hadn't fully understood the snippet of conversation I had heard in the night, it was enough to know Mum had, at best, kept things from us. At worst, she had lied all these years about how precious we were to her. All this time I had looked up to her; wanted to *be* her one day. Admired her spirit, and her honesty. I almost laughed out loud. And then I did: I let out a laugh that became a scream. All the anger and frustration and worry and fear just came out of me, carried away into the wind. It didn't really make me feel better – certainly nothing had been solved – but it felt defiant and rebellious, and that was enough for now.

When I began to feel a chill through my coat and my thin pyjamas I reluctantly stood up and started dragging my feet back towards the house. I didn't quite feel ready to face Mum, but wasn't sure what else to do, so took a meandering route around the bunker section. My heart almost stopped when I heard a man's voice call out.

"Hey!"

I spun around. A guard was standing beside the bunker's entrance: I had forgotten they would still be patrolling at all hours. "What are you doing here?"

I recognised Ben, the one that never seemed to smile and seemed so much more intimidating than the others.

"Nothing."

"Okay. Just seems like a strange time of day to be wandering about on your own. A bit suspicious if you ask me."

"Oh... I'm not... I mean, I wasn't..." I stared at him, wondering what he was going to do. His dark steely eyes looked back at me fiercely, waiting for me to explain, but I couldn't seem to get any coherent words out. And then, suddenly, his face creased into a smile that looked a bit out of place on his face, and he let out a laugh.

"I'm just messing with you. I don't really think you're out to kidnap our friends in there or anything." He leaned a bit closer, looking serious again. "You're not, are you?"

I shook my head, unsure what to make of him. He fished inside a pocket and I felt sure he was about to radio someone to report me – I wasn't sure who, but I knew it would mean trouble. He was right, it was strange behaviour, creeping about in the early hours of the morning. And it was the guards' job to make sure absolutely nothing befell the visitors on their watch. I started to think of excuses; a bad dream, perhaps, or insomnia.

Ben was holding his hand out to me. It wasn't holding a radio, but a battered-looking chocolate bar. I looked at him and he nodded for me to take it. Gingerly I did.

"It's okay, it's not poisoned."

"Is it real?"

"No! What do you think I am, made of money? It's pretty good stuff though."

"Thank you."

"You can save it for later, if you don't want to get into trouble for having chocolate for breakfast. But if I were you, I'd just eat it now. Destroy the evidence."

I smiled at him as I unpeeled the wrapper and offered him some.

"No, you're okay. That's all for you." He leant forward conspiratorially. "I've got a load more in here," he patted his pocket and I smiled again. I sighed and relaxed a bit as I let the chocolate melt on my tongue. It *was* pretty good.

"So, what *are* you doing out and about at this time?"

I looked down, unsure whether to tell him the lies I had prepared.

"I just couldn't sleep."

"It must be strange, being away from home."

191

"A bit." I tried not to betray any surprise at his apparent empathy.

"Only, you seemed angry, or upset or something."

I looked at him. "When?"

He nodded towards the battlements, where I realised there was a good view of the place I had been sitting.

"When you were shouting at the sea there." I felt my cheeks go pink, and thought about just turning and running back to the house, and avoiding Ben for the rest of the whole time we were there. But something in his expression made me stay. A mixture of amusement and understanding.

"It's okay, you know. We all feel like doing that every now and then."

"I don't. Not usually, I mean."

"Did it make you feel any better?"

I shrugged. "A bit, I suppose."

"Really? Because – tell me to keep my nose out if you like – but you don't look much happier than when I saw you stomping out of your house just a while ago."

"Do you normally spend your time watching people and spying on them?" He looked at me with those stern eyes and I wondered if I had pushed it too far. I would never have spoken like that to a virtual stranger normally, but everything felt upside down and it seemed to make me bolder, and less wary of saying the wrong thing. Then he smiled again and shrugged.

"It's kind of my job."

"I suppose it is." I slumped against the wall.

"So, want to tell me? I mean," he checked his watch, "I've still got a bit of time to kill here before end of shift, so…"

"It's nothing really. Just something I overheard."

"Uh oh." I looked at him questioningly. "I mean, things you overhear never usually tell you the whole picture. You know that don't you?"

I let out a little laugh. "It was pretty clear, this time."

"Go on."

"Basically, Mum was talking to Dad on the wall, and they were saying it was a huge mistake to have kids, I even think that might be why Dad went away, apart from just for his job…"

"Ouch."

I looked at him gratefully. "Exactly!"

"What else did they say?"

"I don't know really. I mean, I didn't stick around to find out."

"I see."

"What? What do you see?" I took a big bite of the chocolate and talked with my mouth full, not caring how I must look, caring only that someone was listening to me offload. Someone who wasn't my mother or my sister or my mother's best friend. "Because, I've been trying to make sense of it all."

"Well, it's like I said. You didn't hear the full story. Don't get me wrong, it's pretty bad, what you did hear, but it's out of context, isn't it."

"I can't see how it could be explained away. I mean, they were pretty clear…"

"I think you've made your mind up to be cross about this without really thinking it through."

"I've done nothing *but* think it through!" I accidentally spat some chocolate onto the sleeve of his uniform. "Sorry!" I said as I tried to rub it off.

"You've stewed over it. That's not the same thing."

"Hmmm."

"By my reckoning, you're either right, and your parents never wanted you and have been bearing the burden of having to put up with you for years…"

I stared at him. "Or?"

"Or," he looked at me. "You've got it all wrong. You'll only know for sure if you actually talk to your mum!"

"I know. It's just…"

"You're enjoying your sulk?"

I pulled a face, not knowing how else to respond. We stood in silence for a bit, looking out across the compound. I could see a few other figures walking about, patrolling the other buildings. I felt lighter. The sense of resentment was still there, simmering under the surface, but talking to Ben had made me feel vindicated in some way. Heard.

"You're actually quite friendly really, aren't you." I told him.

"Don't go telling everyone."

"It's okay, no one would believe me anyway."

"You cheeky wee… Now, scoot off back home before your mother accuses *me* of kidnap."

194

Despite Ben's advice I spent the day avoiding Mum, and Shelley too. I felt bad ignoring my little sister but just wasn't in the mood for her chirping, and didn't want to snap at her. I could tell Mum noticed, from the sideways looks she gave me when she didn't think I saw, but I supposed she just thought I was still in a dark mood about the hopelessness of the world. Of course, I was – it sounds trite and self-absorbed to suggest the overheard conversation could in any way overshadow that. But I was ten years old, after all, and what went on in my own small world still felt as big as that which affected the world at large.

That evening at dinner time I had no choice but to sit with them. Mum broached the subject of talking to Dad and I tried to act as though I hadn't expected it.

"He'd really like a chat with you. Especially to talk to you about how you're feeling at the moment."

"Why, so he can tell me we're definitely doomed?"

I know now that I should have just told her that I'd overheard them, and that that was the reason I was really upset. She could have tried to explain it all then and there. But at the time I didn't feel there was any explanation that would make any of it better, preferring instead to carry my discontent around like some sort of martyr's cloak.

But then events took a turn which almost made me forget about it all.

Chapter 26

After our latest meeting with Seraphina it became clear the Thulians were not going to let the climate issue go. Despite Professor Ivanov's attempts at a cover up – or at least a twist on the reality to take the emphasis away from us – the truth was out. Or part of it, and the ETs were relentless in discovering the rest. It wouldn't have taken them long – the evidence was all around, they only had to know what they were looking for.

If there was any embarrassment that the facts about animal life on Thule had been uncovered thanks to questions raised by a five-year-old, rather than by the experts who had been working on it for several weeks, I didn't hear of it. I suppose, like me, they were getting used to being outsmarted by my little sister.

A conference was called between the head researchers and the Thulians to discuss it in more depth. Mum reported back that someone had jokingly asked if the Thulians were expecting some giraffes and kangaroos to attend, too.

"I know it sounds ridiculous to us," she'd replied, "but you have to remember they have no species hierarchy. No one creature that's put itself above all others. Perhaps they've got the right idea?"

She'd been met with a wry laugh.

All the same, Mum was asked along to the meeting, and promised to report back.

It took place in a large room at the centre of the building that we hadn't been into. It had once been used as a sort of lecture hall, and had an area in the middle which was surrounded by tiered rows of seats, a little like a miniature amphitheatre. As well as Mum, who was there as always as the interpreter and negotiator – peacekeeper, should one be needed – was Professor Ivanov, our friend Dr Ling, and Dr Iain McGregor, a resident climatologist. Several others attended too who I had heard of or knew by acquaintance. The Thulians, both present, had chosen to sit at the desk in the centre of the room, giving the effect that they were teaching or delivering a lecture, but also that the scientists, doctors and researchers were surrounding and looming over them from above.

I thought it was more the former.

Alek began with a speech welcoming the Thulians to Earth (again), and re-iterating what an honour it was to have them there, taking such an interest in our planet. It may have gone over old ground, but it seemed necessary to remind everyone in the room that this was a peaceful, mutually beneficial arrangement.

The tone of the meeting was formal, and Seraphina added to this by standing to address the room.

"We thank you for your hospitality and openness. There are still many things about your planet that we do not understand, and we would like to discover more."

"As always, we are very happy to answer your questions, if we can. Although even then, I'm afraid some of it may still be a bit baffling," answered Ivanov. "I would like to pass you over to Dr McGregor."

The doctor stood up and nodded to make himself known, and waited for the first question. It seemed that, in asking Iain

McGregor to speak that day, with his no-nonsense approach, Alek had decided candour was now the way forward after all.

Seraphina began to speak.

"Many animals on our home planet are extinct, due to not evolving quickly enough to deal with the changes in atmosphere and climate. We notice this is happening here, but cannot see why it is the case. You have few volcanoes, a relatively ambient temperature and atmosphere, and varied enough environments to support biodiversity."

"This is true," said Dr McGregor after a slight pause. "And there are many factors that have led to mass extinction." At this point he tapped a button, and onto the large white wall were projected images illustrating the grim facts of the decline of the species, highlighting mostly the land mammals, but also showing changes in the insect world and marine life. It ended with a view of a desiccated rainforest.

"So," clarified Seraphina, "rising temperatures have affected the weather system, melted much of the ice in the northernmost areas, and affected food sources for many creatures?"

"Yes."

"I have also been informed that the melting ice has caused sea levels to rise, resulting in loss of land masses, flooding and coastal erosion around the planet."

"That's right, yes." For a moment it looked as though Dr McGregor's presence was going to be redundant after all. But then the key question came.

"What has caused the temperatures to rise so quickly?"

"Well," the doctor referred to some graphs and charts that were in front of him. "The climate has been changing since the beginning of time, with warmer and colder periods lasting thousands of years. So while some of the changes were perhaps natural, it is true that this time most of them can be attributed to human impact. For the past hundred or so years the fuels we burn, the transport we use and the trees we have cut down have contributed to a rise in harmful gases which have built up in the atmosphere. It is these gases, known as 'greenhouse gases', which have warmed the planet, with the consequences you mention."

"And many more, too."

"Um... yes," he admitted, casting a quick glance towards Alek.

"And you say this has been happening for one hundred of your years," Seraphina pressed.

"At least."

"Longer?"

"Possibly. We've known about it for over seventy years, I would say."

"Our calculations show that the energy from your sun and the strength of the wind here would create enough power for all of your electric items."

"Er... I'm not sure about 'all'. But we do use solar power and wind turbines to generate electricity. We also have nuclear power as a clean alternative to coal and gas."

"But it hasn't been enough?"

"No, I suppose not."

Seraphina glanced down at Sylvian and something seemed to pass between them. A silent message. It was still unclear how much Sylvian understood, but she sat upright, looking alert and seeming to absorb it all.

"We are also interested in the trees on your planet."

"Oh... yes?" Iain McGregor, an unshakeable, stoic Scotsman, was starting to look a little uncomfortable.

"We do not have such plant life on our planet. But you have mentioned that the cutting down of them on Earth has added to the problem of the warming of this planet."

"That's undeniable, yes."

When my mother reported back later, she told us that the atmosphere began to feel like that of a courtroom, as though the human race were on trial. But the Thulians had not shown a hint of aggression, or even criticism, remaining impassive, merely stating and asking for the facts.

Iain tapped on his tablet and produced more images. "Trees have been cut down for their wood, and the pulp made into paper, for thousands of years. The wood is used for fuel and building. However, as the human population has grown, so has the demand. And added to this is the cutting down of huge areas of forest and rainforest to make way for cheaper, more productive crops, and cattle grazing."

"Cattle?"

"Cows. Farmed for their milk, which we rely on as a food source, and – less so, in modern times – meat."

"So are these trees not important?"

"Well... yes. They're vital. They provide habitat for a wide range of species, from insects to birds, reptiles, larger mammals and primates. They also absorb one of the harmful gases described earlier – carbon dioxide – and release oxygen into the atmosphere."

"This we have learnt. And when they have been cut down in large numbers this has led to extinctions, and also released this harmful gas."

"That's right." He gave a little shrug, as if to acknowledge the madness of it all through their eyes.

"So how long ago did this stop?"

The doctor hesitated and looked around slightly. "I'm sorry, did what stop?"

"The cutting down of trees."

"Um... the clearing of forests and rainforests has been greatly reduced, but many trees are still cut down on a daily basis."

"But you have alternative fuel and building materials, we have seen this for ourselves. Correct?"

"Yes."

"There is adequate space elsewhere to grow crops and keep enough cattle to provide the food needed?"

"Well, I think so. I mean... it's not something..." He trailed off awkwardly, and there was a short silence while Seraphina waited for him to finish his sentence. She held his gaze in that steady way, until he dropped his eyes down and began fumbling with his tablet. When it was clear to her that he wasn't going to respond in a more satisfactory way, Seraphina continued.

"Humans also know of the problems caused by the mass clearing of those forests you showed us. But still it continues."

"Yes," Dr McGregor answered after a slight pause.

"Why?"

As Mum relayed this exchange to us it was difficult to believe that Seraphina had shown no hint of judgement. Her words were undoubtedly confrontational, but the tone was calm, measured. It was difficult to decipher her intentions in a language that was so new and unfamiliar to her, and we had no way of knowing how emotions manifested themselves – if in fact they even did. But my mother was sure that it was simple curiosity, and a genuine desire to understand, which drove their questioning, and not an attempt to reprimand or rebuke. I doubted if this made Iain and the rest of them feel any less like naughty children.

The doctor cleared his throat.

"Again there are many factors," he answered. "When the warning signs were first recognised, we felt we had longer to act than we actually did. Many measures were put in place, but they were often less convenient or more expensive, and so were not favoured or regarded as practical alternatives."

"Expensive?"

"Er... costly; needing more money."

"Ah, money. We have heard of this but do not fully understand it."

"It's the currency we use to buy and sell... to trade. To buy the things we need. It is what we earn when we work. I am, in fact, earning it right now." He let out a nervous chuckle.

"So everyone who works – or contributes their skills and their labour – does so for money?"

"Well, primarily. We need it, you see. To pay for our homes, power, food, water…"

"Without money you don't get the things that you need? To stay alive?"

"Well – no."

"May we see some of this money?"

"Well you see, it's not something you can handle. A few years ago it was; it was made of metal and paper and we would carry it around and physically exchange it for items. But now it is all virtual. Meaning it is kept in banks, online. And we can access it that way, or less often with these," he took out a bank card from his pocket and held it out for the Thulians to see.

"Virtual. So this money is not real?"

"No, I suppose not, if by 'real' you mean you can see it or touch it. But it's very real to those who have lots of it. Even more, I suppose, to those who do not."

"Thank you, Dr McGregor. We will prepare further questions. This is interesting to us because we do not have such a thing on our planet."

"Of course. And that, in return, is very interesting to us."

At this point Alek stood up to ask if the meeting could be brought to a close, or revisited later, as they had gone a little off topic. The Thulians agreed, asking if they could speak to an expert on the subject of currency and economics at another time.

Despite not having an active role in that meeting, Mum was exhausted afterwards. Largely on Iain's behalf, who admitted later to feeling somewhat pummelled – and relieved when the subject had moved on to something as 'benign' as money.

"It's as though every time they hit on a big topic, it leads to even more," Mum told us. "I can't see how their curiosity can be satisfied in *ten* years, let alone one. There's just so much for them to know. And we've barely touched on what we'd like to know about Thule!" She sank onto the sofa, took off her shoes and reached for her glass of wine.

"I suppose their grilling about the climate issues are done with for now, at least."

But about that, she couldn't have been more wrong.

Chapter 27

Further meetings were requested. It seemed that the Thulians were going over and over one aspect: the fact that humans had not only been complicit in the destruction of their own planet, but had been unable, or unwilling, to stop it. Mum was called in to try to pacify them. But it was an impossible task; there just weren't any satisfactory answers to give.

There was a discussion held in their quarters, this time just with Seraphina, Mum and Iain McGregor. Sylvian, though present, was elsewhere – they were told she was transmitting communications to the pods in orbit. Reporting back, just like we were.

Everything about this meeting felt less formal; in fact, Mum said it was almost as though Seraphina was trying to explain their apparent obsession with this one topic. To give the reasons why they simply couldn't let it go. She started by telling them a bit more about their home planet, clogged with fumes from the many volcanoes that constantly spewed out toxic smoke. While their gills helped to filter much of it out, many species had not been so fortunate and had succumbed to the gases.

Although she now spoke excellent English (and pretty good Chinese and Spanish, according to the researchers that spoke with her in those languages), she still had limitations. While her vocabulary was remarkable, it was the subtle expressions and descriptions she lacked. But she still somehow conveyed a deep love of her home. It sounded like a beautiful place, with its deep orange earth and rich vegetation, and its blue green lakes. Mountain ranges jutting into the sky, disappearing into the clotted clouds. She told them how, when the fog thinned, they could see the sky and all its colours: blue, red, pink, even yellow sometimes. She spoke of the other strange creatures that lived alongside them, having survived the poison, all living and working and contributing together. Something about the way Seraphina spoke gave away a deep sadness for the loss of each species, as they lay slowly dying, with nothing that could be done to save them.

"So," Seraphina spoke in her calm and practical way, "On our planet, we do not live apart from the natural world. We are a part of it and it is a part of us. We rely on each other to survive. So it is difficult to understand why a species would choke a planet deliberately. You have nowhere else to live, is this correct?"

"It is. And we do understand your confusion," answered Mum. "It is hard for most humans to understand too. I think because there are so many of us, the impact was just too big."

"So there are too many humans."

"I suppose you could say that. But it's not really that simple…"

"And still more are produced every day."

Iain intervened, perhaps sensing Mum did not feel qualified to give an accurate response.

"That's right. Even though the birth rate has dropped dramatically in the past few years, with improved health care and medical treatment, our life expectancy just keeps growing."

"There are all these people, yet no one could stop the damage."

"Many tried to stop it," answered Mum. "We did our bit, but it just wasn't enough."

"Many. Not all?"

"No. Not all. Some just... carried on. In fact, most of us did, really. We were used to the convenience of driving petrol cars and flying in planes, and the ease of buying things we didn't really need to replace others that just got thrown away. It was... easier, just to carry on."

"And now? Will people stop?"

"No. I'm afraid not. Now that it is too late, many people see even less point in trying."

"Too late?"

Iain McGregor jumped in. "Well... yes. The damage is irreversible."

Seraphina held his gaze for slightly longer than was comfortable. He looked steadily back, as Mum had taught him. Rather than being rude or confrontational, this seemed to be customary; polite, even.

"What does this mean?"

"That the climate has been irrevocably altered. We are in a sort of downward spiral where the Earth will continue to heat up and the effects – extreme weather, drought, wildfires – will continue to worsen."

"Many species have gone. What will happen to humans?"

"We don't really know. I suppose – hope – we will adapt, like you have on your planet."

"Can the planet continue to survive, with or without human life?"

Iain hesitated. He glanced at Mum with a barely perceptible frown.

"Er... well, yes. I suppose it could," he answered. "It would more likely be better off, actually."

"Thank you for the information."

Realising they were being dismissed, Mum and Iain exchanged the Thulian farewell and left.

The news about the so-called 'climate conference' was the headline of most of the news sites (as indeed had all things Thulian been, for many weeks). There were reporters questioning the point of the meeting. What right, they asked, did these alien beings – guests, who had been made very welcome – have to grill us about our planet? Was it actually any business of theirs at all? Although some media outlets argued that they were well within their rights, and it was about time we were held accountable, these were, unfortunately, in the minority. And so, as is so often true, the louder voices were listened to the most.

And then there was a news story that focused on the fact that our Thulians had developed gills to help them breathe in their 'inhospitable climate'. The article hinted at the idea that they had come to Earth to occupy it and live here instead. Although it wasn't a new theory, the 'evidence' presented meant it was the tiny spark – all that was needed – to ignite uproar among members of the already nervous population.

The rumblings that had never quite calmed turned into more protest marches, more stories spread on social media making wild claims, more people interviewed on discussion programs speaking out against the visitors. The message was clear from those groups: the Thulians' time here was up. Surely they had learnt enough by now? If they were only here on an information gathering mission, why hadn't they given any indication of when they would go home?

On the ComET base at Fort Leigh we were somewhat cut off from the outside world, despite the constant communications. The only, narrow, road to the base ended at a heavily guarded gate. Other guards stood at various entrances inside the base, stationed there twenty four hours a day. We were protected in our bubble. But of course news still seeped through to us, in our little house. It all felt unreal somehow, as though while we were here, the rest of the world as we had known it had ceased to exist.

The Thulians, after a flurry of meetings and interviews, had gone quiet. Holed up in their bunker for several days, the only contact they had was with the essential team, the doctors monitoring them and those bringing them their supplies. Mum said they were working on something in there, sending a far higher level of communications to the other pods than usual. But no one had yet managed to decrypt any of the messages.

One evening we were eating in the mess room, and I was picking at my food sullenly as I had done now for several days. If I had been in a better frame of mind I would have congratulated myself at being able to keep up this mood for so long. Mum was not so impressed.

"Right, missus, I think we all need a change of scenery. We've been cooped up here for weeks now and you girls have hardly seen any of this beautiful country."

I made a sort of 'hmph' sound, but felt reluctantly pleased at the proposal.

"Ooh, where can we go Mummy?"

"I'll ask some of the locals on the base. Iain is from near Glasgow so may not know the area that well, but most of the guards are from around here so I'll get some recommendations."

"You should ask Ben," I blurted. Shelley and I had seen him around a few times since our meeting, and I had waved and sometimes talked to him. If my sister thought our sudden familiarity strange she didn't say so, and before long she, too, was chatting away to him in her easy manner. He showed none of the sternness or impatience that had made me so wary of him, and I began to wonder if I had imagined it.

"Oh yes, he's local isn't he," answered Mum. "He will know just the place."

True to her word, on Mum's day off two days later we were up and packing a backpack. She had borrowed some walking boots from someone and deemed our scruffy old trainers up to the task of a bit of hill walking. She had been lent one of the Land Rovers for the day (it was manual drive only, but Mum preferred that anyway), and, as one of the guards waved us through the gates and she accelerated along the track, it was difficult not to feel a thrill.

Some of my consternation from the other night had dulled; I was never one to hold a grudge and usually forgave easily. But the knot in my stomach tightened every time I thought about what I had heard and tried to make sense of it. I knew it was silly to be so cross with Mum and not even tell her why, but a part of me was worried that if I did she would have no explanation, and would just confirm what I thought to be true. That Shelley and I had both been a terrible mistake. Worse, that we had caused conflict between our parents and maybe even ruined their lives. The sensible part of my brain told me she had never shown any sign of this: in fact, quite the opposite. But it's not always the sensible part of our brain we listen to. And so I continued to simmer.

Despite myself, I had to admit to enjoying the moment. We were always spending time together – we were rarely apart, especially lately – but I could hardly remember the last time the three of us had been on an outing like this. And here; taking in the huge, wide skies and the freshest of air, the impossibly bright green hills patched with red, pink and purple heather. I had enjoyed our time at the fort. Admittedly, there were times when boredom threatened, especially now we had explored it as much as we could, but I was usually occupied with school work and taking in the general buzz of being there. The thrill and excitement of it all. But still, to be away from the confines of the base felt immensely liberating.

After an hour or so of winding across the hills, Mum pulled off the road onto a wooded track. After bumping across a tiny bridge beside an isolated house, she parked the car in a seemingly random spot in the woods. In response to my doubtful questioning, she produced a complicated-looking paper map, and we followed her as she set out walking purposefully.

The path led through the woods, and seemed to go on and on. Then, suddenly, there unfolded before us a huge, bright blue loch, stretched out below like a sort of shimmering mirage. One moment I was looking downwards at my feet crunching over the gravel, and the next I looked up and there it was, as if it had appeared by magic. We all stood for a moment, taking it in. The surface was perfectly calm, reflecting the hills and the patchy blue sky above. Ever since our arrival in this country, I had felt myself taking a large, deep breath when I looked out over the landscape. There was something unique about it, and it occurred to me now that it was the light.

When the sun broke through the clouds, its light seemed somehow more golden than anywhere else, lending a sort of clarity to everything.

We followed the path down and along as it wove along beside the water. None of us spoke; Shelley ran on ahead choosing pebbles to throw into the loch, and Mum and I were lost in our own thoughts. I found myself looking upwards and all around as I walked, unable to take my eyes away from the giant hills and the peaceful water. There was hardly a sound apart from the odd splash of a stone and Shelley's shout in response. It felt like there was no one else left on Earth but us.

As I looked further ahead I could make out a structure that I hadn't noticed before: a house, painted dusky pink. It had been invisible, blending perfectly against the backdrop, but now we were closer it stood out, proud and clear on the loch's pebbly shore.

"Come on!" called Shelley, spotting it at the same time, and we both ran towards it. It felt good, carefree, to be running like that, as fast as I could, as I had hardly done since I was little like my sister. As we got closer we saw it was quite large, perhaps larger than than our home in Dorset. The weathered stone showed through the paint in places, and the walls in some areas were crumbling. But it looked solid, as though it had been there for many decades. The white framed windows, although lacking glass, looked quite new. On one side a turret-like tower clung to the wall and stretched up into the sky, complete with a cone-shaped roof like some sort of fairytale castle. And it did feel like it was from some lost age. We walked around it as Mum caught us up, wondering who might have lived there. I allowed myself a little fantasy that it was our house, the three of us, and we had a big open fire and paddled in the waters of the loch every day. We would live there and pretend that all the troubles of the outside world didn't exist.

"This place is beautiful isn't it," said Mum, joining us. Around the front of the house, on the loch side, was an opening that once held a door. We walked inside and saw it was just a shell, and we could look up and see the rafters. Light poured in through the gaping windows but also created large shadows. There was a sudden flapping sound that echoed loudly around the house as a small dark shape rushed out of the door. Shelley screamed and I laughed, although it had made me jump too.

"Just a pigeon, silly!"

We walked a bit further along the path and climbed a short way up the hillside so we could take in the view. Mum produced a blanket and flask and various other packets, and we feasted on soup and sandwiches. I looked around me at the world spread out below us, so large and open, and I sighed contentedly.

"That's better," smiled Mum. "I've hated seeing you so sad these past few days."

I said nothing, biting into my sandwich.

"I wanted to bring you girls here so you can see that there's still beauty. And hope."

"You really believe that?" I said bitterly.

"I do. I have to."

I wanted to let her have her peaceful moment, and to just pretend along with her. But I also wanted to hurt her a little bit. To make her feel the way I was feeling.

"But how long for, Mum? It's already far warmer here than it should ever be. And I bet there are no fish left in that loch. The only reason we're not seeing many other effects is because we're up high. You only have to look at how the cliffs and walls have eroded back at the fort."

Shelley, giving up on lunch, had wandered off to clamber further along the hillside.

"Have you been researching, to worry yourself about all this?"

"But it *is* a worry, Mum!" I looked at her and felt all the tension of the last few days well up, and was annoyed to feel tears about to do the same. "It's real! I can't just ignore it, even if you can. That's what your generation and the ones before it have done and it's just made it all worse for us."

Mum leant forward to put an arm around my shoulder. I fought the urge to let her hug me and edged away.

"I don't want you to have to think about all this," she said. "No matter what happens, all that matters is we have each other. You two are my whole world."

"Hah!" I spat out, looking at her in disbelief. "Right! So you don't regret having us, then?"

It was as though I had hit her. She sat back a bit and just looked at me, stunned.

"No." She answered at last, her voice barely audible. "Never. Why would you say that?"

I got up and brushed myself off. "I didn't say it, Mother. *You* did."

My heart was hammering with a mixture of the anger I felt, but also the thrill and disbelief that I had let it out so

214

vehemently. I couldn't remember speaking to her like that before, and I fought the guilt that began to creep over me. I walked away before she could question me, unsure of the words I could use to answer her.

Mum packed up hastily, and we started to walk back the way we had come. From some metres ahead of them I could hear Shelley protesting that she had wanted to walk all the way around.

"That would take us hours, darling. Let's head back to base, we can come back here another time."

"Is it because Faye is in a big fat mood?"

"No. It's because it's time to go."

The walk back to the car felt longer than it had on the way there. I kicked at the stones on the path, feeling sorry for myself and a little bit guilty that I had ruined our day. But there was no going back now: the words had been said. And anyway, she deserved it for lying to me all these years. My mind jumped backwards and forwards between these points, irritatingly repetitive. When the Land Rover finally came into sight I walked over to the passenger door and waited sullenly for the others to catch up. Mum passed me as she went to load the bag and Shelley's muddy trainers into the boot. She stopped and put a hand on my arm.

"We are going to talk about this tonight."

I didn't want to look up and see the concern in her eyes, so just nodded meekly and got into the car.

Chapter 28

The track that led back to the fort seemed endless. But as we got closer to the end we could see something was wrong. Blue flashing lights bounced off the trees. It was mid-afternoon and the sun was still bright, so we didn't register them as quickly as we might have. Mum was almost at the small bridge when a police officer waved us over. Blocking the gate and parked haphazardly around the perimeter fence were several police vehicles and ambulances.

"I'm sorry, you'll have to turn around," the officer said when Mum opened the window.

"But… I work here. We're all staying here. What's happened?"

"I'm afraid there's been an incident – you won't be able to come inside just now."

As they spoke I stared ahead. There was black smoke pouring up into the sky, but I couldn't work out where from. Half hidden from view behind the guard station I could make out a fire engine. A couple of helicopters clattered overhead, adding to the drama. It felt unreal, like we were on a film set.

"Is anyone hurt?" Mum was asking.

"I can't give you any information yet. I'm sorry – your best bet is to turn around and try to find somewhere else to stay with your wee ones. Are you able to do that? And more information will be available when we have it."

"Okay. Yes, I can find a hotel for the night. Thank you." Mum sounded slightly breathless.

"Mummy what's happening?" asked Shelley as Mum swung the car around the narrow turning circle and then started to reverse.

"I don't know darling. Let's just find somewhere to stay and then I can hopefully find out."

We found a tiny hotel, after driving around for a time in search of a town large enough to hold one. It was a pretty place, the street lined with the characterful old grey and apricot stone buildings that had once been so typical of the area. The town looked deserted and rather old-fashioned, although it was obviously clean and well-kept. Mum parked the car on the empty street and we opened the door and entered gingerly. The silence made us feel like intruders. Inside felt like a reconstructed room in a museum – dark wooden panels and furniture, patterned wallpaper. A large clock ticked gloomily on the wall. When Mum rang the bell at the check-in desk I jumped at the sudden noise. We waited for several minutes.

Eventually, an older woman appeared. She was very smartly dressed and looked rather formidable, but when she spoke her voice was warm and friendly.

"Can I help you, dears?"

"Yes, I'm wondering if you have a room, just for tonight."

The lady stared at us for so long I wondered if she was all right. And then she spoke in a burst. "Oh dear! Oh gosh. I'm ever so sorry but this place hasn't been in business for years now!"

"Oh! It's just… the sign outside."

"Yes, I keep meaning to take that thing down. I am sorry. You're better off trying that big modern place down by the airport."

"Right, well, thank you very much."

But something about us must have made her call us back as we reached the door. Perhaps it was the fact we had no luggage, or maybe we just looked as lost as we felt.

"Wait! Perhaps I can do something. It'll be nice to have guests in the old place again. And I do keep it nice, out of habit, really."

Mum thanked her warmly. Despite the place being empty, she chose just the one room for all of us and, although it was a little cramped, there was comfort in being together. We had stopped off on the way and bought some supplies for a 'bed picnic', as Shelley called it. It all should have been quite exciting, but I only had to look at the worry on Mum's face to know it was far from it.

My sister and I flopped onto the double bed. Shelley called out to switch on the TV, and Mum handed her a strange black gadget covered in buttons.

"You'll need the remote."

We shared out food, barely paying attention to what we were watching – a good job, because Shelley couldn't stop changing the channel – while Mum sat in the small arm chair by the window and tapped her smartwatch.

"Hello, Alek, it's Helen, I'm just calling to check you're all okay, and find out what's happened. Call me back."

She tried a couple of other people, and then resorted to checking online. Her face turned a sickly shade of grey as she looked at her screen.

"Faye, can you put the news channel on?"

"What is it, Mum?" She came to sit next to us as I grabbed the remote from Shelley and fumbled with the buttons. The TV was ancient and I wasn't even sure if it would have any up-to-date channels. But sure enough, we found the news.

There were various banners and headlines all over the screen, but the largest one read 'suspected terror attack on ComET base'. There was footage filmed from a helicopter of the large plume of smoke we had seen earlier. It was difficult to make anything else out through the black haze.

"...unclear as of yet what actually happened," said the reporter, "but it is being suggested it was a deliberate act. There was a large explosion which is thought to have damaged one of the main buildings used for the research. Several casualties have been reported but it is unknown if there are any fatalities. Of course, the big question is whether the Thulians have been injured in the blast, but there's no word on this yet. Firefighters are working on the main building to get the blaze under control, but as far as we know, due to strict security measures, everyone that was inside is accounted for. We're going over now to Sally Duke, our reporter on the scene. Sally, what can you tell us..."

Shelley was wide-eyed with shock. "It's *blown up*?" I put my arm around her.

Mum looked helplessly at her watch.

"Why isn't anyone calling me?"

We watched the news report for a bit longer but it was clear there wasn't much more to report as, after a few snippets of other news, the bulletin just repeated the main facts we had already heard.

219

Mum's watch buzzed and she quickly tapped the screen.

"Amy? Oh, thank God you're okay... What the hell happened?" We listened, trying to interpret the one-sided conversation. "Where are you? ... okay. Well, you go back in and get back to me when you feel up to it, it doesn't matter what time it is. Thank you for calling... yes, I'll keep trying too." Mum rang off and took a deep breath. "Amy's at the hospital, she wasn't inside the building but close enough to be hurt. She's okay though I think – they're just checking her over."

"You should go there if you want to, Mum. We'll be okay," I said with a bravery I didn't really feel.

"No! Thank you darling but I can't do that. It's one thing leaving you both alone a few buildings away at a heavily guarded army base, quite another in a deserted hotel in a strange town. I'd rather stay here, Amy will call back later."

We spent a tense few hours with the news on in the background, gradually being fed more and more about what had happened while we had been out for the day.

"...Obviously very secure, so any eyewitnesses will be personnel from the base itself. But the police are saying they believe a UAV, or drone, could have been responsible. The building hit was known as the control hub, and it housed the research labs and other important rooms."

"Thank you, Sally, sorry to interrupt," said the man reporting from the studio. "We're hearing now that there were thirteen casualties, nine of whom were researchers working inside at the time. We believe the other four to be army personnel there to guard the base. There are around fifty people stationed on the ComET base at Fort Leigh, including the guards, but as we've heard the explosion took place at around lunch time, and so many of the scientists and doctors at the base were, fortunately for them, on their lunch break in another building."

I thought of Ben – I was sure he had been working that day. I hoped he was all right.

A little bit later Amy called back. Mum went out into the corridor to talk to her because Shelley was dozing off. We had turned off the lights and the volume on the TV was low, but its flickering screen cast a ghostly glow around the room.

Mum crept back in looking shattered, and whispered to me, "Amy isn't sure where Alek or Ernst are, along with all but one of the four guards – Mya, who's been discharged, thankfully. They were taken away in the first ambulances and she can't get any news of them because she's not related. Some of the others are there with cuts and bruises, but most have been sent home already. It seems we had a lucky escape." She rubbed at her eyes and I gave her a hug. I thought about Professor Ivanov, stocky, formidable and, surely, indestructible, and about Ernst, so serious about his work while being so warm and likeable. And I remembered how kind Ben had been to me that morning, despite his gruff exterior.

"They'll be okay, won't they Mum?"

"We've got to hope so. But there's good news, too. The Thulians are fine, they were far enough from the blast and, anyway, the bunker would have protected them and all the others who were inside. Not really a surprise as that's what it was designed to do. But a relief, definitely."

"Yes."

And it was – I had been anxiously waiting to hear about them, too. Although it wasn't clear yet what exactly had happened, someone had set out to bomb the base, and it didn't take much thought to work out who had been the target. It was frightening to think that this place that had felt like home – safe, protected – had been targeted like this. A thought suddenly struck me.

"Is our house okay? I mean, I know it doesn't matter because we're safe, but..."

"Yes, I think so. It was far enough away, too. Those old houses were built solidly, and it's looking like quite a precise attack on that one area."

"It's a good job the others like their food so much. Going to the mess room for lunch saved them," I said, hoping a flippant remark would help ease the tension.

Mum smiled. "Well, I suppose that's true."

Gradually the truth filtered in as we sat there through the darkening night. The further into summer we got the later the sun set, so that even though I knew it must have been getting close to midnight there was still a slight glow on the horizon. Mum kept telling me to get some rest but I couldn't. Partly because I didn't think I would be able to sleep, but also because I didn't want to leave her sitting there alone in the dark, watching the news and waiting for someone to ring.

It turned out that the blast had indeed been caused by an exploding drone – or UAV, as they called it on the news. I felt sick as I thought about the buzzing above us over the past few weeks. We had become so used to them, seeing them at first as a bit of a nuisance but later barely even noticeable. While no one had yet owned up to the act, it was being attributed to the Planet Protectors, or PP, a vigilante extremist group that had branched away from the original Protectors when they grew frustrated with their mild beliefs and lack of action. Threats had been made by them before, intelligence sources stated, and the senior members had been on a watch list for many weeks.

"So much for that," Mum murmured testily.

I finally fell asleep. I wasn't sure how late Mum sat up till, but when Shelley woke me in the morning, she was still fast asleep. We had no clothes with us but the ones we had been wearing yesterday, but we'd bought toothbrushes on the way over so I did my best to get us washed and ready for the day. When we came out of the bathroom Mum was awake, but she looked like she hadn't slept at all. She had reached for her tablet already and was scrolling the screen.

"A few messages from Amy," she said by way of greeting. She read them through and sighed deeply, sitting forward in the chair.

"Okay, so she's heard about Alek, he's got concussion and a broken arm, plus some internal bruising, but he's going to be all right. Thank God."

"That's amazing, Mum."

"But we don't know about Ernst yet. Apparently he was in surgery yesterday but that's all she's found out."

"Can we go back there now?" Asked Shelley. "I want to see Seraphina."

"I don't know yet, Shelley. They have to make sure it's safe first. Hopefully we'll find out later."

There was a polite little knock on the door.

"Hello, it's Mary. The owner." We opened it. "Sorry to disturb you, I was just wondering if you wanted the full Scottish breakfast this morning or the full English?"

She must have wondered why we all looked so overwhelmed. I think, at that moment, we were all struck by the normality and the simplicity of life outside our crazy world, as well as the kindness of her simple gesture. Also, speaking for myself, I hadn't eaten properly since the soup on the hills of the loch yesterday, which felt like weeks ago rather than mere hours.

Downstairs in a small dining area, Mary buzzed around us pouring tea and apple juice.

"Did you hear about that terrible business yesterday with the bomb?"

"Yes, we did."

"And to think all that happened just down the road. It's awful to think how some humans can be towards others."

We ended up enjoying Mary's lovely, warm hospitality for another day. It was a shame her place had been put out of business, swept off the map by the larger hotels, because she obviously relished the role of host.

Mum spent much of the day on the phone – returning Frankie's worried calls, speaking to Amy and making several other calls – while Shelley and I tried to entertain ourselves. Any interesting shops within walking distance were long gone, and with all our tablets and toys at the house it was difficult to settle to anything, so after a short walk through the quiet streets, we mostly watched TV.

"We can go back in the morning," Mum told us, interrupting an argument between Shelley and me about what to watch. "The other buildings are all safe."

In the morning Mum paid up – with that strange back-and-forth pantomime that adults often perform as though they're too polite to accept money (Mum won, as far as I could tell, from Mary's "Oh no, that's too much!") – and we drove back.

It was a sorry sight. After Mum showed her security pass and the car was checked over, we drove through the archway and past the mess building. The main control building was a smoking wreck; a skeleton filled with rubble. The ground around it had been cleared hastily but there were still piles of broken glass and fragments of brick. Clear sheeting had been placed over it to protect what was left, and there were several people in white suits clambering around it.

We wearily opened our front door and flopped onto the sofa as one, just sitting there for a few minutes in silence staring at the wall. Everything in the house looked and felt so intact, so normal, although I was sure I could smell smoke in the air, hinting at the destruction just outside the door.

Mum went to make coffee and we were settling back in – feeling like we had been away for weeks – when a couple of police officers knocked at the front door. Mum spoke to them in a low voice and I heard one of them say "… a few questions…"

"I'm just popping out for a bit, girls. I won't be far away, just in the mess building, okay?" And she was gone.

Shelley and I sat there in silence for a few seconds.

"Why did they arrest Mum?" Shelley suddenly wailed, revealing the toll the last twenty-four hours of tension had taken on her.

"They didn't!" I tried to comfort her. "It's fine, she's just talking to them. She'll be back in a minute, she said so."

But it felt like hours. When Mum eventually returned, much to Shelley's delight, she looked reassuringly calm. But we grilled her anyway.

"It's fine, girls. They just wanted to know where we were the other day; why I chose that day of all days to go out. I just told them it was pure luck."

"They don't think you had anything to do with it do they?"

"No, of course not. The PP group has come forward and said it was them, anyway. I think they just have to question us all in case there's anything they've missed."

But the strain on her face betrayed her composed exterior.

The next visitor we had was more welcome.

"Amy!" cried Mum as she peeped her head around the door. She ushered her in and sat her down carefully as though she were an invalid. Indeed, she had a nasty looking gash above one eye held together with steri-strips.

"I thought you said you weren't injured?"

"It's just a few stitches," smiled Amy. "Nothing compared to some of the others."

"Come on, now. You were in an explosion, it must have been terrifying."

"It was." Amy admitted. "I only popped out to grab a coffee. I should have been inside with the others!"

"Thank God you weren't."

"I was walking away, across the courtyard, and I just felt a sudden… sort of punching feeling, and then I was on the ground. I didn't have a clue what had happened, I don't even remember hearing the explosion. It was afterwards that was the worst bit, when I managed to get up and I saw the building collapsed and smoking."

Mum put an arm around her.

"Is there any more news about Ernst?"

"He's in intensive care. 'Stable', is all they'd say – doesn't give much away." She took a deep shuddering breath and lowered her voice slightly. "He was stuck inside, Helen. They had to dig him out of the rubble." Mum closed her eyes and they both sat in silence for a bit.

"And Alek?" Mum asked softly.

"Getting there. Desperate to come back, of course, but they want to keep him in for another night. He's up for talking if you wanted to call him."

"I'm not sure he'd want to hear from me right now. He was still annoyed with me about the whole divulgence of information thing."

"That's all history now, surely?"

"I'm not so sure." Mum passed Amy a cup of coffee. It was the real instant stuff, not the powdered fake stuff they were used to, and she had been rationing it, despite it tasting a little 'fusty'.

"What about the damage?" Mum asked now.

"Well. That's not such great news. All the research labs, the samples and everything, have been destroyed. The stupid thing is they were targeting the Thulians, but instead they've managed to set us way back in our understanding of them!"

Amy sipped her coffee.

"They didn't account for how greedy our lot are, either!" She continued, smiling weakly. "As soon as lunch time comes, off they go!"

"Good job too!" Smiled Mum. "And at least our ET friends are safe."

"Yes. Thank God. I can't even imagine, if they'd succeeded…"

"I know."

"Luckily they were completely clueless about the layout of the place. Either that or they knew the ETs sometimes go into that building and were just counting on them being there. The whole fort's been made a no-fly-zone now, of course; no drones or helicopters unless they're ours. And there's extra security at the gate."

"Yes, I saw."

Amy looked at Mum. "Are *you* okay?"

Mum put down her mug and rubbed her face with both hands. "Me? I wasn't even here."

"No, but…" Amy nodded towards us, and Mum gave a slight nod back.

"We could have been. I mean, don't these psychos *know* there are kids here?"

Amy put her hand over Mum's, "I doubt it, actually. It's not been all that well publicised. Not that that's any excuse of course."

"No. It's not."

"Why did they do it, Mummy?" Mum drew Shelley towards her,

"It's not anything we could ever understand properly because we would never do something like this. But the naughty people seem to think the Thulians are going to hurt us, so they wanted to hurt them instead."

"Seraphina and Sylvian wouldn't hurt us!"

"*We* know that, because we see them all the time. But I suppose these people are afraid of them, because they're so different to us. They think the Thulians want to take over our planet or something ridiculous like that."

"That's stupid."

"The truth is," said Amy, "common sense tells us that if the ETs *were* planning something like that they would just have been aggressive from the start. And I doubt something like a little bomb would have been able to stop them."

"So what are you going to do?" Asked Mum. "Now the lab has gone?"

Amy sighed sadly. "I don't know. I suppose we need to wait and see if anything can be salvaged, and then just start it all over again. Take new samples, re-run the tests. All of the data we had already recorded will be safe, so that's something. And there are still the samples that were sent out to other labs."

Amy stayed for dinner. None of us felt like going to the mess hall that evening, with its gaps at the tables, and the quiet sense of shock among the walking wounded and those unscathed. Instead we ate on our laps and watched a film, a lightweight comedy Mum had liked when she was a young girl. At some point in the evening a bulletin came up on the news app that several of the ringleaders from PP had been arrested, and she and Amy clinked glasses with a muted 'cheers'.

Chapter 29

Over the next few days, life got back into a routine. As the remains of the lab building were being assessed and cleared, they stood as a constant reminder of the attack. But everyone got on as best they could. All the researchers that were on their feet and well enough worked together to set up a temporary lab within the mess building, upstairs where there were some large disused rooms. The original samples were ruined, valuable equipment destroyed, but there was still data to analyse and ETs to monitor. A stream of deliveries brought supplies to facilitate that, and it felt like a defiant stand was being taken. Life was going on.

Every day the Thulians underwent a rigorous health check and examination, during which samples were taken, to ascertain the effect of our atmosphere on their bodies over a long term period.

Now that the rubble had been cleared, work began on repairing the damaged building. It was thought at first that the whole thing would have to come down, but enough of the structure remained for it to be restored. The fact that it was of historical interest was a factor in this decision, but this also made the reconstruction more complicated. Gradually scaffolding was put up and the necessary supplies brought in.

Around this time, we discovered that the terrorists had deliberately timed the blast to coincide with our being off the base, as they had indeed been aware there were children present. I suddenly remembered Faiza's interview, when she had mentioned Shelley naming the ETs. I wondered at first if this news would make my mother feel better, as I knew she felt terrible guilt about supposedly putting us in harm's way by bringing us there. But I soon realised the opposite was true. In fact, she felt somewhat culpable, having left the base in the first place and apparently providing the terrorists with an opportunity. On top of this was the unsettling feeling that they had been watching us, and tracking our movements somehow.

Alek was released from hospital, his arm in a sling, as determined as ever to keep the project on track. The blast had inspired in everyone a new motivation to keep going; to prove these so-called Planet Protectors wrong. Several trips were made to the hospital to see Ernst, but whether he knew they were there no one could say.

The morning Alek came back he gathered everyone in the courtyard. Although still a looming figure, he looked somehow depleted, less imposing. I realised he was dressed more casually than I had ever seen him, and wondered if that was why. 'Everyone' included Shelley and me, but the atmosphere made the scientists who worked directly with the Thulians too nervous to bring them back out into the open just yet.

"We've suffered a huge shock here at Fort Leigh," Alek called out from his makeshift plinth that was part of the reconstruction site. His voice, deep and expressive and tinged slightly with his native Russian accent, carried across the open space. This, along with his stature, gave him the stage presence of an actor (helped along, probably, by the fact he practically *was* on a stage), and we all listened closely. Even Shelley was still and silent. "A direct attack on us and the ComET project as a whole. But we are not going to let cowards who fly explosive drones into buildings, targeting innocent people, stop us. We are going to carry on with our work. It is important, and life changing… *world* changing. Finding out as much as we can about these visitors while we're honoured with their presence is now more vital than ever." There were shouts and scattered applause. "We need to fight back with our knowledge, our skill and expertise. For each other; for all of those who were injured. For Doctor Ernst Bauer!"

In different circumstances it was the sort of motivational speech I could imagine my mother gently mocking, or at least being a little cynical about. But as I looked around at the strange sight of all the grown-ups applauding, cheering and hugging, I saw tears in some of their eyes, including hers. And I realised this attack had affected everyone on a deep level, but it had also made everyone more resolute; more connected.

And then – with less of a fanfare – Ben was back. Shelley and I were playing outside and I looked up and there he was, at his old station by the bunker, a slightly comical white bandage covering the top of his head and holding a patch over his left eye. He looked up and saw me, and gave me a salute. I smiled and nodded at him, and then Shelley spotted him and ran over to interrogate him. I went to join them.

"Just a wee bash on the head. Probably knocked a bit of sense into me."

"What about your eye? Can't you see?"

"No, not any more. But it's okay, I've got the other one."

I stared. "Have you really lost your sight?"

"Apparently so."

"I'm sorry, that's awful."

He waved my concern away, "I'm alive, that's what counts. And I can get myself an eye patch. Or a false eye, and look even scarier than before!"

Although I felt bad about it, I couldn't help laughing along with him. It was such a relief to see him standing there, making daft jokes.

The explosion may have caused a distraction for a time, but it wasn't enough to sway the Thulians from their mission for information. Particularly that related to the state of the planet, and the human impact on it. Every day more questions were asked, and the researchers were busy in their new quarters compiling the answers that were sought.

Meanwhile, in the outside world the shock waves caused by the nature of the attack, which spread across all camps, had quietened the angry voices. However, eager to keep the fragile peace, some – including the opposition party in our government – were asking why the other pods still needed to be in our orbit, hovering above us somewhat threateningly. We knew they were there so the Thulians could communicate with them, a last link to their home planet. But many voices in the press were asking what it was that was actually being relayed back to them, and expressed discomfort at our inability to find out.

And, of course, there was no way of knowing. Without speaking their strange language or understanding how the signals were being sent, let alone how to intercept them, no one could offer reassurance that the messages weren't of a sinister nature. Mum was tasked with broaching the subject one day when she went in to visit the Thulians. She brought it up straight away, with no preamble; a method she always preferred, and which worked well as they had no experience of tact or bumbling politeness, and were often baffled by any attempts at it.

"There is some concern about the communications with the other Thulians. Those up in space," she told them.

"Concern? Why is this?"

"Some people on our planet do not like that the signals are kept secret from them. They fear... that you may be plotting an attack or giving information that makes the human race look bad. This is not my opinion, but that of some of our world leaders and others, too."

Seraphina paused to take this in. It was the first time suspicions of anything but peaceful intentions had been openly suggested to them.

"The signals are not kept secret from your people," she answered. "They are simply not understood by them."

"Yes, that is true. But the result is the same."

"Then we will tell you everything we say. We have no secrets."

"Thank you, we are very grateful. I think because we are not advanced enough to understand your language, some people lack trust. I am sorry, as I say it is not how many of us feel, but we have found that if these people are not happy then the problem may get worse. They may spread this opinion to others."

Seraphina had started, whether unconsciously or deliberately, to mimic some human characteristics, and here she gave a very slight shrug, holding her long fingers out at her sides.

"All we can do is tell you what we are saying."

"I appreciate that. Thank you." Mum started to get up to leave, when Seraphina spoke again.

"I am interested in what sort of attack it is thought we would be plotting."

Mum settled back into her seat, contemplating how best to reply. As usual, Seraphina's companion was in the background, busying herself with something or other. When Mum looked closely she could see, along with the tablets they'd been given, books and photographs spread out in front of Sylvian. My mother remembered these had been requested, and someone had had to go into the archives at the old library in the city to dig out all the printed matter, which had been stored away in their basement years ago. She supposed pictures on the internet had been no substitute for the actual photos, and knew both Thulians were eager to travel further and see more of Earth, when and if it became practical. They had actually been fascinated with film and photography since their arrival, not apparently having anything equivalent to it back on Thule. This was a shame: photographs of their strange planet would have been very valuable indeed.

Mum cleared her throat and sat forward slightly.

"We humans are often fearful of things we do not fully understand. And we have been story tellers since the beginning of our time on Earth. There have been many stories told about aliens – beings from other planets – destroying us so that they can take over Earth."

"Destroying you? How?"

"Well... all sorts of ways. Bombs, guns, lasers. The stories differ, but invariably the human race ends up wiped out. Extinct."

"Bombs. This was what was used here. To try to kill us," Seraphina gestured to herself and Sylvian. Mum was surprised – they hadn't explicitly told the Thulians that they were the target of the attack, mainly because they weren't sure how the information would be received. Seraphina had either worked it out for herself, or somehow overheard it being spoken about. Mum saw no point in denying it.

"That's right."

"And guns, what are these?"

"Weapons. Used to shoot, and kill."

The Thulian sat for a minute and studied my mother. This habit, of staring whilst apparently contemplating what had been said, had unnerved many who came face to face with them, but by now Mum was used to it and met her gaze in return. She told us once that when she did this she was careful to make her expression as blank as possible, with no hint of a smile or a frown, as she didn't want it to be misread.

"These are made, by humans?"

"Yes."

"Why?"

"That is a very difficult question. The first humans made weapons to hunt animals, for food and clothing etcetera. But also, humans have been at war with each other, on and off, forever. Weapons were also made to fight in these battles. Before guns and bombs it was spears and swords. But also they are used for defence; many feel they need them to protect themselves and others."

"War? We know about this, but do not have anything like it."

"Nothing? No conflict at all?"

"Arguments? Yes, but never resulting in death."

"Well, wars are more than an argument, usually. A whole belief system or nation's freedom can be at stake. But I see how it may look to you, coming from a largely peaceful planet where species mingle together in harmony. We could learn a lot from you, I think."

"Yes. It is strange to us, that humans purposefully harm one another."

"Do you really not have any sort of crime at all on Thule?" Asked Mum.

"Anyone who does anything that you would call a crime, would be banished from our society. They would have to look after themselves; build a shelter, find food. There is no... motivation for this, and so it happens very rarely." While Mum contemplated this, Seraphina spoke again.

"Another thing that is strange to us is hunting and killing animals for food."

"No one really hunts anymore. There is no need, when we all live close to large shops where we can pay for meat, which is farmed and slaughtered for us. Although, eating meat is now disapproved of, and so harder to find. It was once far more widespread, eaten with every meal almost, but now it's rare to find people who eat it at all. Do none of your species eat meat?"

"There are several smaller, ground-dwelling creatures which feed on the dead."

"Oh – like the insects, here on Earth."

"Yes."

"There are other species here that kill and eat other animals. They are called carnivores. So it is just a part of nature; the way they have evolved."

Mum loved these conversations with Seraphina – it was easy to see how much, in the animated way she would relay them to us later. It was a pleasure for her to share all the things about our home planet that were so ordinary to us and embedded in us. And she loved the way the conversations could be so unpredictable, meandering along and covering so many unexpected topics, from the mundane, to the obscure, to the profoundly important. It was as fascinating to her as it was to them; seeing and discussing aspects of our existence through unfamiliar eyes. At the same time, though, they wore Mum out. She would return home exhausted, having had to stay alert throughout the exchanges, to make sure the information was clear and accurate. And Seraphina certainly knew how to grill someone: her questions were constant and relentless.

In this instance, many of the concerns of the outside world were pacified. The revelation that the Thulians had no concept of war, let alone harboured destructive desires against us, went a long way in convincing most. But there were still those who would never trust the visitors. After all, they would argue, even if the ETs were apparently being open in revealing their communications to us, without knowing anything of their language, how could we be sure we were being told the truth?

Chapter 30

The fear and the uncertainty caused by the attack made my previous melancholia seem childish and insignificant. I could hardly mope about feeling sorry for myself when people had been injured, especially when poor Ernst was lying in a coma. I hadn't forgotten it completely, but it was in the background: a niggling feeling of something unfinished and unresolved.

It was addressed unexpectedly around a week after the attack. Mum was called in again to answer some of the Thulians' questions and, knowing Shelley and I had been a bit lost and struggling to focus on very much, she asked if we would like to come along and listen in, like we had done before.

We were in their quarters again. They hadn't left the bunker since the attack, caution dictating that they remain there for now. We followed Mum inside and all exchanged the Thulian greeting, before my sister and I sat down to one side. It was testament to the way the relationship had built up that there were no longer any nerves or anxiety about doing or saying the wrong thing, no formalities to abide by any more. We just entered the room as though we were regular acquaintances, confident they would not object to our being there.

And indeed they didn't. The two figures stood there, serene as always, holding Mum's gaze. After some communication with each other – that haunting, multi-tonal whine – Sylvian nodded and left the room.

"Today I would like to speak again about the population problem here on Earth," began Seraphina. Shelley watched her carefully. How much of the conversations my little sister ever properly followed I wasn't sure – there were often aspects that lost me, especially when they had to keep stopping so my mother could explain different terms and expressions to them. But I think it was enough for her just to be there, to be able to simply observe this being whom she considered her friend.

"That will be fine. I will do my best to answer, but wouldn't it be better if Iain were here? As he is our expert on climate."

"No. You will be acceptable for now." To most people this would have sounded like a slight, but was intended as nothing of the sort. There was a pause as they gazed at each other in that strange way, which still looked a little confrontational from a human's perspective, before Seraphina spoke again.

"Humans admit they have overcrowded the planet. But still they continue to reproduce. We would like to understand why."

"Like so many of these questions, the answer is complicated," answered Mum. "Restrictions on birth rates were put in place in a couple of our larger, most populated countries. One child per family, in one case. Another went even further, and tried to stop people in certain age groups from having children at all. Assisted conception – IVF and so on – was outlawed in places. But it just caused resentment and distress. And it was seen as a huge violation of human rights. There were protests and objections around the world. Plus, it is so hard to enforce such limits on people. What should happen to a family or a couple who breaks the rules, either intentionally or otherwise? Across the world, most countries are very proud of their liberty, and know better than to try and restrict the freedom of their people."

"But the people know the problems with your planet. Reducing the human population is the best solution."

"Perhaps. This is not for certain – there could be, in theory, enough resources and food for us all. Yet people are starving, as famines and droughts are common. Child-bearing has been discouraged for this reason, but imposing restrictions and punishing people has been proven not to work. Also, the birth rate has fallen quite sharply naturally. Iain has provided you with the data I think? This has been due to a drop in fertility rates, and also people making the free choice not to reproduce, or to adopt children instead, which has been made far more accessible than it once was."

Mum paused and considered her words.

"The thing is, Seraphina, we are just another species. And like other animals, we have a survival instinct, an urge to reproduce, if we can. I realise we're far from endangered, but that instinct doesn't just disappear." She closed her eyes for a moment before gesturing towards us. "I agonised over my decision to have children. I knew, better than many, the impact and strain extra people are putting on this planet. I have felt – and been labelled – guilty and selfish. And it's true: I am. But it wasn't just a simple decision; it was a desire. A need within me. And my justification – to myself and to everyone else who questions me – is that I am bringing up these girls with great care. They are growing up to be good, kind people who can contribute something, and make a difference to the world, however small."

I watched her as she made this impassioned speech. I had never heard this justification before, but it made perfect sense. It explained everything to me, her 'missions', her intense, ever-present love. What didn't make sense were the words I had

241

overheard. They just didn't fit with this person I knew, with the kind of mother I knew she was.

"But if this trajectory continues," Seraphina was saying, "that world will no longer be habitable when they are adults."

Mum stared, and let out a breath as though she were winded. "We don't know that. There has to be optimism, still. The planet will always be here, we surely just have to try and make the most of it. Adapt to survive, like you. Protect what we have left."

"What will change? Humans have known these facts and ignored them up until now."

Mum stopped and sighed. She looked down at the floor for a long time.

"You are right. We have messed up, Seraphina. That is the sad truth. I cannot explain it or justify it." She looked up sadly and met the Thulian's gaze.

"Then it is true. It is too late." Seraphina nodded slightly and turned away.

"But… is there nothing we can do?" Mum sounded desperate.

But she was already retreating; the exchange was over.

We talked for a long time that night, my mother and I. It was like being back at home when we would sometimes have a movie and snack night after Shelley had been put to bed. But this conversation was long overdue. I finally admitted to overhearing part of her conversation with Dad, and told her that that was why I had been so unhappy. Mum hugged me tightly for a long time.

"Why didn't you come and talk to me? I've always said you can tell me anything."

I found I couldn't really explain it to her. The guilt for listening in the first place; the fear of upsetting her; the anger and sadness at feeling rejected. I said nothing and just shrugged instead.

"So, tell me now. What went through your head when you heard all that? What *did* you actually hear?"

"It sounded like you and Dad were arguing, saying you wished you hadn't had us. I was angry with you – it felt like you've been lying all this time, telling us how precious we are to you."

"And is that still how you feel? Now you've had time to think. And after what you heard me saying today?"

"I don't know. I don't think so."

"Well, that's still not great."

"I know *you* wanted us. But Dad said we were a mistake. Is that why you fell out? Why he left?"

"No! He *did* want you, very much. It's exactly what Seraphina was saying today though – from a purely practical, scientific point of view, it's probably true that the planet is full. But when you choose to have kids – and if you're lucky enough to be able to – you're not thinking practically or scientifically. It's true what I said today, about bringing you up to be the amazing people you are. Your being here will benefit the world, not cause a problem for it!"

"No pressure then, Mum."

She squeezed me tightly. "Only a bit!"

"And what about Dad? There was obviously something you didn't agree on about us."

She sighed the sigh she did when one of us asked an impossible question. We didn't see it often because she was always resolved to tell us everything. But clearly she was finding that hard to keep to now.

"I told you about his job; about how committed he is. I mean – it's his lifelong passion. And he's carrying around so much anger and frustration about it all. It's easy for everyone else to carry on as usual and try to ignore the truth, but he's right there, on the front line. He's seen the devastation for himself."

"I know all this, Mum."

"So I really had to convince him that having kids was a good idea. He knew it was what I had always wanted right from the start, and he wanted it too. When you were born he was ecstatic. But I suppose a part of me always knew it was on me; I was the main parent, his mind was on other things. He'd always been completely honest about it – the conflict he felt. So I didn't complain or resent him, because I had what I wanted. You."

"Well… that's great, Mum, but what about Shelley?"

"He loves her too, of course he does – he's always saying how she's fiery, just like him, when they chat."

"What, twice a year?" I scoffed, only half joking. Mum smiled wryly, but then became serious again.

"I report back to him an awful lot. Send him all those photos and videos. I know he's not exactly… present. But I didn't think it really bothered you?"

"It doesn't. I hardly know him so don't really miss him. It sounds bad, but I don't think he'd mind me saying that."

"It's not a conventional relationship, is it…"

"But I'm not stupid, Mum. I remember that Dad left when Shelley was only just born."

"Yes. That's when the original job in South America came up. We knew it wouldn't end there and that he'd have to travel a lot more, so we just came to an agreement. It was all very simple really, he'd been away so much already. We'd become more like old friends than a couple, anyway."

"So he didn't go because Shelley was an accident?"

"No. She was a lovely, welcome surprise. Fatherhood just wasn't for him – not the hands-on, committed type. I know that sounds awful, but it's not his fault. He never misled me or pretended otherwise. He loves you both very much, but his job has always come first. Before me, before anything. I hope that's not hard to hear."

I shrugged. "It isn't. I mean that – I know I should feel abandoned or neglected or whatever, but the truth is I don't. I just hated the thought that we weren't wanted, or that we were the reason you and Dad split up."

"Do you still think that?"

"No. But you'll have a job convincing Shelley when she's older."

"Let's hope not. I'm dreading the teenage years as it is."

I felt a lot better. Even though Mum had more or less admitted that Dad hadn't been the one that wanted us, it didn't seem to matter so much now. Far bigger things were happening in the outside world, but even without those I knew that all along I had Mum, and one parent was enough. Dad was on his crusade and that was fine too. More than that: I was proud of him.

Chapter 31

The news came the next morning, exactly a week after the attack. Ernst had succumbed to his wounds. He was dead.

I had never known anyone that had died before. He had been younger than my mum. I remembered the way he had scooped Shelley up onto his shoulders to see the Thulians on break-out day, and how he was so tall that she had towered above everyone and got the best view. And how he had confessed to me about feeling nervous of being on television in front of millions of people. Snippets of that interview were being played back over and over now on all the news sites and channels, and all I could think about was how he would have hated it. Some of his colleagues on the base used to joke good-naturedly that he lived up to his name, and would call him 'earnest Ernst', as he was so serious and committed to his work. But he had been such a kind man too, patiently answering all of our questions, and making Shelley laugh sometimes with silly answers.

Amy was hit hard by the news. She had been to see him only the day before and, while there had still been no improvement, there hadn't been any indication that he wouldn't make it through the night, either. We were all in shock; the blast itself had affected everyone. The jagged shell of the research hub was a stark reminder every day. You couldn't walk around the fort without seeing it; even at night it was silhouetted ominously against the faint glow of the sky.

The mood had been defiant, almost falsely upbeat, in the past week, since people had picked themselves up and figuratively brushed themselves off to carry on. But now it was sombre again. The fifty or so people that had been living and working on the ComET base for the past couple of months had been bound together in a unique way; guards, scientists, doctors, children alike. No one could quite believe that one of our people had been so cruelly eliminated. One day he had been there, walking among us, with no inkling of what was to come. The next, he had been in the wrong place at the wrong time. He was in the part of the building that had been struck, parts of the wall and roof collapsed on him, and there he had lain trapped under the rubble. Conscious or unconscious we didn't know, but we all hoped it had been the latter. I couldn't get the image out of my mind, of him lying there helpless, waiting to be rescued before he bled to death or suffocated under there. I had tried not to dwell on it too much, but now he was actually dead the thoughts marched their way in and invaded my brain.

His parents had flown over to be by his bedside, and now they were taking his body back to Germany for his funeral. Alek went to the hospital to see them, to tell them about how valuable his work had been and how much he had loved it. Similar to the words spoken by the comrade of a fallen soldier who had fought bravely for his cause. But Ernst had not been a soldier; his parents had had no idea he was walking into danger when they waved him off. I imagined how excited he would have been, how full of ambition and enthusiasm at being chosen to work on the coveted ComET project. How proud his parents must have felt.

I knew these were quite morbid, in-depth thoughts for a nearly-eleven-year-old to have. But the adults around us were suffering, and the concept of death had never felt so close – or so real – before. I suppose a part of it, from a more selfish perspective, was the slight relief of the survivor. The feeling that it could have been any one of us.

After the memorial service, when the grown-ups got together to drink to Ernst's memory and share anecdotes late into the night, everyone started to focus again on the project. It felt important not to let Ernst's work be for nothing. We all knew that, had he walked back onto the base with Alek and Amy and all the other lucky ones, he would have got straight back to work. He had been interested in the next stage of the project and had already put himself forward to be involved.

The idea had been raised before the attack – probably by the Thulians themselves, but supported by the likes of Ernst and my mother, among many others – that they should be bringing this section of the project to a close so that the ETs could travel elsewhere. This also brought up other questions: where should they go? Who would accompany them this time? How would the security aspect work?

But Alek seemingly had something else on his mind.

I knew something was up when he came over to speak to our mother. They usually only spoke in the offices or the lab, or chatted in the mess building. He had never come over to our house before. When I responded to his knock at the door he looked more serious than usual – it was clear this was not an informal visit. He barely acknowledged me, but gave a brief nod and said he was there to see Mum.

Shelley and I had being doing our homework, and we retreated upstairs. But as soon as we got to our room I put my fingers to my lips and tiptoed back downstairs to sit in the usual spot at the base of the stairs and listen. Shelley came too, more out of imitation than interest in what was being said. I gave her a look that was meant to be threatening: keep quiet, or else.

Mum had seemed as surprised as I was at the visit, and this peaked my suspicions further. I was hidden behind the wall in my hiding spot, but this meant that I couldn't see them either, so had to be content with listening.

"...Apologies for intruding on you like this, Helen, but I've got some concerns."

"Oh? About the Thulians?"

"Who else? Yes."

The chairs scraped back as they sat down, and I heard Alek thank her for his coffee.

"What's happened?"

"I've just been going over the latest conversation between you. I'm still concerned about this fixation they have with climate change. You'll remember that I was against going into it too deeply in the first place."

"Because you though they wouldn't be interested. Biscuit?"

"That's right. No thank you."

"But they are. And I convinced you that it would look bad if we were to try to withhold information."

"And I agreed. But I think we're coming off rather badly as it is."

"Probably, but there's no other way to dress up the facts, is there? It's all true."

"Perhaps a bit too true."

Mum let out a sigh of frustration.

"Well it's done now. What would you have us do next?"

"I think we need to watch them. Very closely."

"For... what?"

"As I said, that last conversation was concerning to me. When they were talking about the population size causing problems. They said, and I quote: 'reducing the human population is the best solution.' Then later on they went on to tell us we had left it too late. What do you think they meant?"

"Exactly what they said, Alek! I know I'm a huge hypocrite here, but they're right!"

"Undisputedly. But what I mean is, what are their intentions, do you think?"

"Intentions?"

"It all sounded very... final. As though they've heard everything they need to and have come to some sort of a decision. And what is the other one doing in the background all the time? I've got to admit, it's making me a little nervous."

"Alek, for God's sake, you're starting to sound as paranoid as one of those bloody Protectors!"

There was a silence – I could sense the tension through the wall.

"That was uncalled for," Alek said, his voice cold.

"It was. I'm sorry, I didn't mean that. I've just been getting frustrated with all the hate and suspicion being spread on the news. We've seen the damage it can do."

"I agree. I've seen it first hand, don't forget."

"Of course. I know."

"But at the same time we can't ignore the signs. I realise they have shown no violent intentions towards us, made no attempts to attack or subdue us. But with those bloody pods hanging about above us it feels like they're biding their time, somehow. You can't blame the public for being… paranoid."

"I do understand. But I disagree. I've spent a lot of time with Seraphina and I can honestly say she's a gentle, peaceful being – they both are. They don't understand war, or this insane need to possess or control that us humans have. That's probably why it's so hard for people to understand them; they're so different."

"All the same, Helen, I'm going to increase the guards and restrict the ETs' movements. Put this travel plan on hold. We need their transcripts of those messages they're sending out, and we need them now."

"… Alek… how are we going to explain this to them? Don't we risk angering them further, if indeed your instincts are right? And if *I* happen to be right, we're causing conflict where there doesn't need to be any!"

"That's where you come in, Helen. Conflict management. I'll need you to explain it to them in a way that…" Mum made a shocked sound as she realised what he was asking of her. "I know, and I'm sorry. But I'm under pressure too, from Downing Street and the Ministry of Defence, no less. And, let's face it. It is what you're here for. Thank you for the coffee."

He got up and walked out of the house, leaving the door open as he had found it, before Mum could say anything more.

Partly out of defiance, and partly because it was such a delicate task, Mum took her time preparing for her conversation with the Thulians. However she approached it, it wasn't going to sound good. She said little about the exchange with Alek – it was almost as though she knew we had heard every word. But I could tell she was quietly simmering at being forced into behaviour she didn't agree with. She also knew she had little choice. It was the nature of her work, and it wouldn't have been the first time she had found herself in such a situation. It just seemed that this time, there was far more at stake.

In the event, Seraphina appeared to take the sudden travel ban quite well. Of course, it was always difficult to tell exactly how she was feeling, but on hearing that they would have further restrictions imposed upon them, she was as composed as ever. She also willingly provided Mum with her translation of their communications, which revealed nothing that wasn't already known. This, unfortunately, carried little weight with those determined to suspect the worst, but it was something. The tech experts had been working on decoding the messages ever since the Thulians first arrived on Earth – with their full co-operation and assistance – but still with no success.

I later discovered that Mum had told a lie to soften the impact. She told the ETs there was a suspicion that another attack was being planned, and therefore the increased security was for their protection. It was risky – no one had lied to them yet and it was unclear if they could somehow sense an untruth, as they had sensed mine and Shelley's presence once – but it explained their calm reception of her news. Also, she was following the instruction Alek had given, so he was hardly in a position to object to her methods.

What most of us didn't realise yet was that another, more underhand operation was being planned.

Chapter 32

There was something else that I sensed Alek would not have approved of. Instinct told me to keep it from my mother, too, partly because I didn't want her to be implicated, but also because I was worried she, too, would put a stop to it. I had sneaked in, on two occasions, to see the Thulians unaccompanied. Of course they were heavily protected and guarded around the clock, especially since the attack. But one day I had been walking back alone from the mess building, and had gone over to chat to Ben – the other guards must have been patrolling the other side. For some reason I was talking to him about our previous meetings with the ETs, and he had flippantly suggested I pay them another visit there and then. I rolled my eyes and laughed, sure he was joking.

"Seriously, they must go mad with boredom in there. And it's not like they don't know you."

"I'll get into trouble. So would you!"

"I doubt it. You're not exactly a threat now, are you. And who will find out?"

"What about the cameras?"

"They're only used when there are meetings. It's for their privacy."

And so in I went. The first time I crept in and stood at the edge, terrified they would be angry. But Sylvian had been there, and had turned around as though she had been expecting me, and just gave me the bowed head, palms together greeting. I returned it, but then turned and left, reluctant to intrude. The next day I went back, and was relieved to see Ben there again. This time he just winked at me, looked around and opened the door for me. And this time I stayed longer.

I stood close to the entrance again, as though waiting for a signal to go further in. It was their private quarters, after all. This time I saw them both, and they stood to greet me.

"Welcome," said Seraphina.

"Thank you. I hope it's all right to be here. I just… wanted…" I was painfully aware that it was the first time I had spoken to her completely alone. It felt strange; forbidden. If I thought about it, of course it probably was.

"Come and sit down."

"Really? I mean, I shouldn't get too close, should I?"

"We will one day leave here and travel elsewhere. Your doctors tell us we are no longer in danger of exposure."

I went over and took the seat close to her and looked around, seeing the cramped quarters from their point of view for the first time.

"I'm sure you'll be glad to get out of here." I said, and then remembered that they had just been told their release was to be delayed indefinitely.

"When it is safe, yes."

"But you just said it *was* safe?"

"We are safe from contamination. But there are still those who wish to destroy us." She spoke impassively, and it was difficult to know how they felt about being the target of strangers' hatred and mistrust.

"Yes. I am sorry about what happened."

Seraphina spread her hands. "We are unharmed. Some of your people were not."

"No. It must be difficult to understand us humans."

"This is why we are here. To learn and understand."

"You could be here a hundred years and still not figure us out!"

I meant it flippantly, forgetting humour was not well translated.

"We have much to learn."

"I just meant we're a bit strange. Humans, I mean. I don't think we even understand ourselves. I think you're amazing," I gestured towards Sylvian. "Both of you. You've already learnt lots of our languages, you know so much about our planet already. You make even our cleverest scientists seem a bit slow! Not that they are... I just..." I trailed off, feeling a bit silly for nervously chattering on. I sounded more like Shelley than myself.

"Thank you. We find humans very interesting. You nurture, you have strong emotions, you help one another. But you also destroy things around you, hurt and even kill."

I felt a need to stand up for the human race, to try and explain somehow, despite agreeing with her – we were contradictory, flawed beings. But weren't we just animals, like all the rest?

"Animals have to fight, and sometimes kill, to stay alive. To show they're the strongest, or to get food. Or defend themselves."

"Yes. But have your species not evolved from this? Placed yourselves above all other animals?"

I wasn't sure how to argue with that. But we chatted for a while longer, about lighter subjects – school, and books, and TV programmes I watched. They were surprisingly easy to talk to – and I included both of them in that, even though Sylvian wasn't actually speaking. She still seemed a part of the conversation somehow; I was sure she could understand every word. They were so, genuinely fascinated by everything I said – it was a new feeling. I felt like I could sit there and talk forever.

But I realised I might soon be missed, and didn't want to be caught and get either myself or Ben in trouble, despite his assurances. I had overheard Alek, after all, and feared being on the wrong side of him. Or worse, making things more awkward for my mother. I thanked them and left, but knew I had to try to get back and talk to them further. It was wonderful to see them without all the formalities and restrictions and monitoring that was always forced upon us.

Just a few days after her own conversation with Seraphina, and the same day as my second, secret one, Mum was bewildered to be called into a meeting to arrange another 'outing' for the ETs. It contradicted Alek's outburst at our house so much, she was at a loss for words. Although, not for long – if she had kept her frustration to herself at home before, she showed no such restraint this time. When she arrived back she was no clearer about what was going on than she had previously been.

"It makes no sense. Honestly, Faye, whatever job you end up with it always seems the people in charge are making it up as they go along. God knows what all that was about the other day when Alek came round."

I remembered the light in Seraphina's eyes when she had talked about travelling. "Isn't it good that they're letting them out again?"

"Yes, of course. But it contradicts what I was told. Worse than that, I've gone in there explaining they can't go out because... well, because they can't, and now I'm going to look like I don't have a clue what's going on."

This time, the Thulians were actually leaving the base for the first time. They were being taken out for a drive; a condensed tour of the Highlands that would take the best part of a day. There were strict rules to follow; they were under no circumstances to leave the car, and they would travel with an entourage of security and unmarked police vehicles. The trip was arranged very quickly, despite the complicated logistics behind it. Far quicker, in fact, than the simple walk around the base had been.

"It's almost like they're rushing it through," said my mother.

And yet, the arrangements this time were far more complicated. A large convoy of vehicles was ideally needed to ensure the Thulians' safety, however this would also draw unwanted attention from the public, the media and any more sinister forces. So a line of five vehicles left the base instead, a mixture of Land Rovers and other, more ordinary vehicles, with the only unusual features being the darkened rear windows and the missile-proof glass. The Thulians were to travel in the middle car, sandwiched between the other four.

Mum wasn't due to accompany them; instead Amy, as the chief doctor, was to travel in the car behind with a tablet to monitor their vital signs and ensure no health emergencies occurred. The rest of the cars would be taken up with security – I heard talk that the bodyguards that would be put in the car with the Thulians themselves had previously worked for the Royal Family, which impressed Shelley and me no end.

Another precaution taken was a second convoy, also of five vehicles, but this time containing only human passengers. A decoy, which would leave around an hour earlier and take a different route. We realised later what a huge operation it really was; hundreds of marines, some in camouflage and some in civilian clothes, all armed, lined the route at various intervals, blending in with their surroundings but ready to counter attack should the need arise.

There were no press outside the gates that day – and of course, no drones spying overhead. Interest in the prospect of another bomb (although never in the Thulians themselves) had slowly waned, but also Faiza, the ComET press officer, had struck a deal of privacy, so that at any time journalists and photographers could be banned from approaching within more than half a mile. As this took in the whole road leading to the base, they were not in sight when the odd motorcade departed. I had been aware of a distant beating, but nevertheless we both jumped as a large, black helicopter suddenly swooped into sight, following the cars as they swept out of the gates and disappeared up the track. This was to follow at a safe enough distance so as not to suggest it was to protect the innocuous-looking vehicles, but close enough should any danger appear.

As we walked back towards our house I heard another vehicle popping over the gravel and approaching the gates, and watched as it came to park close to the ruins of the Hub building. This time it was a black car, with blackened windows. It looked a little out of place, not being an off-roader, but I turned away without giving it much more thought, assuming it was a government official visiting Alek. It wasn't the first time someone important-looking had visited the fort. Besides, Shelley was already running off after declaring a race to the turrets, and I couldn't possibly let her win.

Although from the outside the Thulians' bunker was just an unremarkable concrete structure, and even though they spent the majority of their time inside, knowing they weren't on the base made it feel strangely empty. As though the whole point of any of us being there had gone. Which, I suppose, it had. Shelley seemed to feel as lost as I did, and we spent much of our time in the house catching up on schoolwork.

So when the cars came into sight at the gate again several hours later, I felt quite relieved. I watched the whole rigmarole in reverse, of the safe transference of ETs from the cars to the bunker, and then went over to chat to Amy.

"That was wonderful," she said by way of greeting. "It was quite nice to have a tour of the area for myself, too, as I've never been to Scotland before. It's embarrassing that I've been here so long, yet up until today I've only seen the scenery immediately around Fort Leigh!"

I was eager to know where they had gone and how it had been received by our visitors. I did see a copy of the report made by the ETs themselves of their day, the one they sent to their fellow Thulians up in orbit. It didn't, however, make very easy reading, being so dry, analytical and in places impenetrable:

'Day 39

Travelling in 3rd of 5 4-wheeled vehicles. Power: electric. 18 humans

Across bridge: 26.4 metres (m)

Solid surface, unpaved road: 473.56m

Surroundings: 1427 km² (approximate estimation due to speed of 64.45km/hour) tall plants 'trees', ranging from 12-23m in height

Informed there are 29 species of tree in this area (see appendix 3.4 for list)

Stems of varying thickness and hardness, able to withstand strong air currents (wind). No opportunity yet to test hardness and strength. Can be cut with steel (C + Fe) implement, material 'wood' (Wd)'

All this was before they had even travelled a mile.

"It's hard to say what they think," said Amy truthfully, "but I'm pretty sure they enjoyed the tour."

"Where did you take them? Did you go to the loch we went to?"

"No – we took them to Loch Ness, and drove around the edge, and then down to Fort William so they could see Ben Nevis. It's all just so beautiful, it reminded me a little bit of parts of my home state, New Hampshire. We wanted to take them through the Cairngorms too, but we thought we'd better get back as I wasn't sure how long the Thulians should remain seated in one position. It's not like it was safe for them to get out and stretch their legs, unfortunately."

"I'm so glad they got to go out though! It must have been awesome for them."

"I think so. I mean, I got the impression they really appreciated the tour. They've been desperate to get away and see more, so this was a consolation for your mum not allowing them off the base before now."

I was confused. "But that wasn't up to Mum! She wants them to be able to travel around. It was Alek who gave that order."

Amy gave me a fleetingly strange look, before changing it into a smile.

"Ah well… either way, today was a success."

Chapter 33

I wasn't sure what had woken me. I sat up in the dark, trying to clear my head of the grogginess of sleep. When I went to get out of bed and bumped my foot against the wall I remembered suddenly that I wasn't in my own bedroom at home. Shelley let out a snore in the other bed but didn't stir. Then I registered what had woken me: there was a long, steady droning sound like a distant alarm; a fire or intruder alert. Something was wrong.

I got out of bed and went down the stairs as quickly as I could without making too much noise. Outside the moon cast an unearthly glow on the buildings and the distant firth. I was only wearing pyjamas but there was hardly a chill in the summer air.

The sound was louder now – a two-tone high-pitched whine. It seemed familiar to me. It wasn't loud, but somehow filled the air, and it was impossible to work out where it was coming from. And then with a jolt I realised where I had heard it before: it was the voices of the Thulians.

I turned towards the bunker and ran.

More people were up, now – I could hear voices and saw two of the guards that had been stationed outside, standing in the shadows. The number had been doubled since the attack, to protect them and, apparently, us. The others must be inside. I crept closer.

"Back to bed now, Faye." I jumped – it was Ben.

"What's going on?"

"Nothing for you to worry about. Off you go, back to the house."

At that moment I heard Alek's voice from inside. Ben and the other guard turned around, and I hastily sneaked around the back to hide. The wailing sound seemed to be fading away, but it was still in the air, mournful and desolate.

"Something's riled them, that's for sure. Any idea?" I recognised Iain McGregor's voice.

"None." It was Alek. "Get Helen would you? We need to sort this out."

"I'm here," Mum's voice gave me a jolt – I didn't know when she had got up and come over. "I could hardly be sleeping through this. What is it that's troubling them?"

Before Alek could answer, the voices stopped abruptly, leaving a strange absence in the air. The grown-ups all started talking and moving off. I waited in the dark, listening to make sure they had gone.

Slowly I moved out of my hiding place. The door to the bunker was unguarded for the second time that day. I took one last look around, although it was difficult to see much in the shadows, and started walking towards the door. I wasn't sure what I was thinking of doing, I just wanted to see if the Thulians were all right.

"You can help us." The voice startled me. It was coming from just inside the entrance to the bunker, at the top of the steps. And it was unmistakably Seraphina's. I hesitated.

"Faye. Please, come here."

I felt my legs move my feet forwards without really giving them any definite instructions to do so. I blinked as I stepped inside. The lights here were always dimmed to protect the Thulians' delicate eyes, but even so it was bright compared to the night.

"Er – hello." I knew I should make my excuses and go back to my bed and pretend I hadn't heard anything. I thought of my sister sleeping, perfectly unaware. But those sounds had been so haunting; so full of distress. And she said she needed my help. So I stood there and waited to hear what she had to say.

They were both there, standing just inside, staring at me with those huge, searching eyes. Seraphina reached out a long fingered hand.

"We need your help, Faye. We are leaving here."

"What, now? But why?"

"It is dangerous for us here now. You must help us to get out."

"I can't do that – not without knowing why. Has something happened?"

"Someone came into the bunker while we were away. They took things. Tried to destroy things."

"What? Are you sure?"

I thought about Alek and the things I'd overheard. Was this the whole reason for the day trip that day? There had certainly been something suspicious about it: the speed at which the arrangements had been made; Amy's belief that my mother had been behind their extended confinement. Perhaps the Thulians were right to be afraid. Alek did seem to be losing his trust in them, and nothing my mother said to him had made any difference.

Suddenly I heard the voices of the guards approaching us.

"Quickly," I whispered. "This way."

I led them outside and glanced around quickly before running back towards our house. I couldn't hear if they were following me but kept on going. I knew that, when I got to the house, I would turn around and if they weren't there I would just go back inside, and act as though this had all been a dream. Perhaps it would have been better if that had happened. But instead I reached the front door, and turned to see them standing behind me. It didn't seem as though they had been running at all.

Some instinct told me to grab some supplies. I'm still not sure why – I suppose I thought the Thulians would need things: water, food, blankets. I picked up the bag we had taken the other day, still not unpacked, and threw an assortment of extra things inside. Just at the door I caught sight of our security passes, made for us on the night we arrived. They were lying on the kitchen counter, where we had left them. We had never used them – I wasn't even sure if they worked. I grabbed mine. Back outside, the two tall figures were still standing there, calmly waiting for me. Their strange skin seemed to absorb what light there was, so that they blended into the darkness.

"What do you need me to do?"

"Get us outside the gates."

"And then what?"

"We do not have time to explain. They will notice we have gone very soon."

265

I gave a sort of a shrug and a nod, and started walking towards the gates, keeping to the shadows. Apart from the odd guard, there was no one around. I couldn't understand where they had all gone – possibly to meet and decide what to do. Maybe Alek was explaining what he had done, and why. We made it there in good time, still with no indication that anyone knew they were missing, yet. At the main gate house I gestured to the Thulians to wait by the gate, but they were already there. I had no idea what was going to happen next – I hadn't had any time to think it through, but there didn't seem any way they could get out unnoticed. The gate was taller than them and, when opened, wide enough to let out a car, with a metal frame and a strong wire mesh.

"Hey, Faye isn't it?" I gasped and turned to see the guard at the gatehouse walking towards me. "What are you doing here, kiddo?"

Quickly I handed my card to the Thulian closest to me – I thought it was Sylvian. But I couldn't see how they could escape now. I walked towards the guard.

"I… I woke up. There was a noise."

"Aye, we all heard it," she said. "Don't worry, it's nothing for you to worry about. How did you end up all the way over here? Would you like me to walk you back to your house?"

"Um…" I looked towards the gate but the Thulians couldn't be seen. I thought I saw a slight glint that could have been one of their eyes, but other than that they were perfectly blended into the night. "Yes please."

I followed her, glancing back towards the gate every now and then.

"Here you go," she said when we reached the door. "Safe and sound. Will you be okay for now? I should get back to the gatehouse."

"Yes. Thank you..." her name suddenly came to me. "Tilly."

"That's okay. Sleep well, now."

She started to turn around before stopping, and looking at me with a slight frown.

"What's this?" Tilly touched the strap of the backpack. I had forgotten I was even carrying it.

"Oh! I just brought it... my teddies are inside!"

There was a pause while I contemplated the stupidity of what I'd just said. Teddies! There was no way she'd think I was such a baby as to believe that. But she smiled.

"Right! Okay then. You and your teddies had better go inside. Night."

"Night." I watched as she was swallowed up into the dim night, and then started to follow her at a distance. I still had that sense of unreality, as though I really was in a dream and not in complete control of my decisions. All I could think was that I needed to get the bag to the Thulians – they couldn't have gone far, and may need the supplies that were inside it. I waited as Tilly went back inside the house and started talking to the other guard. Then I crept to the gate. The Thulians weren't there.

I felt around the frame, trying to work out if they had opened it or found a way out. My fingers touched something hot and I snatched them back. There was a hole in the mesh – it was as though the metal had simply melted away. With one last look behind me, I bent down and carefully edged my way through the gap.

The first section of road was the short bridge, and I ran across, feeing exposed and visible. But then I came to the edge of the woods, and as I neared them I slowed down.

"Seraphina?" I whispered as I walked forward, my arms out in front of me to avoid walking into a tree branch. I kept whispering her name, and then just as I decided they must have gone out of earshot and that I should head back, I heard something. A rustle in the trees ahead.

"Is that you, Seraphina?" I had never been particularly afraid of the dark, but now I felt vulnerable; exposed. As though something could see me but I was blind.

"Faye. We are here."

I let out a sigh and followed the voice. They were both crouched by the side of the track, sheltered from view by a large oak tree.

"I forgot to give you the bag," I said, whispering as though we could be overheard.

I took it off my back and gave it to her. She held it, unsure what to do with it.

"It's got supplies in it; things you might need. Just in case you can't get any... seaweed."

"Thank you."

I sat down next to them. The ground was slightly damp and chilly. "Where are you going to go?"

"We know the land well. We are going to find shelter and stay out here now."

"But they'll be looking for you! And how... how do you know the land?"

"We were out here today. When they brought us. We can remember the terrain and have seen a lot of places we can go. We will hide."

"Why can't you just stay at the base? They'll let you out eventually, when they know you're not going to hurt us."

"It is too risky for us now. We were betrayed by Professor Ivanov. And others, we think."

"But... how can you be so sure? I know you said your stuff was damaged, but..."

"The professor arranged to take us out so that someone could go in and destroy our pod. To try to stop us communicating with our people. It did not work, but we detected the... sabotage."

"What was it? Were things actually broken in there?"

"Some inconsequential things. We could sense interference from others, damage that had been attempted by human hands. Attempts to use the devices without our permission or knowledge."

As I tried to take this all in and decide which question to ask first, Seraphina continued. "We were able to transmit a message tonight. It was the exit code, meaning that the others will leave Earth's orbit if they do not hear any more from us in an agreed time. Failure is looking likely for this mission, despite us finding a habitable planet. We were seeking information, but have found out all we can for now."

I didn't pay too much attention to this at the time – I was still considering the fact that someone had tried to sabotage the pod. What had Alek, and whoever he was acting with or for, been trying to achieve? We already knew their technology was far beyond our own. Later, with time to reflect, I went over and over it, and all the other things that were said and done over the following days. And I realised how significant it was that Seraphina and Sylvian were willing to risk being marooned here alone, with no way of ever returning. They were effectively fugitives as soon as they escaped the base, and must have known they were very unlikely to ever be able to speak to their kind again.

I thought about what I'd overheard Alek saying. He had seemed worried, a little angry even, but as dedicated and determined as he was, he didn't seem the type to resort to such underhand measures. But then I remembered the strange car I had seen just after the convoy had left the fort – the one I'd thought held some government official there to see Alek, but which had for some reason seemed strange and out of place. I knew then: I needed to tell my mother about it all.

"Will you both be okay out here? Alone? I'd better go back now." I stood up and brushed myself off, hoping I could find my way back in the dark.

Seraphina's companion had, until then, been watching me as we spoke. It was their way, and didn't unnerve me as it would have if a human did the same. But now she said something to Seraphina, the sound that had woken me earlier on, but much quieter now.

"We would like it if you came with us," Seraphina said.

I stared at her. "Come with you? But why…?"

Before I could finish, lights suddenly flooded the trees around us. Looking back towards the gates, I held up my hand to protect my eyes, dazzled by spotlights. Simultaneously an alarm sounded, a buzzing klaxon piercing the night silence. The Thulians melted into the shadows and I felt a tug on my arm as I followed them powerlessly.

Chapter 34

I had the sensation that we were running, but without my feet beating on the ground. While I was certain we weren't flying, still I couldn't explain exactly how we were moving. I felt the trees and the air rush past me, but I also felt the ground beneath me. I had no idea how long we were moving for; all I felt was that rushing sensation and Seraphina's touch on my arm, strangely cold. She wasn't gripping onto me, but I knew I couldn't have stopped myself – or them – even if I had tried.

And that was the other thing – I didn't try. I knew I was scared, and that I didn't want to be carried deeper and deeper into the woods, away from everything I knew, everything that was safe. But still I didn't try to resist, to yank my arm away, or even to shout for them to stop. Perhaps because I knew it would be pointless.

Finally I felt us slowing down. Gradually, until I did feel my feet running, and then we stopped. I sat down, expecting to be out of breath but not feeling tired at all. Neither were the Thulians. Still it took me a moment before I was able to speak.

"Why did you do that? You could have just left me there."

"We needed you to come."

"But why?" I looked at them both, staring back at me with maddeningly calm expressions.

"For protection. They have weapons."

I was confused. And then the realisation hit me.

"What, so I'm like a… human shield?" They didn't answer. "It's *me* they're looking for! That's why the alarms went off."

"No. Before that, they were looking for us. They were in the forest. We saw guns."

"Are you sure? Why would they be carrying guns? They're desperate to protect you."

"Not any more, we think."

I sank back against a tree trunk, suddenly feeling too exhausted to argue, or to wonder how and when the Thulians had managed to 'see; anyone, when I had been there the whole time. I wished that I had just stayed in bed. I could almost feel the covers around me, and realised I was shivering, craving their warmth. I imagined Shelley in the bed next to me, and then thought of my mother. I knew she must be frantic, if they had noticed I had gone and raised the alarm for me. I felt a surge of homesickness, and realised it wasn't for the house back at the fort, but for my real home, hundreds of miles away. Where I had lived safely and happily my whole life. I closed my eyes.

When I woke up, the sun was bright and I felt warm. I moved stiffly, and felt my mother's soft tartan blanket spread over me. As I emerged into consciousness, the previous night came back to me vividly. I couldn't have slept for very long; the sun was not very high and it must have been way past midnight when I fell asleep. I looked around for the Thulians but there was no sign of them. One of them must have laid the blanket over me as I slept; it was an oddly tender gesture. The rucksack was next to me. I pulled it over and rummaged inside for a water bottle.

"Good morning." I stared up at Seraphina, standing above me haloed by the sun. She had appeared suddenly, as though she had previously been invisible, which I thought could be possible. Nothing seemed to have the power to surprise me any more. "It is what you say to each other, is it not?"

"Yes. Good morning to you." I looked around. "Where is Sylvian?"

"Searching for food. We are not able to eat this," she gestured towards the bag. "You must have it."

"Thank you. But I'm not sure you'll find any seaweed in the middle of the forest."

"Good. We have had a lot of seaweed and would like something different."

"Oh!" Despite all the worry and disorientation, I laughed. "They thought that was similar to your food at home, so have been feeding you nothing else! Isn't it true that you only eat one sort of thing on your planet?"

"We do, but it is much more… delicious."

It struck me that it was very 'human', or even British, of them to politely eat food they disliked, without complaint.

"Do you miss your home?"

"We do. We know we will never see it again."

"But, why not? Surely you might do, one day."

"No. Even if we can get back to our craft, the journey is very long. We will not live for long here."

I let out a gasp as I remembered the vials they were meant to have daily to ensure they could get enough oxygen from our air. The doses had been reduced as they got used to our atmosphere, but I was still sure they needed it.

"Your medication!"

Seraphina turned her head away and leant a bit closer. I wondered at first what she was doing, but then realised she was showing me her neck. The three slits on the side of her neck seemed thinner now, just lines on the skin.

"Your gills… are they closing up?"

"Yes. As we adapt to your climate."

"But isn't that good?"

"It may mean we cannot leave."

"Oh. So you might have to stay here forever." I looked at her for traces of sadness, but couldn't tell how she was feeling.

What do you mean about not living for long?"

Sylvian appeared, as abruptly as Seraphina had, and so she didn't answer me. They really did seem to move soundlessly, and their blue-grey skin was perfectly adapted to melt into the silvery brown of the tree bark. Sylvian was holding some foliage in her hands and offered it to us both.

"Oh, moss. Or it might be bracken, I can never tell. No thank you, though."

I found a cereal bar in the bag and we all settled down to breakfast together, like old companions. I felt a little more at peace than I had before, perhaps because the sun was shining and the birds were chirping so fervently in the trees. It was a beautiful morning – I could almost have forgotten that I was with fugitives, and had more or less been kidnapped by them. That morning it didn't seem quite so dramatic or desperate. Deep down I must have known I was being naïve, but I felt that surely the army would be out looking for me, and would find me and then I could go back to the base, and let the Thulians disappear into the woods safely.

As though I had conjured it up with my very thoughts, the ground began to vibrate with the distant thud of a helicopter. The Thulians responded quickly – faster than it took me to register what the sound was. One of them grabbed me again and it was like the night before, running/floating/flying through the trees. Branches loomed at me and we dodged them at the last millisecond, my feet registered the roots and undergrowth but it was as though I weighed nothing and there was no fear of tripping or stumbling. In the daylight the sensation was even more disorientating, my brain was telling me we were moving at a great speed, but my body was relaxed. It was like we were ghosts; the everyday physics of gravity and motion seemed not to apply to us any more.

When we abruptly stopped I steadied myself on a tree, dizzy and dazed.

"I wish you'd stop doing that."

"It was necessary."

I sank down onto the ground. "Why don't you just leave me behind, next time? Surely you would be faster on your own."

"They will stop searching in a few days."

"No! I really don't think they will! My mum will be worried about me, desperate to find me. And you – you're both very important! They need you!"

"Not any more. If they find us they will kill us now, I think." Seraphina said this calmly, the way she said everything. There was no hint of fear or sadness.

"You said that last night. But why do you think that?"

"This is how humans are. You kill. Each other, other species. Even your own home."

275

"But there are good people. People who are kind, and who care."

"It is not enough." It felt like we weren't talking about the prospect of their own deaths any more.

"So, what's the solution, do you think? What could we actually do?"

"It is very simple. The dominant species must die out."

I met her staring gaze, looking deeply for a sense of meaning, or emotion.

"You mean… us?"

"It will happen naturally, but it may be too late."

"Too late?" I kept staring, and this time she didn't respond. A realisation crept over me. "So… what, you're just going to wipe us out?" Still she didn't answer, she just looked at me in that maddening way. Although I couldn't read her expression, looking into her eyes I saw no malice or hostility. And yet, there she was, casually telling me my whole species must die. She held my gaze and I felt that strange shiver I had experienced the first time I saw her.

Without putting any proper thought into it, I turned and ran.

Chapter 35

I had no idea where I was going. I could still hear the helicopter but it was further away now, and I couldn't work out which direction the noise was coming from. It was different this time – I was actually running, and it felt harder than it ever had before. Could it be that I had got used to that strange method of movement the Thulians used? Every time my feet hit the ground it felt harder, more solid and uneven than ever. Lifting my feet back up again was an effort, as though they were heavier. I could feel my heart hammering in my chest as I got more and more breathless. I wasn't even sure if I was going in the right direction, I think I just had a feeling that if I could find a clearing, I would be more likely to be spotted from the chopper. But there was no clearing – the trees grew thicker than ever. I was slowing down. I gave up and leant against a tree, looking behind me and expecting to see the Thulians standing there, watching me calmly. But I was on my own.

With a jolt I realised I didn't have my bag, and I couldn't remember if I had left it at our camp spot or just now. So I had no water, or food, or warmth. I had no survival skills – we barely left our air-conditioned home in our normal life, let alone learnt how to make fires or shelters, or forage for food. What was the point, when we would never need to?

I looked around and above me at the endless twisted branches and big bright green leaves hiding me from view, and it struck me as funny – no, hilarious – that there were so many trees, when that had been one of the things the Thulians had been worried about.

"Here they all are! Here are your trees!" I shouted, laughing crazily.

There was no answer of course. I was lost. In the middle of nowhere. While it was summer, it was still slightly chillier than at home, especially in the shade. What was I going to do?

And then a thought struck me. The Thulians could have easily caught up with me. More than that, they seemed to have a sense of what people were going to do before they did it – why hadn't they stopped me running in the first place? Were they just letting me go? Or were they somewhere now, watching me?

"Hello?" I realised that, rather than feeling unnerved by the thought, I actually wanted them to reply, to step out of the shadows. "I'm sorry for running away, you can come out now. Hello?"

But they didn't. I felt more alone than I had ever been. I *was* more alone than I had ever been. I sat on the ground and rested my arms on my knees, thinking about what they had said. What had they meant? Were they actually planning on killing us all? I couldn't see how – there were just two of them; they had no weapons that anyone had noticed. Even if they did, how could they kill the whole human race? Especially without harming any of the other species that were left. It didn't make sense. Unless that wasn't what Seraphina had meant at all. When I really thought about it, she was probably right. All the problems on Earth were caused by humans. Had we actually contributed anything to the planet, or had we just taken from it?

I held my head in my hands, thinking how ridiculous I was being. These were *people* they were talking about; my mother, my little sister, my dad. Everyone connected to someone else; a giant network across the globe.

I wasn't sure how long I had been there but I was starting to feel chilled, sitting on the ground. I stood up to move around and try to get warmer, but then it felt like it was getting darker too. I knew it couldn't have been night approaching yet, it must have been the leaves or clouds blocking the sun, but it added to my isolation. My stomach growled at me to remind me it was pretty empty, and I began to feel a bit desperate. Then I listened hard – I couldn't hear the helicopter any more.

I had no idea how long I sat there like that, but it must have been hours because the light actually was fading now as the sun sunk lower. Although I couldn't have had much sleep the previous night, and certainly not the night before that, I was too alert, and cold, to doze off now. And then I saw her. Seraphina, standing in front of me, again as though she had formed out of her own shadow. I wasn't startled by her sudden appearance; I felt no fear at all, only relief.

"How long have you been…?"

She didn't speak at first, but held something out to me. As I took it I felt the softness of the blanket, and wrapped it gratefully around me.

"Thank you." She sat beside me, and was so silent I would have wondered if I had conjured her up, if it weren't for the feel of the warm tartan wool against my cheek.

"Did you mean it? What you said?"

She looked at me, and I could see her eyes shining, beautiful in the night. Although it had been hours since we had spoken, she knew exactly what I meant.

"If your people carry on there will be nothing left." Her voice was musical against the silence of the forest.

"I know. But…"

"It is the only solution."

"I know," I said quietly.

Sylvian appeared beside us, as I knew she would. The three of us sat there in silence for a while. At one point I felt something pressed into my hands, and looked down to see Sylvian had placed some berries and other unrecognisable things into them. I smiled in thanks and began to eat. The food was surprisingly nourishing; the sweetness of the berries and the texture of the roots, or nuts, or whatever they were – I had no idea where they had found it all – filled me up enough to stop my stomach rumbling.

"Do not worry about your mother, Faye," Seraphina said softly.

I looked at her, waiting for her to explain.

"She knows you are safe."

"How?"

She looked at me with those huge, dark, expressive eyes.

"We sent a… message. I am not sure how you would explain it. We can project certain emotions, when we really need to. And so we have sent Helen a calm, reassuring signal, to soothe her mind."

"Just with your minds?"

"Correct."

"And… can you be sure it's worked? Over such a distance?"

"Yes."

I didn't really have any idea what they meant, but it did make me feel better to hear this. Perhaps they had sent their signal to me, too, somehow.

"It sounds like telepathy."

"Telepathy."

"Yes. It's what we call it when you can read people's minds, or communicate without speaking."

"So humans do this, also?"

"Hmmm… not sure. Some say they can, but many don't believe in it."

"And you?"

I looked at her. "I think I'm starting to believe in lots of things I never did, before."

Our second night was spent stretched out together, me lying in between the other two with the blanket over us. I slept surprisingly well, that night – perhaps out of sheer exhaustion from the mental effort of trying to make sense of everything. But also because I felt strangely calm and at peace. It was pleasant, spending time out there with those strange beings. I had never slept under the stars or even gone camping before, much less with two unexpectedly companionable extra terrestrials. I had no idea if Seraphina or Sylvian even slept – if they did it was only for a matter of two or three short hours, for they were always awake when I was. I remembered Ernst on TV telling us the ETs only slept for a short time. It felt like

281

another world and time, when I had been sitting on my bed at home watching that.

The next morning, Sylvian showed me how to forage for those strange plants she had given me the night before. Apart from the blackberries, most of the food was unfamiliar to me – some of the berries were sweet, while others tasted more bitter, but mixed together they seemed to complement each other. There were also some mushrooms, which I should have been wary of, but I completely trusted in Sylvian's instincts for what would sustain me without poisoning me. There were also several strange leaves and flowers she found for me; I had had no idea such variety of food existed for free, growing all around us like that. I didn't suppose many people did. I knew that Shelley would have been delighted by it all, and the thought made me feel anxious again.

"Can you tell my sister, too?" I asked Sylvian, forgetting for a moment that she didn't speak English. She looked at me, and I was amazed to see her nod gently. Not only had she understood my words, she had also known their meaning, despite my not explaining myself at all.

"Will she feel it too? The sense of calm, and know that I'm okay?"

Another nod, more pronounced, this time.

"Thank you."

That afternoon, we saw a deer. I wasn't sure who was more awed by it – even I hadn't seen one in the wild before, and certainly not so close. But Seraphina and Sylvian were transfixed.

We were sitting by another tree, something we seemed to spend a lot of time doing. It was strange at first, just sitting, not even speaking, and of course having no smartwatch or tablet to pass the time. At home I would have been bored silly in a matter of minutes, yet I felt no sense of restlessness at all. It's hard to explain what we were doing – it wasn't as deep or deliberate as meditation, it was simply taking in our surroundings. Listening to the wind rustle the leaves, hearing the different voices of the birds. Watching ants going about their work, flies buzzing between the trees. And because we sat there silently, the deer felt safe enough to wander up, casually chewing on grass and leaves, looking up at us now and then with curiosity rather than wariness. I held my breath, afraid I would startle it. I took in its soft, brown fur with the endearing patches of white around its mouth and tail, its huge ears twitching as it ate.

Then I heard a sound, and it took a few seconds to realise it was Sylvian. I was worried she was going to frighten the deer away, but a strange thing happened. The creature stopped tearing at the grass and looked right at her. She carried on making the sounds, and the deer watched her intently, as though Sylvian was telling her something interesting. And then, the deer 'spoke' back. Or at least, it made a series of thin, high pitched sounds. I gasped slightly and looked at my companions, who seemed no less delighted. Their eyes shone and they seemed to radiate happiness. The exchange went on for another minute or so, before the deer blinked its dark eyes slowly and retreated back into the undergrowth.

"You spoke to her!" I whispered, conscious the deer and its herd might still be close by.

"Yes," and it wasn't Seraphina who answered, but Sylvian herself. I grinned at her, feeling oddly proud that she had spoken English, as though forgetting for a moment that she had just conversed with another species.

"What did she say?"

"They greeted each other. Nothing much more complex than that, but it is very interesting that she understood," mused Seraphina. "It is something our compatriots would be interested to know…"

"You mean… the other Thulians? Up there?"

"Yes."

For a moment she looked sad, and it occurred to me that it wasn't because her facial expression had changed, particularly, but perhaps more that I was learning to read them, like when the deer answered them and they looked so happy.

"Are they too far away for the telepathy? Do you really think you'll never be able to communicate with them again?"

"Yes."

That night the moon, huge and bright, shone clearly through the trees.

"Is your moon as beautiful as that?" I asked in a whisper.

"We have two. They are smaller, and not as bright."

The days passed, and I continued in that calm, content state of mind. We fell into a routine, if you can call it that, of foraging for food and water in the mornings, and sitting serenely by a tree in the afternoons. We had several more 'visits' from various creatures, robins and red squirrels, several more deer, a couple of foxes, even a badger at one point, which I was sure had been declared extinct, at least in Southern England. There were only one or two more instances of 'speaking', though, and those only with the deer. The Thulians were keen to find out why this was – whether the smaller animals simply couldn't understand them, were too timid to talk back, or weren't advanced enough to communicate with other species in that way. The foxes and a couple of the squirrels did look as though they understood, or were interested in, what Sylvian was saying. It struck me as a huge wasted opportunity that they hadn't been able to take their longed-for trips to other parts of the world, where they could have tried communicating with larger, possibly more intelligent beings. They could have acted as go-between, given us more understanding of the animal kingdom than ever before. I thought of my nature documentaries, and how delighted the naturalists would have been with such an opportunity.

All the while we were travelling, slowly and steadily, deeper into the forest. I still thought about Mum and Shelley, of course, all the time, and hoped they were still sure of my safety. Although I knew I had to – wanted to – get back to them eventually, for now I felt a need to stay where I was, just for a while longer.

It occurred to me one morning, with a slight twinge of anxiety, that I didn't actually know how long we had been out there in the woods.

"I've lost track of time, I wonder how many days it's been?"

"6.4 Earth days," Seraphina answered calmly. I nodded, neither surprised nor concerned it had been so long. We hadn't seen or heard any sign that we were still being searched for, and it was easy to let myself imagine that they had called off the hunt, and were allowing us – or me – to return when ready. Despite the enduring serenity we seemed to live in, I did have an unwelcome niggle in my mind that, of course, that couldn't be true. Even if Mum wasn't feeling desperate, and was sure I was alive and well, she would still want to find me. And as for the Thulians – what would actually happen to them if Alek and the others caught up with them? Would they simply return them to their bunker and allow the project to continue as before? It was hard to believe, and besides, I knew the Thulians were unlikely to want that, now their trust had been broken.

Chapter 36

It was on the tenth day that something changed. When I awoke at daybreak, there was no sign of the others. I wasn't concerned, I just thought perhaps they had risen early to start the search for food. It was, however, unusual for them to leave without me. I started to hunt for firewood – more to pass the time, really, as it was warm enough not to have lit a fire for the past couple of nights, and we would only have to carry the wood with us.

When they appeared, they seemed different, somehow. Distant. I couldn't say how or why, it was just a feeling I had.

"I wondered where you were, when I woke up," I told them. Neither answered, and I told myself it was because I hadn't asked an actual question.

"Did you go and get food?" But their hands were empty. Seraphina shook her head.

"Faye, the time has come for you to go back."

It took me a few seconds to understand her.

"Back... to the base?"

"Back to your family. To your kind."

"But why now?" I felt conflicted. I missed my Mum and Shelley terribly, and despite the reassurances that they weren't worrying for me, I worried for *them*. And there was so much I had to share with them about our time here – with anyone who would listen. I felt I had learned more and grown up more in these few short days than I had in a whole year.

But there was also a part of me that didn't want these days to end. That wished for this calmness and simplicity to go on indefinitely.

"You mother is worried about you."

"Even with the... the signals you're sending?"

"Yes. They are no longer working. Something is blocking them."

"Blocking them? Like what? Are we too far away, or...?"

"No. The... telepathy works with anyone you have a connection with. Someone you have spent time with or who you..."

"Love?"

She looked at me, and I felt a sensation creep over me. It was as though I were thinking her thoughts, and she was experiencing some sort of realisation. I held her gaze, like a true Thulian myself, and it felt like she was allowing me access to her innermost feelings. A shiver ran through me and my skin tingled, like the first time I had looked into those eyes. So strange, and yet so familiar. She was beginning to understand – to feel – human emotions. And in turn, I was understanding her. That eerie magic, that voiceless communication I had witnessed between them.

Seraphina was telling me that my mother needed me. The communication was no longer enough – it was too vague a feeling for her to cling on to any longer, and now she needed clear evidence. She needed to see and hold me to really know I was safe. I nodded, and felt tears on my cheek as I pictured my desperate, frantic mother. It was as though I had suddenly woken from a dream. How could I have thought she would be calm, and accept that I had disappeared without a trace for all these days? Seraphina was right: of course I needed to get back.

"But how am I going to get back? I don't even know where we are."

"We will guide you."

"Thank you, but won't that mean they'll find you, too?"

"We will be cautious."

And so we began the journey back. There was none of the quiet ambling, pausing to look at various flora and fauna along the way, that had characterised the last few days. While we weren't quite speeding along at the rate we did on that first night, we moved swiftly and purposefully through the forest.

Just before dawn the next day, we reached a clearing. Seraphina and Sylvian sat down on the edge, still inside the treeline so they could stay concealed, but directed me to its centre. I turned to face them, realising we had reached the end of our journey together.

"Thank you Seraphina. Sylvian." I placed my palms together, closed my eyes and bent my head to my fingertips. I felt soft, cold hands envelop my own, and opened my eyes to see Sylvian had stepped towards me, and bowed her own head down to lay her forehead on mine. I felt a rush of joy – this was how the Thulians responded to their greeting. All this time we had simply been repeating it back to them, and now I was the only human on Earth who knew that this had been the correct practice all along. Seraphina and I repeated the gesture. Or perhaps it was just their way of saying goodbye? I swallowed back a sudden sob.

"Won't I ever see you again?"

Neither of them answered, but only looked down.

"Well, thank you for everything. I'll tell them all how you looked after me. And taught me things, and... spoke to the deer!" I was properly crying now, trying to speak though my sobs.

"I hope you can both be safe, and left alone."

"Thank you, Faye. You have also taught us so much. May you be safe and happy for the time that is left."

I stood for a moment, looking at them both, before Seraphina gently pushed me.

"You must leave us." And suddenly, they were gone.

And then I heard what she had heard. Soft voices, heavy feet.

I sat there wrapped in my blanket, waiting for the people to approach. It felt like an age before they emerged through the trees, shapes in the early morning gloom. Their footsteps sounded so loud after days of stepping lightly, like the Thulians. There were two of them; as they got closer I could see it was a woman and a man.

"Here. I'm over here." I stood up awkwardly, my legs stiff. The man reached out a hand to help me.

"Faye? Thank God. Are you hurt?" His voice sounded peculiar to me, strangely out of place.

"No, I'm fine."

The other soldier – for that was what they were, I could make out their camouflage uniforms now – nodded to him and he backed off a little into the trees.

"Are you alone, Faye?" asked the woman. I nodded. "My name is Jess, that's Andy. You're safe now." Andy came back and shook his head at Jess, as she sent a signal via something on her wrist, I assumed to tell everyone I had been found, alive and safe.

"We're going to take you back home, now," Andy told me. "But before we head off, are you okay to answer a couple of very quick questions?"

"Yes."

"Were the Thulians here with you this morning?"

I looked at him, and felt myself shaking my head. They exchanged a glance.

"When did you last see them, can you remember?" Asked Jess, her voice kind but urgent.

"I'm not sure. I'm sorry."

"Hey, that's okay. Let's get you back now."

They walked me through the woods, shining their torches around despite the growing light, as though they were looking for something. Jess was talking to me, to reassure but also, I thought, to assess my state of mind.

"You gave us all a fright there, Faye. Your mum is going to be very relieved to see you. That's all been a bit of an adventure for you, hasn't it. Are you thirsty? Would you like some water?" I took the bottle gratefully and gulped it down. It tasted sweet and delicious compared to the water Sylvian had been finding for us. As Andy moved the torch around I was looking, too, finding myself hoping that Seraphina and Sylvian had had enough time to get away.

We eventually got to a track where a jeep was waiting for us. I climbed up into the back seat, feeling oddly clumsy and out of place. Andy drove along the bumpy track for a while before turning onto a tarmacked road. It was completely light now, and the sun was an orange ball of fire peeping through the trees.

"How far away are we?" I asked.

"Not far now," answered Jess. "You were about five miles from the base."

I sat back, a million thoughts racing through my head. I wondered how far away we'd actually been, before we'd started back. And I tried to picture what the Thulians were doing now. Something told me they were safe, for now. Perhaps I was getting signals from them. Then I thought about Mum and Shelley, and realised I'd be seeing them in a matter of minutes. They must have heard the news that I'd been found, by now. A jolt of guilt hit me as I realised what Mum must have been going through, these past few days, while I was having a pleasant time gathering berries in the woods. I hoped she'd understand, when I explained it to her. I hoped I could find the words *to* explain it all.

I remembered my promise to Seraphina.

"They didn't hurt me, you know. They looked after me – they even walked me back to where you found me, to make sure I was..." I bit my tongue. I always was a terrible liar, and now I had given away the fact that the Thulians had, in fact, been close to where I was found.

Jess didn't acknowledge my mistake, but turned round and smiled at me. "That's good. But there's plenty of time to talk about all that, just relax now and we'll get you home."

And on cue, I recognised the white barriers of the bridge just up ahead. I felt strangely apprehensive at the reception I was about to get. And then I saw my mother, standing just apart from some other people, looking strangely small. My little sister clung to her side, watching the car approach.

They were at the door, pulling it open as I wrenched at my seatbelt. Mum didn't say anything, but wrapped me in a suffocating hug. Then I felt Shelley's thin little arms too, hugging us both so that I was sandwiched between them. I felt like I had been away living in the woods for months, rather than days. When they stepped back to look at me I was suddenly conscious of my filthy, torn pyjamas and wildly tangled hair, and realised I must look like I had, too. I knew I must stink. I hadn't noticed it while out in the forest; Seraphina and Sylvian certainly hadn't seemed at all dirty.

There was a group of people – only five or six, but it felt like a crowd – who all seemed to want to ask me questions at once. I recognised a couple of familiar faces but didn't really register them. Everything suddenly felt very surreal, as though it were this that was the strange part, rather than me vanishing into the woods for days. Mum stepped between me and them, and spoke firmly.

"Faye is going back to the house. I realise some of you need to speak to her, but she's coming home to bathe and rest. You can talk to her there, one at a time."

After thanking Jess and Andy, we walked back to the house, several others trailing behind. Mum ordered them to sit in the kitchen, and then brought Shelley and me up to our room. She crouched down in front of me as I sat on the bed, and stared at me. Her eyes were red and bloodshot. Shelley was still clinging to me as if she was afraid I might not be real.

"I know this is all very overwhelming, my darling. But Alek is going to need to have a quick word with you. I will be there with you the whole time, and you don't have to answer any questions you don't want to. Also – and I'm afraid this won't be very nice – but Amy is going to examine you, just to check you're okay. I promise I will stay with you then, too, if you want me there."

"Okay."

"Now, while it's just us, are you really all right?"

I nodded, suddenly feeling the urge to cry for the second time that morning. Mum reached up and hugged me again, and I felt my resolve leave me as tears rushed up to my eyes.

"It's all right, darling. You've had a terrible fright. We all have. But you're home now, with me, and I will keep you safe." She held me as I sobbed, Shelley's grip on my arm was even tighter. They thought I was crying through sheer fear, and relief at being safe. But, while I did feel relief, I was also crying for them; the ordeal they had been through. And for my friends and the thought I may never see them again.

"It's okay, Shell, you can let go now," I said, wiping my eyes.

"No way," she answered, wrapping her arms around both of us. I laughed through my tears.

"I'm okay, Mum, really. They didn't hurt me, I promise." Mum held me and looked at me again.

"Good. I had a feeling they wouldn't, but when they took you I just didn't know what to think. And you were out there for so long..."

"They didn't take me. Not really. I wanted to help them."

She stared at me for a few seconds, her gaze almost as probing as the Thulians'.

"Well, we can go over all that in a minute with Alek. The main thing is you're here now, safe."

Alek's questioning wasn't quick. He kept asking the same things, going over and over it.

"So Lieutenant Buchanan tells me he saw you by the bunker and told you to go home. You remember that?"

"He means Ben," said Mum softly.

"Oh… yes, I think I told you that."

"And then a few minutes later you were caught at the gates by Lieutenant Reid… Tilly."

"Yes."

"Doing what…?"

"I had some supplies I wanted to give Seraphina. In case she needed them."

"So you know about this, then." I tried to hide a sharp intake of breath. Alek was holding out the security pass I had given to Seraphina. He turned to Mum, who looked equally surprised. "It was found on the ground next to the damaged gate."

"Yes," I answered in a small voice. He said nothing, but waited for me to say more. "I thought they might need it to get out."

"So you knew they were escaping. Not only that, you helped them. Or tried to – it would have been no good to them. It's a child's pass. It doesn't work unless a guard at the gate authorises it. But you didn't know that, of course."

Mum stepped closer to me and took my hand, but said nothing.

"No." I felt rather pathetic, and thought I may as well tell him the rest – or some of it. "I met them both outside the bunker just after I saw Ben. Then I ran back here to get that."

"So at this point were you planning on going with them?"

"No. I mean – I didn't plan to go with them at all."

"So you were taken against your will?"

"No! Not really…"

"Alek, I think we need to let her have a break," Mum interrupted. "She's been through so much and I think she's getting a bit muddled."

"Right. Yes, I suppose that would work. How about twenty minutes?"

Mum scoffed slightly. "She needs food and rest, Alek. About eleven o' clock should be fine."

"I'm afraid I can only give you an hour – I'll see you then. Welcome back Faye. It's a relief that you are safe."

Mum sighed but didn't argue, and ushered everyone out of the door. I caught Amy's muttered words to her on the way out: "All fine, no visible bruises or marks and she's adamant she wasn't harmed." Mum nodded and smiled gratefully.

"Thank God for that, I thought they'd never go!" She smiled, leaning against the front door as though worried another tide of people would try to come in.

As Mum set to work making us all breakfast, I took in my surroundings, familiar and strange, all at once. The heat of the house felt oppressive after the days and nights spent outside,

296

and I pushed the front door back open, and the windows too, to allow what breeze there was to circulate. It was a relief to be home, in familiar territory with Mum and Shelley. But I felt separated from them, somehow, by my recent experiences. I wanted nothing more than to relay it all to Mum, but felt suddenly exhausted. I wished there was a way I could convey it to her without actually having to find the words: like the Thulians and their telepathy.

"Mum... you know you said you had a feeling I was okay? That the Thulians wouldn't hurt me? What did you mean?"

She watched me as she stirred mushrooms. "Well, just that, really. I was worried about you, and that got worse as the days went on. But knowing what I do about them, I knew they wouldn't deliberately cause you harm. What did worry me was that you'd become separated and might be on your own out there, scared and lost. We couldn't even track you because you'd left your watch..."

"But did you feel kind of... calm about it? Not as worried as you normally would be?"

"I... don't know, really. I did come out and look for you, you know. Several times."

"Did you?" I wasn't sure why but I felt surprised – I hadn't thought about her trying to to find me, even though I knew that's exactly what she would have done. But Mum misunderstood the reasons for my questions. She stopped what she was doing.

"Yes, darling! I hope you don't think I didn't care! I was frantic, especially..."

"It's okay, Mum! I know! I'm sorry – I was only asking because of something really amazing Seraphina said, and did."

297

And I told her all about their unique way of communicating. Mum was fascinated.

"That explains a lot! It was so strange, my brain was telling me my daughter was missing, and that I should be panicking, but even though I was worried sick I could still function, somehow. I slept well, didn't really lose my appetite. I'm so glad I know why, I thought I was losing my mind."

She served up the food – she had gone all-out. I looked at my plate, full of toast and beans, mushrooms and scrambled egg, and realised I was ravenous.

"Real eggs? Where did you get those?"

"Ben knows someone near here with chickens. He heard you'd been found and brought us these."

She called Shelley and the three of us sat in silence for a while, eating. I could tell they were both desperate to ask questions, but were holding back for fear of overwhelming me. It wasn't like my sister at all – I assumed Mum must have instructed her not to bombard me. But the food was fortifying, and I was as eager to share as they were to hear it.

"They're amazing, Mum. They knew how to look for food, and we all sort of communicated, in the end. Even Sylvian. I always thought she could understand everything."

It was like a signal for Shelley, and the questions began about what we'd eaten, where we'd slept – she wanted to know it all, and was especially fascinated by the 'magic' communication. Eventually Mum had to intervene, and my sister gave up and left the table.

"We would both love to hear all about it, when you're ready. But you're about to be grilled again by Alek, so you'll need your energy for that! Would you like a shower before or after? You should have time."

I put my knife and fork down, suddenly full.

"Mum, do you know why they ran, that night?"

"Well, that's something Alek's hoping to discover. Did they tell you why?"

"He knows!" I shouted out. "It was because of him!" Mum frowned, waiting for me to explain. "He sabotaged their pod, somehow! I think they were trying to stop them communicating with their kind, in orbit. That was why they were crying out in the night."

"What? How do they..."

"They just knew, when they got back after that day trip. The whole thing was a trick, Mum. A way to get them out so someone could go in there and wreck stuff."

She put her face in her hands as though trying to make sense of what I was telling her, but didn't say anything.

"He doesn't trust them, Mum. I don't think he has for a while. I could tell Seraphina and Sylvian felt threatened out there, like they were being hunted. But it's stupid, because if we let them, and worked with them, maybe they could help undo some of the damage we've done, or at least stop it getting worse? Seraphina was saying the problems have all been caused by humans, so the only solution was... well, for us all to die out. But I know she didn't mean it! She was probably just angry they'd tried to destroy the pods..."

Something in the corner of my eye made me look towards the open front door. There was nothing there, but I was sure I'd seen a movement or shadow.

299

"I'm not sure about that, either…" Mum was saying.

"What was that?"

She followed my gaze and got up to go and peer out of the front door. Her face dropped at whatever it was she saw out there

"Alek…" She muttered. And she suddenly ran out the door.

"Where are you going?" I called after her.

Shelley, who had been absorbed on her tablet in the lounge, came in. "Where did Mum go?"

I grabbed her by the arm. "Come on."

We didn't have to go far. Alek had obviously been on his way over, and it looked like he and Mum were arguing. We stopped several paces away, cowed as much by Alek's calm, authoritative tone as by the anger in Mum's voice.

"…Basically tricked them!"

"It wasn't like that, Helen. We needed to gain back some control of the situation."

"Oh really? And how 'in control' are we now? You don't even know where they are!"

"We'll find them, sooner or later."

"And then what? Because Seraphina is pretty convinced they're both going to be killed."

"Is that what she said to your daughter? What else did she tell her?"

"That doesn't matter right now, Alek. I want to know the truth, for once, because you've obviously been making some pretty shifty, top-secret decisions. I thought it was odd, suddenly arranging an excursion for them! How stupid was I, trusting you."

"Now, come on…"

"So are you going to kill them? Is she right? Because I trust her instincts more than yours, right now."

"That's completely up to them, and how they respond when they are found."

"How are you expecting them to respond? Lasers shooting from their eyes? Because they have nothing out there, Alek, no supplies – certainly not any weapons."

"Are you sure about that?"

He looked around, suddenly aware they were being overheard. Quite a crowd was gathering – a few of the researchers were edging forward awkwardly, unsure whether to intervene. But just as my mother was about to respond, we heard engines. A long convoy of army vehicles started to drive out of the gates; jeeps and armoured cars, even a truck, all packed with people in camouflage. We could see many of them were armed.

"What's happening?" asked Mum. "Are you mobilising the army?"

"They're already out there searching for them."

"Yes, but this looks like a lot more than a search party."

"Sir," one of the soldiers called to Alek as he walked over. "Operation Buzz is underway."

"Thank you Jack."

"Buzz? What's Operation Buzz?"

Alek looked at my mother, and then turned to me and held my gaze for a second or two. An anxious shiver chilled me, despite the heat of the sun. And then he walked away.

Chapter 37

"Mummy, what's happening?" Shelley asked on repeat, following her about as she marched back to the house and began turning it upside down looking for things.

"Not now, darling," she muttered. I tried to occupy my sister with her toys, even offering to play with her, but she knew as well as I did that things had escalated. Although, I wasn't sure she knew exactly how. It was clear to me: they were going to capture and kill the Thulians. From the grim set of her mouth as she opened cupboards and banged doors, Mum seemed to be of the same mindset.

"Mum, what are you going to do?"

She paused for a second.

"Do you know where the bag is?"

"The backpack? I... took it. It's in the woods somewhere."

"Of course. It's okay, I'll just use my pockets."

From the cupboard under the stairs she fished out an old wax jacket that I'd never seen before; it was huge on her.

"Someone must have left it behind," she said. "It'll be just right."

"Mummy, what's *happening*?"

She finally stopped and turned to us both.

"I'm worried they might try and hurt Seraphina and Sylvian, sweetie. I'm going to try and find them both, before the army does."

Shelley started wailing at the first part of it, and the second was addressed to me.

"So they were right to be afraid?"

"I think they were in danger the moment they escaped. Now there's the belief they pose a threat to us, too."

"Then... it's my fault."

"No, darling, it's not. They would have escaped even if you hadn't been there."

"But I distracted the guard. I helped them get away."

"It doesn't matter. I think they would have found a way anyway. That stupid sabotage destroyed their trust. Besides, there's more to it now."

"What do you mean?"

Mum sighed. "Alek overheard us just now, talking about what Seraphina said about humans needing to die out."

"What? So does he think they want to kill us all? Because of what I said?"

"Not because of what *you* said, Faye. Because of what Seraphina told you."

"But she didn't mean it like that! And now everyone knows what she said, and it's put them in danger!"

Mum held me gently by the shoulders.

"None of this is your fault. But I need to help them now. Can you remember roughly where you were when you were found?"

"No, we were miles away though. About five, the soldiers said. It took a while to get back."

"That's okay, I'll take a car. No one will notice in all the chaos."

"Mum! Listen to me. I don't even know which direction we went in! I wasn't paying attention."

"It's okay, I can ask Jess, or Andy, or someone else will know. You told them the Thulians had walked you back, so they can't have gone too far. And Alek knows that, too."

"Please don't go. The army is out there with guns!"

"Exactly, that's why I have to find the Thulians. Before they do."

"Mum... isn't it the Special Forces? No offence, but they're a bit more highly trained than you. How are you going to get to them first without being hurt yourself?"

"I'll be careful. All I know is that I have to try. And you're right, they *are* highly trained. They're not going to mistake me for a seven foot alien."

"It's not funny."

Mum crouched down and hugged us.

"It's broad daylight, I'll wear bright clothing. Look!" She held up a hideous bright pink cap she'd found in the same cupboard.

We stood at the door and watched her go, looking slightly odd in her oversized jacket and lurid hat. It was hardly inconspicuous, but she was right. There was too much going on for her to be noticed; the threat was deemed to be outside. She climbed into a spare Land Rover and drove out through the gate, which opened when the scanner recognised her face.

"It's okay, Mummy will be fine," Shelley reassured me, and I had to hug her for being the bigger sister yet again.

But it was a fraught wait. All the grown-ups were preoccupied, and no news filtered through to us. It was as though Shelley and I had been momentarily forgotten. Around an hour after Mum left my heart and stomach gave a sudden, unpleasant lurch. I ran to the toilet, sure I was going to throw up my breakfast. I felt breathless as my heart thumped painfully. Leaning my head against the wall and breathing deeply as the beats gradually settled back down, I knew the panic and uncertainty must be getting to me. I went outside to breathe in some fresh air. Dark clouds were gathering, momentarily blocking the sun and promising another dramatic, fiery sunset that evening. But all I could do was will the Earth to slow down for few hours, to give Mum enough light to search by, and my friends the chance to get further away.

But we didn't have to wait until sunset. The sun was still high in the sky when everything started happening at once. Crunching over the stones, the vehicles started to return in a broken up convoy. We ran outside to look, scanning them for the car Mum had taken. Soldiers and scientists were milling about, going in and out of the gate house and the replacement lab building. Faces were stern and set; difficult to read. I saw Amy and ran up to her.

"Doctor Ling! Have you seen my mum?"

She gave me a hug which both surprised and worried me. She had always been kind to us, but in a reserved way. She hadn't ever hugged me before, and it gave me a sick feeling of foreboding. She eventually released me, and it was as though she had only just realised I had asked a question.

"Your mother? Isn't she here?"

I let out the breath I had been holding. While I had been hoping for news, the fact that Amy didn't even know my mother had left the base meant that she also didn't have bad news about her.

"No. She went out to try and help the Thulians. To protect them from the army."

"She... what?" I studied her face properly for the first time since she had come over to us. Her eyes looked haunted, as though they had witnessed something shocking. Her hands were on my shoulders and I could feel them quivering.

"Amy... you're shaking! Come to the house, I'm sure Mum won't mind me using the kettle to make you some tea."

She allowed herself to be led towards the house, Shelley and I on either side. It was as though we were the grown-ups, and it was hugely unsettling. Every adult on the base was specially trained and educated, at the top of whichever game it was they were in. And yet, here we were, guiding one of them along as though she were an invalid, shell-shocked by some terrible event I dared not think about. At the time I was mainly consoling myself that it didn't have anything to do with our mother. She was still out there, somewhere. Perhaps in some sort of danger or perhaps making her way back to the fort right now. Either way: at least whatever had shaken Amy like this had nothing to do with my mum.

I looked back to check the doctor was steady on her feet, and something over her shoulder caught my eye. It was the larger of the trucks, an ugly old thing with a bulky cab and canvas-covered trailer, rumbling back through the gates. I stopped to watch, and even now I don't know why I didn't just turn around and keep on walking into the house. Because if I had, the thing that I saw wouldn't be forever branded into my mind. As the truck parked, several military personnel surrounded it. I could see the canvas coverings being pulled back, and then Alek appeared with a couple of the other scientists to help them drag something out. I think I knew before I saw it. In fact, I think I knew as soon as I saw Amy's face. A stretcher, not long enough for the thing it was bearing, covered crudely with a mixture of tattered tarpaulin and rough blankets. As it was dragged out of the back of the truck I saw the awful sight of two, long, graceful legs hanging lifelessly off the end. The large feet with the odd, gecko-like toes. The once blue-grey skin now a sickly shade of deep green.

I wasn't sure who started moving first, but my sister and I were both running towards the truck, shouting. Shelley had realised at the same time as me, I thought later when I went over and over it in my head. I had felt her hands clinging to me, heard her calling out, but I hadn't registered it until hours later. She got there slightly ahead of me and grabbed the blanket that was covering the end before any of the grown ups could react quickly enough to stop her.

There she was, her large, expressive eyes closed forever. My friend, Seraphina. I wished I could have said that in that last glance she was as graceful and beautiful as ever, but awful wounds disfigured her face and body. Her blood, thick and dark, covered her upper body and parts of her face. Bullets had shattered her skull. Too late, I shielded Shelley from the sight as we turned away, but not too late to see the second body being lifted from the truck. Both of them. Eliminated in an instant. All for the crime of being curious, and concerned, and clever.

Chapter 38

The news escaped quickly and the public reaction was instantaneous and strong. There were marches in cities around the world; crowds of people expressing the anger and disbelief that we also felt. Some marches became out of control, violent even. It was reminiscent of the protests from months before, when people on the other side, who wanted no part in accepting the aliens, made their voices heard so strongly.

Those on the other side of the debate were not silent now, either. More sickening in some ways even than the murders themselves – because 'murder' was how I and many others saw it – was the reaction of the so-called planet protectors, whether the more militant or peaceful branch I didn't care. They partied in the streets, waved flags and banners, hugged each other and danced around. Celebrating the brutal deaths of these harmless, gentle people I had come to think of as friends.

And it became clear, in a matter of days, that we had been right: the Welcomers and the majority of the soldiers and scientists; Amy, my mother and sister and I. Because as we were still reeling from the actions of the people right there on the base, who had been following orders from our very own government put under pressure from the likes of the planet protectors and the more hostile cities and countries around the world, there was news that stunned us all. The other pods, having hovered patiently and silently above our planet for so many months, simply disappeared. I read the headline, and with a jolt recalled Seraphina's words about the agreed exit signal. They had sent the pods away themselves.

The Webb telescope scanned the vast abyss of space for signs of the other Thulians, but with no success. Even the main ship, which had been identified somewhere in the vicinity of Mars just a few weeks previously, was nowhere to be seen. Communications were sent out into the ether to be met with silence. It was as though the Thulians had never existed, but had all been a strange mutual vision, dreamt up by the entire human race.

The disappearance did little to appease those partying in the streets. Still they refused to believe the aliens had had good intentions. Rumours were still strong that the others were biding their time, simply gathering strength before returning with force. To attack us properly, this time. Many of those that had fled to underground bunkers remained in them, just in case.

My mother began preparations to leave the day after the murders. She had returned to the fort less than an hour after we had witnessed the bodies being brought back. By then we were in the house with Amy, and although I wasn't sure then how Mum had discovered the news, it was clear that she knew. She was as upset as we were, but also bitterly angry. On top of the great loss, it struck her that her role there had been pointless in the end. After all those weeks of smoothing things over and keeping the communications cordial and peaceful, ultimately she had been overlooked. Overruled: ignored. I think it was in that moment that she lost a lot of her passion for her work; it was certainly the last big assignment she was ever involved with.

We were booked onto the shuttle train from Inverness the day after that, and Shelley and I spent our last hours wandering about, trying to both imprint the place on our minds and recall the feelings we'd had when we first arrived. We walked the battlements and explored the old nooks and crannies we had discovered and come to think of as our own. But instead of running about, shouting to each other and inventing games, we walked slowly. Running our hands along the ancient walls and staring out over the unforgettable hills. The mood around the place was sombre, as it had been after the death of Ernst. But this time it felt even worse: while Ernst's death had united us and given us purpose, now many people were packing up, some had already left. It was quiet. There was no buzz of activity, no sense of urgency or feeling that important work was being done, ground breaking discoveries made. The project had died with the Thulians. All the remaining samples and data was being collected up and taken away by some government officials, taken no one appeared to know where. It didn't seem like anyone was asking.

Added to the insult was what happened to the bodies. Mum had tried to push for a decent burial, perhaps in the hills they had gazed at so many times. But even her pleas were slightly half-hearted. Sure enough, just the day after they died, at noon, a sinister-looking vehicle resembling a giant hearse, with blacked-out windows, arrived to take the bodies away. Taken for further testing and experiments; subjected to further trauma and indignity, no doubt. Shelley and I watched as the caskets were loaded in like cargo and driven away.

My sister and I found ourselves wandering towards the bunker. I didn't know why – perhaps I felt I needed to see it one last time, although I knew I dreaded going inside and finding it empty. But when we went inside it was worse than we could have expected. It had been stripped bare, anything deemed useful to research packed up and taken away, the rest just discarded. There were no seats, no sleeping areas, no research areas. It was just a bare concrete room. Again I had that sense of unreality, as though none of the events of the past few months had happened at all.

We said our farewells with regret and sadness. The end of the whole experience was not only tragic, but premature. There was a sense of limbo. Many of these people had set aside several months of their lives to dedicate to this unique and world-changing project. Said goodbye to their families and resigned themselves to relationships via the wall. And now they were all going home, many of them feeling they had failed; let down the visitors in the very worst way.

There was no sign of Alek, on that last day. He was around, so we heard, but kept himself hidden; many said, wisely. I indulged in a fantasy in which I ran up to him and shouted, venting all the fury and frustration I felt.

"You didn't even succeed, you know! In damaging their pod. They knew you'd tried, in your sneaky little way, but they still transmitted one last message."

Of course I never did, and never would have, but it was oddly satisfying, imagining his startled expression and my hands clutching at the lapels of his shirt.

As a ten-year-old child who felt powerless and betrayed by many of the adults in control, I thought I hated him. But, as time has passed, and as I have talked it over with my mother many times, I have come to realise that he was doing what he felt was right. He was just following orders from above, from people he supposedly trusted to get it right. No one successfully holds a position of power who bows down to pressure or tries to please everyone beneath them, I suppose. I never saw or heard about him again, and I have often wondered if he regretted his role in the events, or if he stood by his decision as the right one. The governments behind it certainly continued to try and justify themselves, speaking of 'viable and immediate threat', and 'acting in the best interests of planetary security'. But none of those empty phrases bore any relation to the events I witnessed that summer. I suppose I am in a rather unusual position though; I actually lived among the Thulians, spoke to them, saw them living and breathing. Most of the world leaders who decided their fate had never even met them.

Chapter 39

We gradually learned what my mother witnessed and discovered, that day the Thulians were killed. Not straight away, not even all in one go. But eventually. The train journey home was mostly in silence. We slept, stared at our tablets or out of the window, half-heartedly made plans to meet our friends. But we barely spoke. I think like me the others were exhausted – Shelley couldn't even find the enthusiasm to point out any of the sights that flew past the windows. We were drained; of emotion, energy and motivation for anything much at all. This feeling followed the three of us for several weeks after our return. We all went through the motions, returning to school and work, talking to people when we had to. But it was as though we were hollow inside.

Frankie noticed. She was there to greet us as we got off the train, and she hugged each of us tightly in turn. Mum had been telling her everything, from the day the bomb fell, and so no words were needed. It was a comfort, her just knowing. She became our rock, just as she always had been, really. Quietly helping out where it was needed. There was an unexpected moment of lightness when we first stepped into the house, when the sight greeted us of a somewhat lurid blue and pink tartan design on the lounge feature wall. Mum laughed.

"Oh! Wow. I didn't even know we had that in the catalogue!"

"I found it and couldn't resist! But... I'll change it back..." Frankie picked up the controller, but Mum stopped her.

"No way, we're keeping it for at least a week! I wouldn't want to offend you!" Mum hugged her friend, and I heard her say "I needed that! I've missed you."

When we first arrived back at the compound there was another, less welcome surprise. A small knot of reporters were gathered just outside the gates, but we barely even looked at them as we drove through. When I occasionally glanced out of my bedroom window over the next few hours I saw them drift away, one by one. I was grateful that Mum had kept my 'disappearance' out of the news at the time, not because she wasn't frantic, but because, with the army searching for me, there was no need to involve the press or even the police. I knew now that, if those journalists knew half of the story, they would have been rather more persistent.

The 'official' story about the deaths came out in the news over the following days, and I was shocked, but possibly not surprised, that the claim was self defence. It wasn't clear who released the version of events, but there had been, according to the reporters, a 'genuine feeling of threat'. The way this was communicated to the marines in that forest wasn't revealed at first. But then it gradually came out that they had seen a change in the Thulians, a 'warning sign of attack' in the form of a vivid change in colour, from the gentle blue-grey to the dark green that I myself had seen on two occasions, and that had been noted by the doctors the first time the ETs had been examined.

"It was a sign of fear!" I called out to my mother. She looked at me, and I didn't have to say any more. She called Amy on the wall.

"Yes!" Amy exclaimed when we told her. "Ernst and I were working on that theory before he... before he was killed. He'd noticed it too, that their skin tone darkened when they were anxious or under stress. It was green when they arrived here on Earth, then faded when they became more acclimatised. We worked out they must have experienced high levels of anxiety and fear on landing – naturally. Hence the darker skin, and it seems like it happened again when they fled with you, Faye. We didn't ever get the chance to present our findings, and then with everything that happened it didn't seem to matter any more. But now... I've got to set the record straight. We can't have people thinking they were aggressive after all."

We finished the call with gratitude, and promises to visit and call each other often. Although it didn't change anything, and possibly wouldn't have even if Amy and Ernst had been able to mention it sooner, at least it would mean the truth, or some of it, was out there.

That was when Mum started to tell us what had happened. She had followed some inner instinct, that day, to find the Thulians. We wondered if it had been the telepathy guiding her. As we were discussing it I was reminded of the strange attack of nausea I'd had, and the unpleasant thumping of my heart, and I realised that must have been it. The instant they were killed.

"Sylvian had come out into the clearing, probably to check you had been safely found, before she and Seraphina disappeared again," my mother told us. "But the search drones were able to lock on to their location, as soon as Jess and Andy gave the signal you were with them. I've got no idea if they were aware the drones were following them, but I can't imagine they didn't. Perhaps they gave up running. Because when the command came through from Alek..."

"Operation Buzz?"

"Yes. When the marines received that, they didn't have far to go to find them."

"Did you… did you see them get killed?"

"No. But I heard the gunshots. So I can't have been far away. Amy saw it all, I hadn't realised. She talked her way into the guard room at the base and watched it all on the screen. She said she knew, too, that something was about to happen."

"That's where she'd been when we saw her."

"Yes. It was an awful shock for her to see it all like that and not be able to stop it. She'd known, like we had, that there was a threat to their safety, but I don't think any of us really believed they'd just kill them, in cold blood like that."

"But didn't they think there was a risk? Because they didn't know about the skin thing?"

"I'm afraid I don't believe that for a second. It may have been the justification Alek and the others used, but those marines were sent out there with one purpose: to kill."

317

Chapter 40

Life gradually tried to return to normal, although we had forgotten what that meant. We were glad to be back in many ways; I hadn't realised quite how much I had missed Daisy and Aaron. Even the routine of home life was comfortingly familiar – getting up to work at home or to get on the bus to school. It was as though my other life for the past few months had been an aside; a departure from reality. But I came to realise it was the opposite.

My friends were bursting with questions, on that first day back. They had been incredulous when I told them where we had really been, not overseas with my father at all but in one of the most famous places on Earth, by virtue of its strange inhabitants.

It had been arranged that I go back into school at my first opportunity so that I could endure a day of testing and assessment to check just how far behind I had fallen, despite having completed several online exams over the past few weeks. And Daisy and Aaron were waiting for me at the bus stop. Their eager greetings were a surprisingly welcome tonic, an antidote to the heaviness that had plagued me since my journey home. It was nice to fall back into easy conversation with them, and to answer all their questions about life with the Thulians. Talking about my friends, giving them humanity and emotions beyond the robotic beings everyone assumed they had been, had a healing effect. They were even quite sympathetic and understanding, as far as they could be. But as their questions were answered and their attention drawn back to 'real' life, I felt a dissatisfaction I didn't quite understand. I wanted to talk about it, constantly. I found myself asking about their life and hearing their responses, but it was difficult to express a real interest. It wasn't that I felt my experiences were more important or interesting than theirs. Not really. More that I found it impossible to muster up a real enthusiasm for all the things I used to care about so much. It created a distance between us that wasn't immediately obvious.

It felt as though it was this life, the one that had been mine and so real to me, that was the fake one. Here we were, going about our mundane practices, eating, sleeping, working, ignoring. Ignoring the truth that was all around us. We were consuming and creating faster than the planet could manage. We had killed the very beings that could educate us, and try to save us from it. And yet here we were, carrying on as usual, hiding from the truth because it was easier to do so. It was just as Mum had said when I had quizzed her about the way these problems had been recognised and then ignored, way back when it had been possible to stop it. I was as guilty of it as the rest of us. It took me a few weeks of adjustment to even realise.

One morning, over breakfast, I watched my mother and sister, going about their routine just as they had before. Mum caught my eye and gave me one of her looks that told me she saw me. Inside me; read my deepest thoughts. Even if she didn't completely understand them.

"You've been very quiet, lately."

"I suppose so."

"Do you want to talk about anything?"

I shrugged. "I wouldn't really know where to start."

She stood up in her decisive way.

"I know what we'll do. Let's do what we did before and go out for a walk – maybe by the coast. Where was that place Frankie took you?" She picked up her tablet.

"But I've got school work to do…"

"You'll get it done. I think we all need to clear our heads."

And so we found ourselves at that spot again, where we stood on the cliff top and beneath us the sea stretched out forever. It was reassuringly unchanged; even the weather was the same. The sun warmed us from the wide blue sky, dotted with fluffball clouds. The wind was strong but warm.

We climbed down the steps that had once led to the beach, until we reached the fence that had been put up where the cliffs were eroded and the old beach hidden beneath the waves. Mum found a comfy spot in the thick grass on the hillside and beckoned us to sit either side so she could put an arm around each of us.

"Here we are. Things always feel better with a view like this."

"I love it," murmured Shelley, shuffling closer into Mum's protective shelter.

But as I looked around me all I could see was the destruction. I couldn't help it; I saw the beauty of it, but it seemed to make it worse somehow. The remains of the beach could be glimpsed below the low tide, and debris clung to the cliffs where it had been washed up by an ocean too polluted to swim in. The detritus of human life.

"Why are we just carrying on? As though nothing has happened?"

Mum squeezed me tighter.

"Because sometimes I suppose it's easier."

"But it's not, though! Is it?"

"Not for everyone, no."

And that was it. For once my mother seemed lost for anything to say to make it all seem better.

It was less than a year after we had lived at Fort Leigh when the news reports started to warn us. Even I had begun to settle back into life, although I had never forgotten Seraphina, or her words. I still felt cast out from most other people, not deliberately so, but more through choice. My friendship with Daisy and Aaron had faded away – I hadn't noticed it happening at first, but then we saw each other less and less until I struggled to remember the last time. I had started at a new school and hadn't made any firm friends yet. It was difficult to show enthusiasm for the things that excited the other kids: the newest gadgets or apps or platforms. The latest posts from whichever celebrity. It was all empty to me. I had never been particularly interested in these things, but now as I got older it seemed to take on a new significance for so many. The ones that had interests beyond this bubble were either in the tiniest minority or hidden from me, too afraid to speak up.

And then the news came. I still took an interest in it, keeping an eye of my news app every day. It was certainly true that I was looking out for information about the Thulians. Not obsessively, but hopefully. A mention of any strange signals, perhaps, or even a sighting of the craft in our solar system or beyond. Any indication that they still existed, still had hope for our planet and its flawed inhabitants. But the news stripped that away.

It was a Breaking News banner that caught my eye, trailing across the bottom of the screen when the reporters were talking about something else. 'Scientists express alarm at sudden fall in the ocean's oxygen levels.' It was something that many would probably miss, or ignore. I would have done the same myself, just a year or so before. But I searched for more information, and saw footage and images of dead sea creatures floating lifelessly in oceans around the world. These weren't new to me – for years we had seen more and more whales becoming beached, or creatures that had choked on the multitude of plastic or chemicals that filled the sea. But this time it was the sheer volume of the creatures – boats were shown wading through carcasses of every sea creature I could name and many I couldn't. Thousands and thousands of fish, turtles, dolphins, I could even see some octopuses in there. More animals than I knew even remained in the ocean. And, we were informed, this was a gauge of things to come. The oceans were like litmus paper for the rest of the planet. Once things began to go wrong there, it was only a matter of time before it happened on land, in the air around us. The planet was running out of oxygen, and alarmingly fast.

It hadn't been the only stark warning dealt us lately. The last of the Arctic ice had finally melted away, and with it the global temperatures suddenly soared. We knew the planet was hotting up – that had been news long before I was born. But now the problems suddenly accelerated. The rise in sea levels meant rivers had burst their banks worldwide. Smaller coastal towns had been wiped off the map, many bridges simply washed away. A record number of displaced people sought shelter, having been made homeless by flooding and landslides, or fleeing drought and famine. Summer in the southern hemisphere had brought with it fiercer, faster and wilder fires than ever before, devastating huge swathes of land and taking people and wildlife with it. Even where the fires didn't burn, there were deaths from heat exhaustion and dehydration. Crops worldwide had already been suffering – this year was set to be worse than ever, causing further famines across the globe. It was bleak news, echoed by my father who was seeing it all first hand.

Summer was on its way to us, perhaps with less extreme heat than experienced elsewhere, but with the same hazards. Mum mused about a time when she used to look forward to the summer, not dread it. With the news now about the falling oxygen levels, it felt like a large invisible shadow was creeping closer.

Even the experts interviewed on the news were at a loss as to what to say.

"This level of devastation, and the implications it brings… none of this was meant to happen yet for a… a generation or more," one scientist told us. It was a fact repeated daily. This had taken everyone by surprise.

There were adverts for air conditioning units – O2 Boosters – that also regulated the oxygen levels in buildings, and my dad convinced Mum to get one installed early on. She admitted to feeling a bit foolish and neurotic, but within a couple of weeks it was being speculated that the units could be life-saving. While there was the usual mix of scepticism and fear at first, before long they were in high demand and the prices rocketed, and soon they were scarce worldwide, and we were glad we had listened to my father.

In fact, he had been calling us a lot lately. As soon as the news first came through he had got in touch, and he had seemed impressed and perhaps even proud that I had been following the events with some level of concern. According to Dad the news wasn't irresponsibly raising hysteria, as many people claimed, but quite the opposite. The reports were not bleak enough as to what the future held. I was speaking to him more than ever, looking for his take on things, even when I knew it would be far from reassuring.

"What's actually happening in the oceans, Dad?"

"It's not good. Worse even than you're being told, I'd say. For decades now things have been spiralling, with marine heatwaves causing extinctions, along with a huge growth in harmful sea algae and high acidity levels. But this sudden drop in oxygen is relatively new, and is just compounding and snowballing all the rest..."

While this did nothing to alleviate our anxiety, we were grateful to have his expertise, and it at least made us a step ahead, like in the case of the O2 Booster.

"You need to stay in as much as possible," he was saying one day.

"But surely that's crazy? The girls need fresh air."

"Helen – it's not exactly 'fresh' anymore. I'm serious, the air outside is becoming more and more toxic."

"What – everywhere?"

"Some places are worse than others, as is always the case, but soon there won't be anywhere we can go."

"Mark!" Mum snapped, as Shelley let out a moan and buried her head in my armpit. While it was true that our parents had never shied away from the truth, this was proving a time when I would actually have welcomed a few lies here and there.

We all tried to continue our lives, as normally as possible. The threat, though looming and very real, was invisible, therefore easy to ignore. Just as the land was being slowly swallowed up by the rising sea, so the air was gradually, imperceptibly choking us. Some people wore oxygen masks – similar to the masks we were used to, but transparent, and with a slim tube disappearing into a pack that could be carried in the pocket or a small bag – but only those who had heart or lung difficulties. It was a few years yet before they became essential for making any trip outside. So it was easy to live in denial, apart from those unfortunates living in larger, more populated cities or who were already ill and gasping for air. I heard stories of people dropping down in the streets, and in some places the hysteria was at a level even greater than that caused by the arrival of the Thulians, if that were possible. This time, though, it seemed more understandable, even if the behaviour it led to wasn't. Lack of oxygen to the brain was blamed for actions ranging from looting, to violent riots, to murder. I read about a woman who drowned her own children before stabbing her husband and herself, and I felt sick. I switched off my tablet for a while, then. It wasn't as though schoolwork was being monitored very closely – in fact, within five years of the oxygen crisis first being brought to our attention, the schools around the country actually closed their doors altogether.

And yet, I went to university. I am in my final year – with the rather macabre double meaning that phrase carries. Universities don't actually exist anymore – not in the way they once did when my parents attended. Global events have put a stop to the socialising and gathering being a student used to signify, but in recent years the whole point of having a degree or any form or higher education has somewhat been lost. Even so, with many jobs and occupations obsolete, university lecturers still needed to scrape a living, and so for a fee remote studying is still a possibility. Towards the end of my school years and – apparently – the impending end of the human race, it was hardly surprising that I felt more than a little of the usual fear and desperation about what my next steps should be. And I didn't have the interaction with my peers, who no doubt all felt the same. My classroom was my bedroom, as it still is now. Each day I watch lectures delivered by people I have never and will never meet – they could be AI robots. And I submit my assignments to be returned in the same anonymous way. And that is okay, because it is all I have known of university life.

In fact, I have been able to interact and make friends on my course. I am studying English and training to become a teacher, although of course the irony is apparent at every turn. The fact that there are others on this course helps me to realise I am not the only one feeling the way I do. It's not hope for the future – that would be futile. It's a way to alleviate the boredom while trying to do something as normal as possible. Given the chance, if things had been different, I think I would have gone to university and studied on exactly this course, with the same people. I am faking it.

We have relatively ordinary conversations, my fellow students and I. I even have a best friend of sorts – Martha. She reminds me a little of Daisy, my friend from school, sometimes. She has the same slightly sarcastic manner and ability to laugh easily. Just like with the university thing, I can't help comparing my life to the one I would have been living without all this, as though it's there somewhere in a parallel universe. As the Thulians taught us, it's probably possible. But anyway, I think Martha and I would have been friends in that life, too.

One evening we were having a 'social', as we sometimes call it. It's basically like everything else: me in my bedroom chatting or interacting on screen. But it's informal and relaxed and refreshing. This particular day there were five of us, all from my course. Martha, Alfie, Max, Freya and me. We were having a convoluted discussion that had taken a rather bizarre turn.

"This is one of those conversations I'll think about in the future and wonder if it really happened," said Freya. No one so much as blinked at the mention of the word 'future', just like we never spoke about the fact that we were there to learn how to teach a generation that wouldn't exist.

Martha laughed. We were all a bit drunk, I think.

"Well," she said. "Faye knows all about that!"

I frowned and smiled at the same time, wondering what she was on about.

"Why's that, then?" Freya asked.

"Tell them Faye." Then she continued before I could say anything. "She was friends with those aliens that came here."

I rolled my eyes slightly. Martha was the only one I had actually told about all that. It wasn't through any need to be secretive, more because it took a lot of energy, going over it all. She was right to compare it to Freya's observation: all those memories did seem blurry, as though my mind is playing tricks. Like when you look at a baby photo so many times you convince yourself you can actually remember it being taken.

The others were staring wide eyed. "Those skinny grey ones?" Asked Max.

I laughed, "Yes! As opposed to the other ones!"

They all had that look of disbelief I was so used to seeing now, every time anyone finds out. Which was another reason I hadn't told anyone; it drew too much embarrassing attention.

"You were friends with the aliens?" Max was saying.

"Thank you, Martha, remind me never to tell you anything!"

"But it's true, though?" Asked Alfie. He was the quietest of us all. Which was strange because I always thought that would have been me. He wasn't shy, he just didn't say a lot, preferring to listen and take it all in. I think in another world (there I go again) I might have hoped we'd be together.

"I met them."

"And..." prompted Martha.

"...spoke to them quite a lot."

"But, how?" Max asked.

"My mum worked on the ComET project, and we got to live there for a bit."

"Wait!" shouted Max. "You're that kid! The one that named them!"

"No, that was my sister."

They wanted to know more, of course, and much of the rest of the night was taken up with me going over it again. I had to go downstairs and help myself to more of Mum's wine. I didn't mind talking about it – it had been so long since I had, much less to someone who wasn't there. It was interesting to give them my perspective, and to hear theirs. I smiled along sadly with the opinions they had built based on the news coverage. This was the attitude I'd heard from most people. It was as though the Thulians were a distant memory, a strange anomaly from which we had all moved on, rather than the intelligent, thoughtful beings I had known. I found myself skirting around the subject of my days spent out in the woods, telling them as little as possible. It felt like the last thing I had of them, a precious memory I didn't want cracked open or joked about. And I wasn't sure I could find the words to really make them understand, anyway.

"I used to have nightmares about them," confided Freya when they'd finished their questioning.

"Well, they were pretty creepy looking weren't they. Sorry, Faye."

"That's okay, Max."

By this time, the world outside was becoming more and more hostile. Both the atmosphere and the people in it. I didn't make much effort to keep up with events anymore, but it was impossible not to know what was happening. From my friends' discussions and the TV, and conversations between my mother and Frankie or my dad on the wall. It had got to the stage where everyone was being advised, if not ordered, to connect with loved ones and stay home with them, where possible. Emergency centres were set up for people who were alone or had nowhere to go, in old church buildings and schools. While nobody was giving a specific time frame, it was clear the prognosis was bad. At one point someone called round to offer us essential medical supplies. She was a doctor – although it was difficult to see her properly under her breathing apparatus, and she told us staff from hospitals were visiting every house to issue the kits.

Things descended into chaos remarkably quickly, now it was clear the end was close. Services that we relied on and took for granted, like the postal service and rubbish collections, became erratic and less frequent before grinding to a halt. Shops began to run out of food, causing people to fight in the aisles over the last tin of beans or packet of rice. Luckily many people had surplus supplies, stockpiled over the years in case of another pandemic, or through paranoia when the aliens arrived, and now since this latest (and last) crisis, plus there were the vitapills, which gave the body basic nutrition without the need for solid food. Most households had stacks of those – we certainly did – but there was no way of knowing if it was going to be enough. Many reporters doggedly continued bringing us the news where they could, but I avoided it, preferring to hear it second hand from my mother. We all knew it was bleak.

It was the change in Shelley that struck me the most. She was a teenager now, and I couldn't help remembering Mum's flippant comment to do with dreading the 'terrible teens', or something like that. But she wasn't terrible; she was growing into a clever, thoughtful young woman. It didn't seem that long ago that she had been my annoying, perceptive, doll-obsessed little sister. She had always seemed old for her years, and that hadn't changed; there were still times when it felt like she was the eldest. But she was lost, I could tell. She had nothing to occupy her at home beyond books and TV. She should have been going to school, rebelling, hanging out with friends. Instead it was as though she was just waiting for something.

But no one was going out now, not if they could help it. The advice being given was to remain home, even if you were ill, and not to go to the hospital. A few months before the medical kits there had been an emergency delivery of heavier grade oxygen masks to each household so that people could still make short journeys if they needed to, but it seemed safer to stay indoors. The irony was, everyone was using more and more power running the O2 Boosters twenty-four hours a day, contributing to the problems that had caused all this, if the experts were to be believed. And of course, they were right. But did it matter any more?

Chapter 41

When there was a knock at the front door one day we all almost fell off our stools at the breakfast bar. No one apart from Frankie had called at the door since the medics and that was… I was becoming confused, but I knew it was some weeks before. I wasn't sure if the doorbell was working, but it was the sudden urgency of the tapping that made me jump. Frankie had called to warn us just the day before that she'd heard about looters breaking into houses armed with whatever they could get their hands on, to steal food and supplies. Some even from their own neighbours. In fact, she hadn't been home since, after Mum had finally broken down the woman's proud resolve and told her to stay with us. Mum said at the time it was 'for the time being', but we all knew the situation wasn't going to improve, and that Frankie would be here for good, now. (It struck me that 'for good' was a strange expression. It means forever, but there's nothing very good about forever, now.)

Mum gave us a reassuring look now, before hitting the button on the door cam.

Standing there looking up at us, dishevelled and haggard behind his mask, was my father. I didn't recognise him until Mum said his name – we hadn't been in contact with each other for weeks and we had all secretly been a bit concerned about what might have happened to him. The last we'd heard he'd made it over to Australia.

"Mark!"

"Can I… come in?" He breathed. Mum jumped up to let him in, greeting him with a tight hug that betrayed all the worries she had been carrying lately as the lone parent. Seeing him seemed to ignite something in Shelley, too. He may have been a virtual stranger that she knew only on screen, but he was our dad, after all, and his surprise arrival brought hope in an otherwise hopeless situation.

"How did you get here?" Asked Mum, after he had caught his breath and demolished a pint of water and a packet of biscuits. "I thought travel was suspended?"

"It is. I managed to talk my way onto a military aid flight from Sydney."

"But… how on earth…?"

He gave her a wry smile, "you're not the only one in the family who's good at persuading people, you know. Besides, I did actually help. I delivered some supplies to the hospital before I came here."

"Well, I'm very glad you did. We all are. It's just… wouldn't you have been safer over there? In New Zealand? Like you said you would be when the Thulians came?"

"I haven't been in New Zealand for a few weeks now. But the truth is, I don't think anywhere is going to be safe for long." He looked around at Shelley and me. "I'm sorry, I know that's not what you want to hear."

We didn't say anything. But it felt good to have Dad there; even though it had never felt like he was missing, right then I realised how important it was that we were all together.

He'd been there a few days before I asked him the question that had occurred to me when I had first seen him at the door. He had looked so frail and old, standing there stooped over with the mask on, but after some food and water and recycled air he had seemed revived.

"Be honest, Dad. Are you here because you know something we don't?"

He looked over at Mum, who nodded very slightly.

"It's not looking good, kiddo."

"Meaning?"

"We've got six months, a year at best, I'd say."

"Until what, exactly?" I knew. I just wanted to make him say it.

"Another mass extinction."

"Of the human race, this time."

He nodded.

"How is it not in the news? About how long is left, I mean."

"I can think of a few reasons, can't you? It's carnage out there as it is. Better to bury your head in the sand. But it is out there, in the news and the reports. If you read between the lines."

"And if you're a climatologist who understands it all."

"A conservationist. But, yeah."

And he was right. It was there, hinted at, suggested. It was just that no one had come out and blatantly said it yet. What would be the use? It would be like the hysteria generated by aliens descending, only on a much larger scale. Better for the realisation to dawn slowly, on its own. Or, better still, to be in denial. To carry on with life, make plans, go to university for an education we would never need.

So, here we are, counting our last weeks, or even days – there's no way of knowing, and no reason to want to know. It's speculated that the power will go off, soon. Then we won't be able to run the O2 Booster. But the food supplies dropped by the aid workers are holding up – even the vitapills, which we have been conserving – so that's okay. The five of us are passing the time, telling funny stories and working our way through some of the old board games Frankie found in her house. Trying to take our minds off the headaches and dizzy spells we've all been getting but don't dwell on.

A matter of months, even weeks, ago, there would have been news, when it was still reaching us, from somewhere in the world of people fighting to protect their freedom or their beliefs. Showing the passion, determination and anger that makes us human. But here we are now faced with the end of mankind. And all we want is to shrink down and be close to our loved ones. There is, after all, nothing else left to fight for. And certainly nothing more important.

It's hard to explain, but the atmosphere is almost relaxed; happy. Part of it is having Dad here. I've said before that I never missed him, but that was because I never truly remembered him being around all that much. But now he's here it feels like he always has been. And I know he has – just because he was on the other side of the planet, doesn't mean he wasn't thinking about us. I suppose in a way the work he did – or tried to do – was for us.

One day not so long ago Dad and I were attempting to play a game of Scrabble. It's strange to have actual little tiles for each letter; strange to think of someone making them all those years ago. We were just playing to pass the time, like with everything these days, but he was revealing a comically competitive streak.

"I'm really sorry, you know," he blurted.

"That's okay. I don't mind losing really."

"I mean for not being here with you and Shelley."

"Oh, I see. It's fine Dad, really. Neither of us resent you for it. We never have."

"I feel like I missed out on so much."

"Your work is – was so important, though."

"Huh. It all seems a bit pointless now."

"No, Dad. You had to try."

He put down a word that was clearly nonsense, but I chose to ignore it.

"You know your mum had a word with me about what you overheard when you were living in Scotland."

"What are you talking about?"

"You remember – apparently I said you girls were a terrible mistake."

"Oh that! That is ancient history."

"It upset you though at the time, didn't it? And I'm sorry about that. Even though I'm sure I never said it."

I smiled wryly, "you *did* say it. But, like I said…"

"Not about you two! I would have meant the human race. It's our collective mistake to have overpopulated the world, to have become," he waved a hand around, "unsustainable. I always felt like a huge hypocrite for that, which is why, like a coward, I upped and left your mother to it." He held a hand up to stop me as I protested. "But, like your mum, I wouldn't change… you, or Shelley… for anything."

I smiled and gave him a quick hug. "I know, Dad. I understood that pretty quickly. But, you know 'quog' isn't a word, don't you?"

He looked down at the board. "Damn, I was hoping I'd distracted you enough!"

Yesterday – or perhaps the day before – we suddenly realised it was my twenty-first birthday. Mum went and found some wine, although none of us could drink much. One sip made me feel drunker than I have ever been, and it wasn't a feeling I enjoyed, even though the old, familiar taste was good. Perhaps because she felt as drunk as I did, or because the occasion made her sad for the celebration we should have been having, Mum became slightly maudlin, and kept apologising.

"If I'd known, I wouldn't have had you. I wouldn't have been so selfish…"

"Mum! What are you talking about?"

"Dad was right. We shouldn't have brought children into this world. I'm sorry."

"Stop it, Mum! I've had a great life… you've given me a great life."

"But look at us now! I shouldn't have had you girls, only to put you through all this… It was selfish of me, I've loved being your mum, but what's in it for you?"

Shelley put an end to that talk by telling her to shut up, and played some happy tunes on her tablet. Before long, I was glad to see, it was as though Mum had forgotten what she'd been saying, and it became almost the party I should have had.

It would be lying to say we're feeling happy all of the time. I doubt anyone would believe me anyway – we are dying, after all. There are times, like on my birthday, when one of us melts down a bit, struck by the finality of it, the helplessness. From watching the others sometimes I know it's not just me that gets headaches, the sort I've never had before. Paralysing, thought-stopping pains that freeze you in your tracks until they pass. The first time Shelley had one she collapsed, and I saw real panic in my mother's eyes. I suppose it's hardest for her and Dad, because it's their job – their instinct – to protect us. And they can't. Not from this. Mum scrabbled about in the medical kit looking for painkillers, and came across a small packet of tablets that she showed to Dad and Frankie. They looked at each other, shocked, and then Mum tucked the box into her pocket. I wasn't sure later if I'd just imagined the whole thing, but if I didn't I can only think they're some kind of last resort. How they got into the med kit in the first place I don't know – they could have been dropped off with the emergency kit – but there's a strange comfort in knowing they're there.

Occasionally we see the shape of a vehicle going past on the road outside. I looked out once and saw an orange and white truck, a little like an ambulance, and I glimpsed the driver and passenger wearing white suits and masks. Mum speculated they might be from the hospital, patrolling the streets to check if people needed help. But I heard Dad mutter to her later that he thought they were simply collecting and disposing of the dead. The thought gave me less of a chill than I would have expected.

I suppose the worst bit isn't the fear of death – I don't actually fear it at all, despite the fact that I should have years ahead of me. There's nothing we can do to stop it, that was true even before all this. It's something we have to accept. I suppose I'm a little afraid of the pain we might feel – we're already experiencing some of that. But even that doesn't seem too frightening, because I really do think that it will be like falling asleep, maybe even without the knowledge that it's for the last time. No, the real fear for me is that I might be the last one left, and that death might cruelly elude me for minutes or hours or days, even. I'm wondering if we're all thinking the same thing but are too afraid to say it.

The water went off today. We're not sure if the problem is permanent or not. We have our supply of bottled water, but it feels like one more step. I'm carrying on writing for as long as I can – but it's strange, wondering if there'll be anyone left to read it.

I'm starting to forget things, now, becoming clumsier – I've noticed it in the others too. So I'll have to stop this, soon. But I just wanted to say, don't see this as a sad ending. I'm trying not to – whether it's the strange euphoria that engulfs me now and then, or whether I'm just facing facts. It will sound strange, but I do have hope. Not for us, of course – it's too late for that. But for our planet. It's like Seraphina said – it isn't going anywhere, it will survive, despite our best attempts. Nature will restore itself, in one way or another. There will be a species that survives this, that adapts, of that I am certain. I suppose it's like the dinosaurs – perhaps our time on Earth was just meant to come to an end now, and it's time for another species to have its turn. Who knows, maybe it will be like on Thule, where there are no dominant species, and they all co-exist harmoniously. Or maybe the Thulians will even come back, and live here instead. I can hope. And with these hopes and dreams, I can feel content. Or at least at peace. No. It's not sad; it's the natural order of things.

Once upon a planet there were two young girls who lived with their mother. Three of billions like them. Humans, who filled this planet with love, laughter, music, stories, knowledge, technology, war, injustice and hatred. Who brought about their own destruction, in the end.

Acknowledgements

Well, I finally did it! After solemnly proclaiming, at the age of around nine, that I was going to be a writer, and spending two decades writing a story that really wasn't going anywhere (but that wouldn't, and still won't, leave me alone – so watch this space!) this one landed out of the air, while I was doing my far less glamorous real job.

So I ought to thank the inspirational Tim Peake, who commented on the podcast I was listening to that day, about the possibility of alien life, thus planting the seed of a story in my head. And I also mustn't forget the legendary Sir David Attenborough for… well, for everything he has ever said and done, really. But his eye-opening book *A Life On Our Planet* (2020) was also very helpful and informative in the writing of this story.

While researching this book (and what a lot of very random internet searches it generated!) I came across many useful and fascinating sources. Some from people I was already familiar with, some newly discovered. Carl Sagan, whose quote fits so perfectly at the start of this book, has of course written countless words of infinite wisdom, of which I only managed to scratch the surface. His book, *Pale Blue Dot*, published in 1994, grabbed my attention with his assertion that humans are not the all-important beings we believe ourselves to be.

I have already mentioned Sir David Attenborough, but along with the book I found his series, *A Perfect Planet* (2021), to be a beautifully filmed (as indeed all of his documentaries are, of course) insight into the delicate balance of our ecosystem.

Other inspiration and thought-triggering goodness came from the fantastic artist and writer Oliver Jeffers' TED talk, *An Ode To Living on Earth;* the fascinating online event *Climate Change: The View From Space* (featuring among others the previously mentioned astronaut, Tim Peake); various reports found on the WWF website (www.panda.org), a specific one being the Living Planet report, and discussions on tipping points on www.carbonbrief.org.

This book was a 'lockdown project' for me in late 2020, so was inevitably affected by global events. In my keenness to get the story out and my excitement at actually having finished writing a novel, I first published it in March 2022. Eagle-eyed readers will see the words 'revised edition' at the start of this copy, however. The drawback of being an independent writer meant I didn't have the wise, experienced eyes of a professional editor. But I did take on the feedback of friends and family, and found myself thinking of ways I would have liked to expand or change the story. So – drawback though that may have been, the advantage of indie-publishing meant I could simply re-write it and re-publish it. So here it is. For those who did not read the original, the main story is the same, but told… better! (I hope.)

Now I've explained all that, and if you're still with me, I'd better get on to thanking people I actually know.

My wonderful late mum, devourer of books, who was one of the few people who took that nine year old me seriously. Thank you. And my lovely family and friends who were too nice to refuse me when asked to read the first drafts of the book – David (Dad), Melvin (second Dad), Julie, Richard and Char. Thank you for your time and invaluable feedback. I wish I could name everyone who has supported and encouraged me, but that would make for a very long list, so please know you have my gratitude.

And of course there's Stuart, Archie and Finlay, who keep me crazy, and happily put up with me while my head is in the clouds. Love and thanks always.

Printed in Great Britain
by Amazon

21439881R00202